STRAF

World War II. The Russian Front. A doctor risking his own life to find an antidote to a particularly virulent strain of virus suddenly finds himself on the other side of the fence, forced to kill instead of to save lives when he is thrown into the inhuman conditions of a punishment battalion under the brutal command of a cowardly sergeant.

Also by Heinz G. Konsalik in *Tattoo*:

HIGHWAY TO HELL

DOCTOR OF STALINGRAD

THEY FELL FROM THE SKY

HEART OF THE SIXTH ARMY

THE LAST CARPATHIAN WOLF

STRAF BATTALION 999

Heinz G. Konsalik

Translated by Oliver Coburn

TATTOO

A TATTOO BOOK

published by

the Paperback Division of

W. H. ALLEN & Co. Ltd

A Tattoo Book
Published in 1977
by the Paperback Division of
W. H. Allen & Co. Ltd
A Howard and Wyndham Company
44 Hill Street, London W1X 8LB
Reprinted 1977, 1978

First published in Great Britain by
Aidan Ellis Publishing Ltd 1976

Printed in Great Britain by
Hazell Watson & Viney Ltd, Aylesbury, Bucks

ISBN 0 427 00300 8

1

Julia Deutschmann took trouble over her appearance that morning. People made concessions more readily to an attractive-looking woman than to one who looked haggard and care-worn. She did not have much to do, for she was beautiful anyhow, despite the shadows round her tired eyes and the paleness of her lips; a pencil to her eyebrows, a touch of rouge on the lips, some powder, a hundred brush-strokes over her curly black hair, which she wore loose, without slide or comb. The simple dress was cut to emphasise her figure, the high-heeled court shoes matched the colour of the material. As she slipped into them, she remembered that it was Ernst who had chosen them. For a moment she stayed motionless, the memory flitted over her face like a glimmer of light, and was then extinguished.

She straightened up and gave a last appraising look in the mirror. Then she went.

The guard outside the Army High Command in Bendlerstrasse, Berlin, read the short note she handed to him, slowly and attentively, as if there were more there than three miserable lines, an impersonal summons to an interview with General von Frankenstein.

In the main entrance of the big building complex she met a staff officer, a young lieutenant, who on seeing her saluted with a click of his heels and volunteered to take her up to the second floor. They halted outside a big oak door at the end of the corridor: a gate which seemed to lead into another world.

Into the world which would decide about Ernst's fate: alien, unknown, full of riddles.

Near the door was a plate: General von Frankenstein.

The young lieutenant bowed a little stiffly. "The General will see you directly. I shall announce you in the front office. May I have your letter, Madam?"

Julia gave it to him. The lieutenant with the eager, pallid face and dreamy eyes disappeared into the office. Quite soon he came out into the corridor again, slightly stiffer, more formal and reserved, and also, Julia felt, less self-assured than before. "Just a few minutes longer. You will be called."

He turned and went. His gleaming polished boots creaked. No salute now, no "Madam". That's how it is then, thought Julia, wryly; the name Deutschmann is enough to turn him to ice.

She sat down on a rough uncomfortable bench in the corridor and waited. It was not till half an hour later that the heavy door opened, and a young secretary's head appeared.

"Frau Deutschmann?"

"Yes." Julia stood up.

"The General will see you."

General von Frankenstein came three steps towards her as she entered the wide room. Then he stopped abruptly, like a wound-up doll when the clockwork has run down, and gave her a nod. "Dr. Deutschmann?"

"Yes, General."

"You have submitted an appeal for clemency for your husband?"

"Yes."

"On what grounds?"

For a fleeting moment Julia was overcome by the crazy thought that the General's voice creaked like the boots of the lieutenant who had brought her here. "He ..." she said haltingly, "he was arrested because of a mistake, condemned to service in a penal battalion—I don't know where he is now."

"It was not a mistake," the General grunted.

"But ..."

"Please allow me to interrupt you," said the General, bowing slightly: a veteran Prussian officer, a cavalier of the old school, who had been taught in his cadet days that one should behave politely and correctly towards ladies in every situation; that was the tradition. And Julia was obviously a lady—even though Dr. Ernst Deutschmann was her husband. You could see a thing like that. When you are young, you consider almost any woman a lady. But not when you are in your late sixties, even though you still have as much spunk and as much blood in your veins, by Gad, as would make you a match for that young whippersnapper of a lieutenant. The hint of a smile played around the General's screwed up mouth—for a general smiles, he does not laugh.

"You are, after all, a doctor, Madam," he continued, "and you must understand something about these things. It was not a mistake. I am not relying on my own observations, but on correct scientific analysis by recognised authorities. I myself am unqualified in these matters. We never act irresponsibly, Madam; that would not be in keeping with the tradition of the German Army. We have examined your husband's case conscientiously, and the result given was unequivocal: self-mutilation by infection with sta … sta …"

"Staphylococci," said Julia.

"Precisely." His voice now sounded cutting and abrupt. He turned away and went back to his massive desk. The dark red stripes on his trousers flashed as if he were walking through a sunbeam slanting into the room through the curtains. He stopped behind the desk, bending over slightly, and propping himself on its top with both fists. Julia's eyes travelled up from his blue-veined, brown-spotted old man's hands, over the light grey coat gleaming with silk—the Iron Cross, First-Class, from the First World War, red lapels with golden stylished oak-leaves, over the bony, immobile face, to the pale blue red-veined eyes under the furrowed brown and white hair like a prickly brush.

Looking him in the eyes, she said: "It is just because I am a doctor and have helped him in his work that I know you are wrong. What he did is something you wouldn't find very many others doing. He wanted to help others, and that is why he made a test on himself. That is the truth. But then … then he was locked up like a criminal and convicted. That is why I have submitted an appeal for clemency."

"It could have been worse," said the General impatiently. "Listen, Dr. Deutschmann: your husband was a pretty well-known scientist. Consequently, we exempted him from military service as long as it was possible. When it was no longer possible, and he had to enlist, he infected himself with this ... er ... illness. That is quite clear. Self-mutilation. And as regards his service in a penal battalion ... it is a unit of the German army. He must make good in this special unit, then he will go into another. So, he has got off, I must say, very lightly."

"I have heard," Julia began again, although she knew that her words and anything she could say would bounce off this man like a ball off the wall, "I have heard that this Battalion 999...."

"What have you heard?" the General interrupted her.

"That the people there are treated very badly... like criminals ..."

The General raised his hand imperiously.

"He is a soldier," he said coldly. "You should not believe these rumours. There is no mollycoddling in the German army, we have to fight. It is not only your husband who will be fighting. Millions of others have been doing so now for years. That is all I have to say about it."

"Yes," said Julia weakly.

"You see. Your appeal is superfluous. Battalion 999 is an army unit. Whether he goes into that or a different one ..."

"Yes," said Julia.

"There you are then," said the General, closed a file, looked up and smiled again.

Julia went. It was all in vain. She stood outside the big oak door and supported herself on the window ledge. Whether he goes into Battalion 999 or another unit, she thought, he is a soldier, like millions of others, penal battalion, he must make good, and if he does, then ... oh, Ernsti, she thought, Ernsti ...! And the long weeks of her despair and futile hopes and the useless fight for him, the endless wakeful nights, the trial, the conviction, the appeal for a new hearing, the fruitless battle against people who had condemned him and who were as impenetrable as the General ... like a rubber wall that gives. Anxiety, fear, hidden allusions on harsh brutal words, and now the last hope crushed for good: all this collapsed on top of her, burying her like an avalanche of dark snow.

2

Friedrichslust Barracks, base camp of Penal Battalion 999, was on the outskirts of the town of Poznan, near Kostritz in Thuringia: a collection of massive, stone huts in bare dismal country.

It was autumn. A slow continuous drizzle came down from the heavy overcast sky.

Sergeant Major Krull was at the turnpike receiving the new arrivals to the Battalion: that is, he was doing what he called "giving them a good going over"

First he offered a casual parting salute to the military policemen who had brought the latest batch of scum, as if to say: don't worry, I'm here and this shower will get just what they deserve.

Outside the guard building he had the four men line up in a row according to height. He wore his cap at an angle, shading his screwed-up eyes. He contemplated the four long and intently.

"Your name?" he asked the man on the left of the row, the tallest.

"Gottfried von Bartlitz," said the grey-haired man. His tired eyes lay deep in their sockets and deep wrinkles went from the nostrils right to the corners of the narrow bloodless lips. His uniform jacket, threadbare and far too big for him, was soaked through. Rainwater was running over his face.

"Aha," said Krull, "a Von. And you're a general, are you?"

"Private," said the tall man.

"And I'm also a private, am I?" asked the Sergeant Major.

"No. You are a sergeant major."

"Right. I'm a sergeant major, and what's more, *your* sergeant major. That's what I've just become. And what are you? What's your name?" This last he bawled but, bending forward with his hands on his hips; the sound of his voice tore through the grey heavy air and broke against the long barrack walls on the other side of the big, white square shining with moisture.

"Private Gottfried von Bartlitz, sir," said the tall man, his face impassive.

"Lie down!" said Krull, now quiet again. When the tall man was lying down, Krull walked round him in silence, pressed his heels down in a puddle, regarding the prone figure for a while, walked round the three others and then with a sharp about-turn faced them again.

"And you?" he asked the second.

"Private Ernst Deutschmann, sir."

"Trade?"

Deutschmann hesitated. Then he said: "Doctor, sir."

"Doctor, eh?"

"Yes, sir."

Krull stared at the haggard-looking man with the high forehead, pale yellowish face and restless, worried eyes, then drew himself up, spat to one side and said at length: "Well, blow me down, the things you hear these days! Doctor, by trade!" He shook his head, then bawled: "You're not a ... doctor now, you're a ... private. By trade and calling! Lie down!"

Private Ernst Deutschmann, doctor of medicine, biochemist, honorary lecturer at Berlin University, distinguished scholar and author of several highly regarded articles in medical journals, lay down on the ground, pressing his heels inwards. "Private doctor!" he heard the Sergeant Major's voice say again. Then he heard the third in the row: "Private Erich Wiedeck, sir."

Then the Sergeant Major bawled something more, but Deutschmann did not understand what it was. He lay with his face on his arms, and felt sick, the rain pricked icily on to the back of his neck, and pattered gently on to his back. He was shivering, but at the same time he felt too hot. There was a round wet pebble before his eyes, and a small wet lost ant was climbing over it. The ant kept going, turned round, ran back; and Deutschmann thought, it will be quite a time before I'm well again.

Then he heard the third man lying down at his side.

Now Sergeant Major Krull stood in front of the fourth man, who was of medium height and just as broad as Krull himself. But what was fat in Krull, in this man was thick swelling muscle. With each of his movements the muscles under the tight patched uniform tunic, clinging to him with wetness, came into play as if they had a life of their own. The massive chest extended far beyond the concave stomach and thick sturdy bandy-legs. The man looked as if he were hewn out of granite, and his face was like an unwieldy lump of clay: a low forehead beneath the cropped black hair; a flattened nose and the chin of a killer. He was grinning. But only the mouth grinned; the rather slanted dark eyes were lifeless and dull like two glass balls.

"My Christ, what a face!" said Krull.

"*And* I've won a beauty contest, the one after yours," said the man. "And by the way, my name is Karl Schwanecke, I've got sweaty feet, and you're the Sergeant Major, and now I'll lie down too." He made a move as if to lie down with the others, but the flabbergasted Krull yelled at him to remain standing. So Karl Schwanecke remained standing and grinned at the Sergeant Major, who said nothing for a long time.

Heaven only knew what he was thinking during those seconds. Probably nothing at all; his brain might have been paralysed. He had never had such a thing happen to him before. Of course there were a lot of trouble-makers in this bloody battalion, a shower of intellectuals and bookworms, and also a lot of criminals who had been shuttled off here. But nobody dared say things like that to him, Sergeant Major Krull, things like … sweaty feet, he thought, and didn't know what to do. So he began swearing vociferously. That was the best way out, and if you did it for long enough, some useful idea almost always occurred to you.

Whatever Krull's weaknesses, he had a powerful voice, and his oaths were terrifying enough to put the fear of God into any recalcitrant soldiers. These qualities, combined with his strict attention to petty details and general severity, were famed far and wide and had eventually landed him in the penal battalion, where he, if, if anyone, would be the man to deal with enemies of the people and such elements.

Until these days of total war people like Schwanecke would scarcely have been stuck in uniform. They were locked up in prison or liquidated, depending on circumstances. Krull for all his experience felt baffled, and because he was baffled, he yelled and swore: with a scarlet face, wide open mouth and protruding, half-closed eyes. His bawling voice filled every corner of the wide square, reducing every other sign of life in the drowsy barracks to complete stillness. But if Karl Schwanecke's grin was a sign of life, that went on, gaping and shameless. When Krull took a pause for breath, there was suddenly a paralysing, almost audible silence, audible through the gurgling of the water in the gutters and through the very faint sound of singing by marching soldiers which came wafting from somewhere out of the dismal, rain-sodden countryside.

This singing was Krull's way out.

With the disconcerting ability of old soldiers to change direction abruptly, he broke off his stream of oaths, looked at his watch, compared it with the clock on the guard hut, nodded, ordered the still grinning Schwanecke to lie down, and then stalked off to the turnpike.

The four new arrivals he left lying in a short, slanting, soaking row, from the tallest to the shortest, from Private Gottfried von Bartlitz to Private Karl Schwanecke.

This was Dr. Ernst Deutschmann's introduction to Penal Battalion 999.

3

They marched through the rain and sang.

Sergeant Hefe stamped ahead of them grimly. He was wet and muddy, and furious at having to stamp through the same mud as the men behind him.

The road stretched far in the distance. It led through the lowlands of the River Warta, through harvested cornfields, past sad birches and melancholy beeches. The grey-brown river ran sluggishly between sandy banks.

They were tired, and it was not time for singing. But they sang because Hefe made them: grey ghosts marching and singing in a grey landscape beneath a grey sky, with wet faces and gaping black mouths, from which the songs about the rose on the heath, edelweiss, rolling tanks and rotting bones, rose wearily, and then sank like the rain drizzling from the sky on the dismal wet countryside.

One hundred and fifty-three men.

"Company—halt!" yelled Hefe. He fell the men out on the left of the road; and looked at the tired, scraggy, filthy mob, who stared back at him apathetically and were glad not to have to sing any more. What a crew!

"You're singing like love-sick skivvies in the moonlight. If I hear any of you singing out of time again, we'll go the whole way back at the double, get me?" He said it, but didn't mean it seriously. Wild horses wouldn't have dragged him back that deadly boring route, and besides it was pretty late, so he ignored, too, the tired "Yes, sarge," from about 20 of the 153 throats.

"Right then," he said, "in a quarter of an hour we march into camp. The C.O.'s there, so don't give me any trouble, get me?".

"Yes, sarge."

"Right then, a song. 'It's fine to be a soldier,' Sing it with feeling, my lads, sing it as if you meant it."

They marched into camp, where they were already expected by Sergeant Major Krull. That late afternoon he invented a new exercise.

He was furious. That is to say, his permanent state of fury had reached a new peak because of Karl Schwanecke and because of the lateness of the marching column. Seven minutes overdue! And the C.O. might be standing at the window, looking at his watch and grinning slyly.

Krull through what he would do with them. "I'll ... I'll ..." That was a far as he got for the moment.

The turnpike went up, the company wheeled left, Sergeant Hefe giving commands in a shrill voice. But right in the path of the column the four new arrivals lay on their stomachs, turning their faces to the side in the direction of the marchers.

Hefe saw them, although too late, and gave the command "right wheel" so as to avoid the men lying there. Slight confusion arose in the colum. This was the moment when Krull saw his chance. "As you were!" he bawled, thereby adding to the confusion. But Hefe saw what Krull's idea was, and decided he could hardly countermand the sergeant major's order. So he continued to give his own loud commands, which rang over the barrack square; and the one hundred and fifty-three men, divided into four platoons, marched over the men on the ground and sang as they marched.

Krull knew he was not risking anything by this. The distances between the men on the ground were small but not too small. If you stepped carefully, you could put your foot down between them—even if the foot was in a huge jackboot. He knew also that the marching men would not tread on them any more than a horse does when it gallops over someone lying on the ground. Still, it was a nice idea, a novelty, a foretaste for the new arrivals, at once a warning and a punishment in advance. Afterwards he was to develop the exercise further and sometimes had the rest of the company march over a platoon, lying on the ground, with strict attention to their keeping in step. As this was almost impossible and the columns regularly began stumbling, it gave him a good handle for further exercises.

The returning company on this occasion were tired and apathetic. Many of them didn't understand what was going on. Many were too tired to lift their feet more than four inches above the ground, and generally they did not see the men on the ground till rather late in the day.

Consequently, all four sustained some painful bruises and the first, Private von Bartlitz, a crushed finger, before he managed to hide his hand under his body.

4

The battalion commander, Captain Barth, stood at the window of the orderly room and watched this spectacle. When the last marchers had stepped over the four men, and their figures, stretched out flat and covered with mud from top to bottom, had become visible again, he turned round. "Your company, Obermeier?" he asked the lieutenant standing behind him.

The lieutenant nodded. "They're coming back from work, digging sand. Not much fun in this bloody weather."

"A tough nut, our Krull," said the captain, and looked out again. When the lieutenant made no answer, he continued, "Just the right man for us, don't you think?"

"Well, I don't know, sir," said the lieutenant.

The company was now standing in the middle of the square in front of Krull. Hefe reported to the Sergeant Major, but Krull ignored him, nodding pleasantly to the hundred and fifty-three men. Then he thrust his thumb between the third and fourth button of his service jacket and began giving one of his customary talks, referring to the lovely picnic they must have had, and how they had probably been skimming stones across the Warta, which must be why they were so late back. Basically, there was little difference in this talk from thousands of other talks being given in thousands of barrack squares all over Europe by other N.C.O.'s to other companies. The men listening here—or for the most part, not listening—belonged to a penal battalion, which was a big difference, though even that did not show too much on the surface. Most of the men in a penal battalion were likely to die, but that went for all service men at this time, although the losses in other units were usually lower in proportion compared with a penal battalion. The difference did show in the uniforms and the food and above all in what the men faced before death: a vast humiliation, mental and physical oppression, hopelessness and despair.

When Krull had finished his talk, he doubled the exhausted men twice to the far wall, made them lie down once and finally ordered them to dismiss. He left the four new men still lying on the ground.

"Now they'll start fighting for the tap," said the lieutenant.

"Why do they need a tap?" asked Captain Barth. "It's raining outside, isn't it?"

"Ten hours hard manual work without any drinking water and having to sing on top of that. They might need that tap."

"But, Obermeier," said the captain mockingly, lighting a cigarette and laying his case open on the table so that the lieutenant could take one, "I thought I had my old cheerful mess companion here, not a wet blanket. You weren't like this in Vitebsk."

"That's just it, sir. There, on the front, I was where I ought to be. But this business here? I'm an officer, not a prison warden." He took a cigarette from the case and lit it with slightly trembling fingers.

The captain looked at him curiously. "Are you sorry for that lot?"

"Aren't you, sir?"

"What?" The captain put his head on one side. "There isn't one of them who hasn't been legally convicted."

Fritz Obermeier stubbed out his cigarette, hardly started, in the big ashtray. "You've seen my company, sir," he said. "A hundred and fifty walking corpses chased to and fro, now being finished off once more by Sergeant Major Krull because they were seven minutes late getting back here. Legally convicted! The little thin man in the first row, for instance, formerly Lieutenant Colonel Remberg, Knight of the Iron Cross, was one of the first officers outside Moscow. In a conference on strategy he said something to the effect that we shall wear ourselves out and bleed to death in the wastes of Russia. He said we should stop while it was still possible or there would be a catastrophe. Now he's here. 'I can't go on with it here any more, I'm not a butcher,' he said—and HQ reacted badly. Now he's shovelling sand."

"Well, he didn't want to be a butcher, and now he's a sand-shoveller," said the captain. "Better that than dead."

But the lieutenant might not have heard his superior's words. "Or the exhausted-looking chap with the bald head and glasses. There, walking across the yard."

"What about him?"

"Professor Ewald Puttkamer. He said the brown shirt was the new uniform and special clothing for grave-diggers."

The captain grinned. "Not bad."

"There are lots of people like that here. But you know that yourself, of course."

"Still, there are criminals as well, eh?"

"Those as well."

"And what are your thoughts about all this?"

"I hardly think it is a German officer's function to take over the duties of a prison warder."

Captain Barth smiled. He sat down in the only armchair and blew smoke from his cigarette up to the low ceiling. From the square, Krull's bawl could be heard through the closed window. He was on his way to the rations distribution.

"Disgusting," said Obermeier.

"Oh, come on," said the captain genially. "War is disgusting. And peace is even more so because then we soldiers are superfluous. You must be more detached, my dear fellow, much more detached. Then you may have a chance of survival. Then it won't worry you any more whether a lieutenant colonel or some genius of a professor and other such heroes are being bullied about by Krull and company and look like—how did you put it?—corpses being driven around. That was it, wasn't it?"

The lieutenant nodded.

Captain Barth rose heavily, yawned, stretched his tall burly figures and straightened his leather belt. Then he looked at the small gold watch on his wrist and yawned again without taking his hand from his mouth. The watch was attached to a white linen wristband, and it was said that Barth changed this strap every day for a snow-white, newly-starched one. Perhaps what was said was a fact, though this somehow did not tally with such a tall, strong man. It would have been more in keeping with the commander of A Company, that ladies' man, Lieutenant Wernher.

When Barth looked up again, he saw Obermeier standing in front of him in stiff official posture. "I ask you, sir, to recommend my transfer to a front-line unit."

"Well, I never," said Barth mockingly, "Just look—a hero! If you'd waited a minute, you could have saved yourself this old Germanic hero's pose." He felt about in his pocket, took out a written order, and put it with the files which covered one part of the desk. "Your company, B Company in Battalion 999, is moving up in the next few days to Russia."

"Russia?"

"That's right. The remaining companies are following at intervals of two days. I shall be going with the last one. Satisfied?"

"No, sir."

"Still not. Dammit, what more do you want?"

"A decent unit. What am I expected to do in Russia with these near-corpses? Can we fight the war and win it with physical wrecks?"

"Win it? Obermeier, you're joking!" Barth smiled contemptuously. "Well, anyhow we've been given a marvellous assignment, you'll be able to show all your hero's courage. An assignment with dates for achieving certain objectives—or else being court-martialled. Not only the boring stupid digging, clearing mines, defusing bombs, clearing of water, hauling ammunition, building roads, clearing away bodies ..."

"And—what's this marvellous assignment?"

"You'll learn soon enough." Barth walked to the window and looked out. On the square Krull was chasing a private to and fro.

"And who's that there? You know your men's life stories, don't you?"

"Lieutenant Stubnitz," said Obermeier.

"Private Stubnitz," Barth corrected him. "What did *he* get up to?"

"In Dortmund he threw a brandy glass at the Führer's picture and called out, 'Here's to the clown'."

"The idiot!" said the captain.

"He was drunk."

"A drunken idiot, then. Why don't you intervene? Why don't you give Krull his comeuppance? You could report him for maltreatment of the troops."

"Where would that get me? A short hearing. Question: what troops? Answer: Penal Battalion 999. What did you do, Sergeant Major? I drew a rebellious soldier's attention to his incorrect behaviour within permitted bounds. Well done, Sergeant Major, carry on with the good work. And *I'd* get it in the neck."

"So you would," said Barth. "You're no fool, are you? Well, now it will be better, when we get to Russia. Soon you'll be released from all your worries and melancholy thoughts."

"Why?"

The captain answered slowly, emphasising each word as if he had had to nail it to the wall: "Because - after - a - few - weeks - you - won't - have - any - company - left."

There was a silence. Then it seemed as if Barth wanted to soften the impression of his words and dispel the shadows of a grim and lurid future which had begun to spread through the room. "The four men lying in the mud there belong to you. They are your replacements. Interesting folk—just right for your collection. The first"—Barth went over to the desk and opened a file he had brought with him—"is Gottfried von Bartlitz, former colonel with the Iron Cross and Oak-leaves, divisional commander, now a private. After Stalingrad he opened his mouth too wide, but what finished him was the business with the order to retreat—he too, they say, didn't want to be a butcher. The second man is Erich Wiedeck. He was a corporal, a farmer in Pomerania, and he extended his leave because he wanted to get the harvest in. That's what *he* says. The third man is Karl Schwanecke, formerly dock-worker but only now and then. Otherwise a habitual criminal, subhuman specimen, one might say. And the fourth, Dr. Ernst Deutschmann—significant name, eh? Self-mutilation. Very subtly worked out, but still it went wrong. And that's it. What's up, Obermeier?"

"What ... What did you say the first man's name was?"
"Why, do you know him?"
"What is his name?"
"Gottfried von Bartlitz. Do you know him?"
Obermeier nodded. "He was once my battalion commander," he said heavily.
"Well now, isn't that interesting!" Barth returned to the window and looked out, as if he hadn't yet had his fill of Krull stalking about and bawling. "You see, that's how it is," he said quietly, not looking at the lieutenant. "Yesterday on top, today underneath, and tomorrow deep under—I mean, under the earth. Remain on top, Obermeier, that's the most important thing, always remain on top. Try to climb higher, but not too high. And forget what these people were before. Forget it, or the same may happen to you one day. These people have lost their past. They are privates in a penal battalion. Privates without weapons. They have forfeited the honour of bearing arms. The only honour they have left is the right to die. Privates - in - Penal - Battalion - 999," he said slowly, as if he had to savour each letter of each word. With a quick jerky movement he stuck his hands in his trouser pockets and shrugged his shoulders. "Survival," he said. "Staying on top, not being an idiot. Got anything to drink?"
"Hennessy?" asked the lieutenant.
"Let's have it," said the captain.

5

Hope is a jack-in-the-box. Even in the darkest despair we suddenly find a grain of hope, hidden at first, but then growing and spreading. Admittedly, it is often a false hope we cling to, illusory and unrealistic, but that doesn't matter. We become stronger through it, it helps us to get control of ourselves and overcome our resignation; and in the end, though destroyed and unfulfilled, it makes us believe in or guess at a way out—the grain of a new hope.

So it was with Julia Deutschmann. The ray of hope she thought she saw after the humiliating and fruitless interview with General von Frankenstein was called Dr. Albert Kukill.

This was strange, for Dr. Kukill was the prosecution's expert witness in the trial: the man with the ice-cold intellect, whose authoritative opinions were razor-sharp and definitive and were considered infallible in all trials. But for Dr. Kukill, Ernst would scarcely have been convicted.

If Dr. Kukill admitted that he had made a mistake, it could mean a revision of the verdict after all, and then there would be no more Penal Battalion 999 for Ernst.

Julia was a doctor herself and knew many other doctors, but there were extremely few of them who would have been willing to admit to a mistake. It didn't seem likely that Dr. Kukill was one of those few. But perhaps if she did things right, if she chose the right words, if she went about it cleverly, if she—yes, if she wanted to help Ernst, it was the only thing left for her to do.

Towards evening, therefore, on the same day as her

interview with General von Frankenstein, she stood outside Dr. Kukill's villa in the Berlin district of Dahlen and rallied all her courage before pressing the bell. She had decided not to try to make an appointment with him first.

Now she stood before him.

He was wearing a smart double-breasted suit, his grey hair was smoothly combed back, his narrow face showed a remote resemblance to a watchful bird of prey. His eyes tallied with that image: they were grey, hard, hooded.

He gave no sign of surprise on seeing Julia Deutschmann; and if he felt at all guilty towards her—or rather, towards Ernst—she thought he concealed it skilfully. But could a man look so calm and lofty if he had a guilty conscience? She became unsure of herself.

He held out his hand to her, as if she were someone he had known quite well for years. He even smiled. When he did this, his face at once lost its hardness and unapproachable severity; and when he spoke, there was an agreeable Viennese touch to his manner and voice. That voice was a versatile instrument, with which he could range from shouting, through professional reserve, to disarming affability.

"You know why I have come?" asked Julia, grateful for the half-darkness in the hall, which would help to hide her trembling hands and flushed face. She tried to make herself calm, but her voice trembled.

"I can imagine, Madam—or I should say Doctor, should I not? We are colleagues, I believe. But why are we standing here? Whatever it is you may have to discuss with me, we can make ourselves more comfortable." He opened a dark oak door and showed her into his lovingly furnished drawing-room, which looked out on to the garden through big French windows. It was an immense garden, full of trees, like a small park. Dusk was just falling on it. Half of a swimming pool could be seen between rhododendrons and lilac bushes.

Dr. Kukill turned on the light and drew the heavy curtains. Then he pointed, smiling, to a large yellow armchair. "Please sit down."

Julia sat down. How on earth did the man manage to go on smiling like that and look so serene, when he must guess what she wanted from him?

"I'd like to talk everything over with you once more," she began. Now she didn't need to force herself any longer; she *was* calm. The man opening a small drinks cabinet was her adversary, an adversary you could only conquer or drive into a corner with cool calculating shrewdness.

"I can't imagine what good it will do," he said, turning towards her. "Bur first tell me what you would like to drink. A brandy? Armagnac 1913? I keep it for my very special guests." He actually said this without a trace of irony in his voice.

"Thank you," said Julia.

Dr. Kukill lit a candle, warmed two glasses over the small flickering flame and then poured out the golden fluid, about a finger in each glass. "There are people," he remarked chattingly, "who grudge me all this, the house here, and the 1913 brandy. It's not the time for that, they say. When *would* be the time, I wonder. Actuaries put the life-expectancy of the present-day European at about 66, and of course with the war it has gone far lower. Tomorrow might be too late. Should one not try to enjoy life today? What do *you* think?"

"I have other things to think about," said Julia.

"Now don't be bitter," he said, smiling again. He held up his glass, examining it against the light, then looked at Julia. "Come on, let's drink—your health."

"I don't know what sort of a person you are," she said. "Perhaps you really don't see anything but all this"—with a slight gesture of the hand she took in the room, the house, the garden, the brandy on the table, and the words he had been speaking. "Perhaps you really aren't bothered by what's going on around you."

"Not very much," smiled Dr. Kukill.

"But there *are* the other things, too," she continued. "Yesterday there was an air-raid and many dead, and today there will probably be an air-raid again and perhaps still more dead, and there's Russia and Italy and death over and over again. But there are also the small things, the apparently small things, which mean life for other people, what they live for."

"I suppose you are thinking of your husband?" said Dr. Kukill.

"Yes," Julia answered, looking him straight in the eyes. "That is my world. Please understand me—I—I don't know where else to turn. You're the only person who.... It was all a chain of tragic circumstances."

"A lawyer might refer to it in that way. We can speak more simply. You would rather call it a mistake, wouldn't you?"

"And you, what would you call it?"

Dr. Kukill thrust out his lower lip and regarded his slender white hands reflectively. "Suppose it really was a mistake?"

Julia jumped to her feet. "And you can dare say that! Your medical judgement destroyed Ernst. It was because of you he was convicted. And now you sit here quite innocently and say 'Suppose it really was a mistake?"

"Please calm yourself. Sit down, Madam. My medical judgement was purely scientific in character. It was well-grounded, it was impartial, it was formed in accordance with the present state of scientific knowledge. As a specialist giving his judgement before a court one cannot operate with possibilities, assumptions, hypotheses ..."

"But we have achieved good results ..."

Dr. Kukill held up his hand slightly. "How many control experiments have you carried out?"

"About thirty."

"And you as a doctor can speak of good results on that number? But let's leave that aside. How does the case look, or rather, how did it look?" He put his fingers together and regarded Julia thoughtfully. He was only half with this conversation, which was futile and tedious: no one could help Ernst Deutschmann. And for a moment he wondered why he was wasting his time on her. But—she was pretty, elegant, well-groomed and courageous. No, more than that, she was beautiful. She radiated a strange charm such as one rarely finds in a beautiful woman, a mixture of intelligence, single-mindedness, pure will-power and helplessness. What more does a man want?—he thought, a little envious of Ernst Deutschmann. What will become of her if he dies in the penal battalion? While he tried to find words to convince her of the hopelessness of her efforts, he was thinking that she would make a beautiful widow, though certainly not a merry one. But she was as good as a widow already.

"Look," he said eventually. "Consider the matter from our stand-point. The day after your husband received his call-up papers, he became ill. Some time later it transpired that he had obtained the pus of a severely infected person and had secretly injected himself with it—allegedly to test on himself the effect of an antidote he had discovered. An infection with staphylococcus aureus of this kind entails years of convalescence, years of unfitness for military service." He spoke the last words slowly and with emphasis. When Julia did not answer, he continued:

"That was something he knew. But this is something we know too, that through such infections, which are mostly fatal, we have lost tens of thousands in this war. Now, I don't want to attribute to him any ideas of suicide. It is quite possible he believed he had found a—a serum, let us say, and that like all, shall I say scientific fanatics or heroes of his kind, he infected himself so as to test his discovery. That is why I observed that his conviction *could* have been a mistake; supposing that it was not a case of self-mutilation to escape military service. A military court, however, cannot take this possibility into consideration. The fact remains that he did, as it were, mutilate himself. That alone is decisive."

"But—I'm convinced. I was there the whole time, I know he was on the right track. We had so little time, things had to be done so fast ..."

"*I* take the possibility into account. But a judge can't. I have already told you: there is no really effective remedy for infections of this kind. And I doubt whether your husband with all his talent is such a genius that he found, alone and unaided, what a whole world of researchers have for years been looking for in vain. That was the judgement I gave the court. It was and is my personal conviction. What interest should I have in getting your husband ... by the way, have you tried for a revision?"

"Yes," said Julia.

"And?"

"I was told—it was an S.S. man ... he told me ..." She faltered as if afraid of what she had to say or of the memory of the man who had told her. "He told me that if the case of

Deutschmann should come up in a court of revision, then the end of that new hearing would be a death sentence."

Dr. Kukill lit a cigarette and said nothing. "Why an S.S. man?" he asked eventually.

Julia shrugged her shoulders.

"And—what will you do now?"

She looked at him. Her eyes were large, dark, feverish. "Is there nothing one can do?" she asked, her voice trembling. She stood up, walked round to the table, and clutched his arm, while he went on sitting there helplessly, caught up against his will in her suffering and despair. "You can do something, I'm sure you can, please, it all depends on you, I know that. Who else can I go to? You can say it was a mistake, then he will come back, come back to me. Oh! my God! Please, please do something."

He tried to calm her, but saw that she wouldn't listen to him, wouldn't believe that her husband was finished, that nothing now could be done for him—not after the bars of a penal battalion had closed behind him. They stood opposite each other, and when he had told her that he could do nothing for her husband, he looked at her in silence and thought again that she had the sort of feminine beauty that suffering and despair cannot injure but only deepen. And a small sharp thought shot through his brain: Deutschmann won't ever come back, and then.... He bent forward gazing at her tensely with a strange excitement.

"Yes," she said after a while, continuing to look at him, through him. "Yes," she repeated, "there *is* a possibility. I was present at all his experiments. I have all his notes. I will go on. I will repeat his experiments. If necessary, even those carried out on oneself. I will ..."

"For heaven's sake!" cried Dr. Kukill.

"... I will prove he was right. Then they'll get him out and let him go on with his work. Then ..."

"That would be—Good God, it could mean your death." Dr. Kukill looked at the woman in front of him, aghast.

"Please let me go now," said Julia.

As soon as she was back home, she threw her coat carelessly over a chair, rushed into her husband's laboratory at the back of the house, and began to put the confusion of notes in order.

Meanwhile, that evening, in Friedrichslust Barracks, Lieutenant Wernher, Commander of A Company, rode across the square, with raincoat thrown loosely round him, a solitary dark figure. The horse's hooves crunched on the gravel. He was on his way to a lady friend, a German-Polish land-owner, a young widow whose husband had been killed in the Polish Campaign.

Captain Barth sat in his room under a standard lamp and read *The Adventures of Tom Sawyer.* His stockinged feet dangled over the side of his chair; sometimes he smiled. Then his face became almost youthful, free and relaxed.

Lieutenant Obermeier drew the black-out blind in front of the window, felt his way through the room, switched on the light, and for a moment was dazzled. He poured himself half a glass of Hennessy and drank it down in a gulp. he had decided to get drunk this evening.

In the sleeping quarters the men awaited the arrival of their Sergeant Major, wondering anxiously which room tonight would satisfy Krull's need for distraction. As was only to be expected, it proved to be the one to which the four newcomers had been assigned.

First of all he found on the floor under the last bed a small flint or perhaps a large grain of sand. He picked it up and without uttering let it drop again. Then he stood in front of a locker and felt around it with his forefinger, without discovering any dust. But he found it on a ceiling beam and a window frame and smeared it on the room orderly standing stiffly to attention. This was the former Lieutenant Stubnitz, whom he had already chased across the square. He smeared the dust all over Stubnitz's face in beautiful squares, without saying a word.

A heavy enervating silence reigned in the room, broken only by the sounds of Krull's steps over the creaking floor and sometimes a contemptuous snort he gave. No one stirred: twenty-two men lay stretched on their backs covered to their chins with damp-smelling blankets, their arms pressed to their bodies—lying "at attention", so to speak. They waited for the inevitable. From the corner came the heavy rattling breathing of Private Reiner, formerly Dr. Friedrich Reiner, Munich lawyer, from 1939 inmate of Dachau concentration camp, from January 1943 reprieved to Penal Battalion 999; he suffered from asthma.

When Krull decided that Private Stubnitz looked sufficiently dust-chequered, he began the locker inspection. From the first locker he only threw the washing-things on to the floor. He emptied out the second almost completely, did not disturb the third and fourth, threw out the underclothes from the fifth, and cleared out most of the sixth. He still did not say a word.

The seventh locker was Karl Schwanecke's. When Krull opened it, he started back. This locker was really staggering. the only things in good order, that is to say properly lined up, were the pictures of naked women on the inside of the door. Krull suppressed his curiosity, deciding some time to look at the pictures at his leisure. He had been intending to inspect the men's feet, but dispensed with this and instead scuffled them out of bed to make them goose-step with "eyes left" past Schwanecke's locker. Then he chased them on to the barrack square for half an hour's noctural gymnastics, a tragicomic collection of figures in white nightshirts with clattering clogs, doing duck-walks, hare-jumps and frog-hops.

By the end three men were near collapse: the asthmatic former lawyer; Deutschmann; and von Bartlitz. Others still managed to totter around, sweating, mud-sprinkled ghostly figures. Schwanecke alone seemed unaffected. He grinned, and swore at the Sergeant Major, for which insubordination he had to perform some extra contortions. But the grin stayed on his face.

Then came a good hour's washing and room-cleaning; so that it was past eleven before they were at last lying in bed again with some prospect of being able to sleep the night undisturbed.

Ernst Deutschmann lay stretched on his back and forced himself to breathe calmly, deeply and regularly. His heart was racing. Gradually he felt better, the faintness dispersed, and the only thing left was a heavy, paralysing weakness, which made his body feel heavy as lead.

In the next bed lay the farmer Wiedeck, the man he had got to know in the military prison in Frankfurt-an-der Order. Wiedeck had been his cell companion, dour and uncommunicative. They had scarcely exchanged a word, although they had been together all the time: in the cell, on the daily walk in the prison yard, and in the workshop, where they nailed the soles of army boots. They had not become friends until a sergeant who did not like Deutschmann's face overturned some boxes full of nails and ordered Deutschmann to pick them again. Siedeck had helped him, grimly and doggedly.

"How are you?" he heard Wiedeck whisper now.

"Better," he whispered back.

"— Bastards!" whispered Wiedeck after a while.

"Don't worry about it," said Deutschmann.

There was another silence, then Wiedeck asked: "What are you thinking of?"

"Julia," said Deutschmann.

"Same with me. Thinking of Erna. Got any kids?"

"No."

"I've got two. No, three now, I hope. Oh, if only I knew...."

"Tell me about it," said Deutschmann.

Then the former Corporal Erich Wiedeck, who had just been expecting promotion to sergeant, began to tell his story. Deutschmann, lying near him, could see growing before his eyes a world quite strange to him till now. He no longer heard the asthmatic's heavy breathing or Schwanecke's snoring. The musty room, filled with sour darkness, faded out and then widened through Wiedeck's whispered, halting words, till it became wide as the expanses of Pomerania.

A light wind flew over the fields of Melchov. It was around midday. A few tractors rattled over the paths. Men with shorn hair, in torn rags of clothing, sat on the bouncing seats. Some women and girls in coloured head-scarves, followed the tracks of the big wheels. These were Russian landworkers, peasants from the Ukraine, the Caucasus and White Russia. They had been trapped like game, pulled out of their beds at night, herded into cattle trucks and brought to Germany to save the harvest which it was said would mean victory.

Wiedeck let some ears of rye slip through his fingers. They were thick, crammed full of grain, ripe for cutting as no crop had been for years. The fields were high with it: eighty mornings under the plough. Rye, wheat, oats, barley, potatoes, turnips.

He looked across at the tractors and the Russians, who were laughing as they came back to the village. It was Saturday and knocking-off time. The weather was good. The sun was there and would go on shining for the next few days at least.

They won't make it, he thought, they can't make it. These few Russians and the women, these few tractors. The harvest will rot in the fields if it isn't cut at once. Then he thought of his wife, Erna, expecting a baby in two or three weeks, with her body so heavy she could scarcely bend, suffering from the sun and the exhausting work. He looked over his fields, the sea of waving ears, and calculated the hours and days it would take to cut it and bring it in before the rains started.

When he returned home early that afternoon, he found Erna standing in the doorway. "Where have you been?" she asked anxiously. "Your train leaves in two hours."

"I've been looking round," he said shortly. He gazed at her, at that heavy body.

"The corn looks fine," she said, taking off her apron. "Come on, have something to eat. And I've baked you a cake to take with you'"

"Who's going to cut the corn?"

"I am."

"You?"

"Of course. And three Russians. When they're through at Pilchov's, they'll come to us. They'll bring the big combine harvester."

"It'll be too late."

"Come on." Erna drew her husband into the house. "There's just nothing else for it. What we *can* bring in, we will. As for the rest ..." She shook her head. "One day even this old war will be over. Then you'll be able to see to things better again."

"It's a scandal the corn should go to waste," he said stubbornly, sitting down at the window in the big kitchen and looking out. Then he turned round to Erna, who was standing at the stove, pouring out coffee. Real coffee, saved from the rare special rations on the cards, for the day when Erich came on leave. The whole kitchen was filled with its aroma. And on the table stood a big currant cake. She had even tied a white ruff round it, as if today were his birthday or some other day to celebrate. By the cake was a bunch of wild flowers—from his meadows.

He turned away and stared again at the land. "I'm staying," he grunted.

"What?" Erna looked at him blankly. She put the jug of coffee down on the table and sat down. "What's that you said?"

"I'm not going."

"So I stayed," Erich Wiedeck told his friend, glad of the darkness, because then no one could see his moist eyes. "I told her my application to extend my leave had come through and that I was allowed to stay as long as I needed to bring in the harvest. But," he said, "that wasn't the only reason I stayed, you see. The doctor had said she must let up before the birth, but how should she let up when I was gone and she had to do everything herself? And then, if she couldn't do it, how would she eat? What would she have got out of the harvest? The fields have never borne so well, and yet she would have starved. Do you understand why I couldn't leave?"

"Yes," said Deutschmann.

"So I stayed and brought in the harvest. I worked like an animal. I hardly slept at all, I was out in the fields from early morning till late at night, and then I also had to do the housework. Still, I got the harvest in." There was a note of triumph in his whispering voice. "I was always waiting for the M.P.'s to come and fetch me. But they didn't come. The only thing I'm sorry about ..." He broke off.

"Go on," said Deutschmann.

"I'm sorry I didn't stay longer. Till Erna had her child. I've got two daughters, so we were hoping for a son. Oh, it must be a son!"

"I expect it is," said Deutschmann. "So why didn't you stay on?"

"After the harvest was in, I felt really scared, it was no good waiting to be picked up, I thought it was best to go. Now I wish I'd stayed. It was hard saying good-bye to her and the little girls. I ..."

"Go to sleep now," said Deutschmann.

"Yes, I'd better. Thanks for listening."

The next day, after they had finished work, the whole battalion got mail permission. The old lags said this must mean something bad coming. Probably going to Russia.

Deutschmann wrote to Julia: "I'm fine, my darling. There's plenty to eat, and I'm not doing too badly for anything else. Except for missing you. How I long to see you again—but for the moment that's only a dream. Anyhow, don't worry about me. Just look after yourself, especially with all the enemy air-raids. Please take care of yourself, sweetheart, I want to find you safe and sound when I come back. Heaps of love from your own Ernst."

Wiedeck wrote: "Dearest Erna, I still don't know how the birth went, and if you're well and if it's a boy or a girl. Please write and tell me. If it's a boy, call him Wilhelm, after my father. If it's a girl, as we decided, it's to be another Erna. I'm all right, except for worrying about you and the kids. But we'll trust God to make everything come right and bring me home quite soon. All my love to you and the kids, your loving husband, Erich."

Both letters were several lines longer than the regulations permitted. But in view of the battalion's future assignment they were allowed to go through.

6

It was obvious something special was going on. Obermeier's company was taken off work and stayed in camp. Also Captain Barth was given a new adjutant.

At first he had gazed blankly at the notification sent to him by the commander of the penal units. "A new addition to our ranks," he told Obermeier and Wernher. "A lieutenant, Heinz Bevern, from Osnabruck. An exemplary character by the sound of him. Hitler Youth leader, passed out of training school with distinction, special merit marks in politics. War service first class, Iron Cross second class. He's arriving today."

"Just what we need here," sighed Wernher. "What we've been looking for all this time."

"He may be a good lad all the same." Barth put the notification in a folder. "Let's wait and see. Anyhow I get an adjutant. Quite a step up, eh? Taking the burden off my shoulders and maintaining contact with the troops. The only thing is, I'm afraid he'll soon be superfluous."

"What do you mean, sir?" asked Wernher.

Barth grinned. "Who will he have to maintain contact with when we've been three or four weeks in Russia?"

"You always look on the black side, sir. May I go now?"

"Is the horse saddled?" Barth asked slyly.

"It has been for an hour."

"Enjoy yourself. Will you stay here and give me moral support, Obermeier?"

Bevern came driving up in a fine old car which had once

belonged to a big land-owner. As he stepped out of it and walked springily to the battalion office, gasps came from the faces peering behind the rows of windows in the huts. Flashing boots, smartly fitting uniform, cap at the right tilt, light grey deerskin gloves, a pistol in its own light brown holster. The very model of an officer. A military tailor's dummy: how the correctly dressed officer should look in service dress.

Barth lit a cigarette. What am I going to do with this dressed-up ape, he thought in horror. He'll be paring his nails while we trudge through the Russian mud.

But Bevern belied his appearance. In fact, when the introductions were over and they were sniffing each other out over a glass of wine, he at once took the offensive. "When I drove into camp," he said, after a quick gulp from his glass, "there was a character with a broom on his hand lolling around near the gate. Is that a Russian, I thought at first. No, gentlemen, it was a German soldier. I stopped and gave him a sharper look, but the degenerate swine still didn't salute. And then—he pushed his finger in his nose and poke it round. Disgraceful. I asked him what his name was. And what do you think he said?"

"What did he say?" asked Barth.

"He said: eh?"

"Said what?"

"He said: eh? Incredible."

"And what *was* his name?" said Obermeier.

Bevern unbuttoned his tunic pocket, took out a piece of paper, buttoned up the pocket again, and read out: "Karl Schwanecke, B. Company. It wasn't so easy to get it out of him. The follow's stone deaf."

"What do you say he is?" Barth could scarcely keep a broad grin from his face.

"Stone deaf."

"He's got better hearing than you or I," said Barth with relish.

Bevern looked very disconcerted. "He's not deaf at all?"

Barth shook his head. "Not on your life. What's more, he's a specialist in house-breaking, petty larceny and rape. He used to be a corporal, though, and showed plenty of guts."

"I'll deal with him tomorrow," said Bevern, his face flushed with anger.

"I hope you'll manage it," said Barth, puffing a blue cloud of smoke towards the ceiling.

"Why shouldn't I?"

"Have you ever served in a—in such a unit?"

Bevern stiffened his back. "Till now, sir, I have been given different assignments."

"Then you will have to change your ideas, my friend. In your own interest. This is not an ordinary unit, it's a penal battalion. You have got men like Schwanecke here, men who recognise no authority except that of their own impulses and desires. No authority, remember: least of all, that of military rank. Then you have people who bow to another authority, that of their ideas, who are opposed both to your—er, I should say, our—ideas and to the criminal instincts of people like Schwanecke. Your authority, Bevern, can't scare that sort of man any more than it can scare Schwanecke and his like. Then there's a third group, people who don't know themselves how they landed here. They are probably in the majority. They include all possible variations, from completely spineless individuals, whipped dogs, who will read your every wish from your eyes—to the ones who beat their heads against a wall rather than submit."

"And are *we* to submit to *them*?" Bevern demanded indignantly.

"I said: change your ideas," Barth answered. "Look at our Lieutenant Obermeier here. His father was an officer, so were his grandfather and his great-grandfather. And he's an old front-line warrior, German Cross in gold, mentioned in dispatches et cetera, et cetera. When he came here, he thought nothing could shake him. After a week he really felt cut down to size. Now he's begun to get his bearings again."

"Anyhow, I'll have this—this Schwanecke's guts for bloody garters when I get him on the square. Just as a deterrent, you know."

"What picturesque language," observed Obermeier suavely. "Did you get it from the latest manual of army slang as written by our Sergeant Major Krull and published for the use of all N.C.O's?"

Barth chuckled, and Bevern did not answer. What a slack, sloppy crew, he thought grimly. Surrender to these swine who were only saved from the gallows out of pity? Change his ideas? Absurd. he looked out of the window. B Company were exercising, hollow-eyed figures with sullen faces and dirt-encrusted uniforms. He looked quickly away again, disgusted. Shoot 'em all, he thought, that would be the best solution.

7

That evening, while Obermeier was in town at a cinema, and Wernher was with his lady friend wondering whether to have some more to eat or go straight to bed, and Barth was sitting by the radio listening to Beethoven—Lieutenant Bevern went round the huts, introducing himself to the battalion in his own way.

First he met with Sergeant Major Krull, who was returning from an inspection. Krull had chased Deutschmann into the latrine again, because it was not yet clean enough for his liking.

While Deutschmann crawled round with bucket and cloths, Krull had stood for a while, hands behind his back, watching the private at work and giving a periodical contemptuous snort. "I'll be back in half an hour," he announced eventually, "and if by then it doesn't look like an operating theatre in here, you'll be washing the whole floor with your face— get the message?"

Fresh from this exercise of supreme power, he met Bevern and produced his smartest salute.

"What's your name, Sergeant Major?" asked Bevern casually.

"Krull, sir."

"Ah, so you're Sergeant Major Krull," said Bevern in surprise.

"Yessir." Krull beamed. His fame had evidently gone before him. He would have been less happy had he known that Bevern was deciding at that moment to have his revenge for Obermeier's crack.

"How much do you weigh, Sergeant Major?" asked Bevern.

Krull looked up at the night sky. The man's nuts, he thought. "I don't know, sir."

"You weigh fourteen stone, Sergeant Major."

"I—don't think as much as that."

"How much do you weigh?"

"Fourteen stone, sir."

"Too much, don't you think, Sergeant Major?"

"Yessir."

"At least two stone too much."

"Yessir."

"You must take it off, Sergeant Major."

"Yessir." And that'll be the end of these stupid questions, thought Krull; but the new lieutenant showed no sign of being willing to let him go.

"Let's start straight away, Sergeant Major," said Bevern, and then raised his voice to cutting sharpness. "About—turn. Double march. One, two, one two."

Krull began trotting with scarlet face and mouth wide open. He hadn't run for five years. His shirt stuck to his sweating body. He didn't understand the world any more. It was incredible. Till today, till this moment, he had thought he stood with the officers on the same side of the fence. And now this dressed-up monkey was putting him on the other side. He gasped. And Bevern's cutting voice kept hammering into his baffled brain: "Faster, Sergeant Major, faster than that. It'll make you fit, get you in proper training, one two, one two...."

Then it was over, and Krull, duly dismissed, staggered off to rest. But for Bevern it was only the beginning. I'll have them all, he thought grimly, the whole bloody lot of them. All those miserable privates. *And* the N.C.O.'s. *And* the damned officers.

In Hut 2 of B Company Bevern saw something which at first left him speechless, as it had done two evenings before with Krull: he discovered Schwanecke's picture collection.

Schwanecke was in fact just decorating his bedhead and

the wooden frame beside it with similar pictures of naked girls.

Lieutenant Bevern came closer. "Aha, it's you again," he said loudly when he was standing behind Schwanecke. The decorator turned round, grinning. "Oh, sir, you shouldn't make me jump like that … Aren't they lovely!"

"You …" Bevern began, but Schwanecke went on unperturbed. "Do you like 'em, sir? The blondie there—she's from Berlin. Smashing, eh? If you like …"—he bent forward and spoke confidentally to Bevern, who started back: "If you like, sir, I'll give you her address, 'case you ever go to Berlin—well, any man can learn a whole heap from her."

Bevern choked. He let the air out of his nose with a hissing noise, and felt round inside his collar with his forefinger.

"Anything wrong, sir?" Schwanecke asked solicitously.

Bevern chased him over the barrack square for half an hour until he was tired and hoarse, but Schwanecke was still grinning; the only sign of his exertions was a little sweat. "You can do that almost as well as my sergeant could when I was a recruit," he said when stood to attention in front of Bevern. "About the address. …"

"Shut your mouth!" roared Bevern.

After another fifty knees-bends Schwanecke was dismissed. His knees were trembling, but he grinned and seemed unperturbed. Inside, however, he had it in for Bevern and, just as much as Bevern had it in for him.

8

Deutshmann was finished with latrine duties and everything else. Till now he had managed to see the absurdity of Krull and the other N.C.O.'s with their bawling and bullying; and this sense of the ridiculous somehow kept him going. But he was physically weakened by the "self-inflicted" illness, followed by the arrest, trial and constant new humiliations. Now he was too exhausted, hopeless, drained, to see the funny side any more. Nor did he even feel anger or bitterness at the moment, only how weak he was and how tired.

After clearing away bucket, cloths and broom and having a good wash, he staggered back to the hut, wanting only to smoke a cigarette and then go to sleep. To sleep for days without moving. His left arm, which he had infected, hurt intolerably. Big scabs had now formed on it, and it had become emaciated to the bone. It would never be quite healthy again.

The weak, naked light bulb spread a dull diffused light. At the long, roughly made table in the middle, some soldiers were playing cards, but most men were already lying on their beds. At one end of the table von Bartlitz, the tall ex-colonel, sat staring at his bandaged hand. A former staff major gloomily worked away with a broom; he was room orderly.

Deutschmann went to his locker and got his cigarette case out of the far corner. It was of black leather, mounted in silver, with his monogram in the bottom corner, a present from Julia. He sat down at the table, opened the case and let it lie in front of him.

"Did Krull make you crawl, eh?" asked one of the card-players, a small thin man called Katzorki commonly known as Ratface; when he laughed, he showed sharp yellow teeth. He had once been a truck-driver in Berlin and a petty thief. It was because he couldn't keep his fingers off things that he had come into the penal battalion.

Too tired to speak, Deutschmann merely nodded in answer. He was too tired even to lift his hand, take out of the case one of the two cigarettes he had saved up for this evening, and light it.

Just then Schwanecke lumbered into the room. "To hell with him," he said, after closing the door behind him. "He thought he could knock the shit out of me, but he's wrong."

"Where is he now?" asked one of the card-players.

"He's tired. Gone to bed. The bastard. But nobody's going to do me down, and especially not him, you bet your life."

"Are you playing?" asked Ratface.

"In a moment." Now Schwanecke noticed Deutschmann slumped in his chair. "What's up with you?"

Deutschmann did not move. Schwanecke walked round the table and stood at his side. "What's up?" he asked again. "Was someone cross with you, Professor?"

Deutschmann raised his hand and groped for the cigarette in the case. Suddenly he saw Schwanecke's big hairy hand, with its broad fingers and short dirty nails, reach for the case and pull it away. He looked up.

Schwanecke turned the case up and down, examined it closely, nodded two or three times, raised it to his nose, sniffed it, and got out a cigarette.

"Please give me the case," said Deutschmann faintly.

"Quite pretty," said Schwanecke, lighting the cigarette. "What will you take for it?"

"Give me back the case."

"I'll give you two of my pictures. You can choose 'em yourself."

Deutschmann heaved himself up and reached for the case. Schwanecke took a step back, stuck the case in his tunic pocket, buttoned up the pocket, stuck the smoking cigarette in the corner of his mouth, and screwed up his eyes at the smoke. "I'll keep it," he said, grinning, "till you've decided what you'll take for it. Three pictures. O.K.?"

That seemed to end the matter for him. He turned round and went over to the four card-players. Deutschmann supported himself on the table, closed his eyes for a moment, tore them open again, and called out desperately, bewildered by what had happened: "Give me back the case!"

Von Bartlitz looked up.

"Whose deal?" asked Schwanecke.

"Werner's … Sit here," said Ratface.

Schwanecke pulled a stool out from under the table and was sitting down, when he felt himself gripped by the shoulder and spun round. Erich Wiedeck had come up silently in his bare feet and now stood before him. Wiedeck's face was flushed. "Give him back the case, you swine," he said.

Schwanecke's grin widened. "Steady now, keep your hands off like a good boy."

Deutschmann got up from the table, took two long steps and caught Schwanecke by the arm. Schwanecke made a slight movement of his hand, like someone swishing away a fly, and Deutschmann fell backwards over a stool, hit his head against a locker, and lay on the floor half stunned.

"You bastard!" hissed Wiedeck, catching hold of Schwanecke's tunic. Schwanecke gave him a quick chop in the stomach, which made him groan and double up like a pocket-knife, then came at him from below with a terrific upper-cut to the chin, lifting him again, so that he too went backwards, crashing against a locker door, and slid slowly to the ground. Schwanecke kept the lighted cigarette in the corner of his mouth, and all the while his grin remained, showing the bared white teeth.

"Vumm—smashing!" cried Ratface, licking his lips with relish.

"Anyone else?" growled Schwanecke. He stood slightly leaning forward, eyes still screwed up from the cigarette smoke, his thick muscular body radiating concentrated energy, suppleness and power. "Anyone else?" he repeated.

"Come and get it, somebody," said one of the card-players.

Von Bartlitz slowly got to his feet and walked in silence

round the table. He stopped two steps from Schwanecke and drew himself up. Wiedeck turned on to his stomach with a groan, tried to struggle to his feet, collapsed again and stayed lying on his face.

"What do *you* want?" said Schwanecke.

"Give him the case back at once," said von Bartlitz.

"Is that it?" said Schwanecke. "You think you're still someone who can give us orders, do you, shorty? Don't you understand yet that you've come down in the world, that you're the same sort of scum of the earth as me?"

Von Bartlitz had listened impassively. When Schwanecke turned round again, he repeated, raising his voice: "Give the case back at once, and apologise to Deutschmann and Wiedeck. Did you hear me?"

Schwanecke whipped round, pulled the cigarette from his mouth and slung it furiously to the ground. "Shut your trap," he cried, "you make me retch, you puffed-up Von. You still think you're the masters, don't you?" He brought a hate-filled face close to von Bartlitz, and spoke quietly now. "Listen, I've always had to knuckle under to people like you. Yessir, yes, Herr von Thingummy, of course, Herr Whatsit, right away, Herr von Whosit. I could squash you with one hand, and I will too." He got hold of von Bartlitz's tunic with an iron grip, raised his other hand ready to strike, and the grin had disappeared from his face. "I'll do it if you don't at once say, Yessir, Yes, Herr Schwanecke. Did you hear me" Yes, Herr Schwanecke ..."

"Let me go," said von Bartlitz hoarsely.

"Yes, Herr Schwanecke," hissed Schwanecke. "I'll give it to you now, if you don't beg my pardon at once and say, Herr Schwanecke."

Deathly silence reigned in the room. It was obvious that Schwanecke meant to carry out his threat. The tall pale man who had till lately been a colonel personified for Schwanecke all the hated power in society which had condemned him from boyhood to mean streets and squalid poverty. He had never yet found a chance to vent his hatred on the wealthy respectable citizens or even, during the war, on the officers and N.C.O.'s who could order him about to their heart's content. Admittedly he made as much trouble for them as possible, but he couldn't take it out of them properly. And now here was one of *them* he *could* take it out of. He could batter that upper-crust face to a pulp and show him and all the others like him who was master in this hut. "I'll count to four," he said. "One...."

"That'll do for now, my lad," came a soft, placid voice from the corner. A young, rather thin, fair-haired soldier walked slowly up to the table, his bare feet padding on the floor.

"Two ... three ..." Schwanecke counted.

"Turn round," said the young soldier in a louder voice.

Schwanecke seemed to hear him for the first time. He turned his head slightly, assessed the new adversary with a quick glance, then turned back to von Bartlitz. His raised hand was clenched tighter.

"Here I come," cried the young soldier, vaulting over the table, and pulled the surprised Schwanecke away from his victim.

"Lay him out, Karl," Ratface squealed eagerly, jumping up; and it seemed as if he and the other card-players might have joined in the fight. But they didn't have time. What followed happened so fast that afterwards no one could describe how the rather slight-looking youngster dealt with Schwanecke. Two bodies whirled across the room, overturning the table; Schwanecke could be heard grunting furiously, gasping for breath; and suddenly there was a shrill agonised scream. Then Schwanecke was on the floor, with the young soldier on top of him.

The winner detached himself, stood for a moment bent over the prone figure, straightened up, and passed a hand through his short hair. "Right," he said.

Schwanecke lay on his back and gazed up at the ceiling. Tears of pain filled his eyes and trickled over his face. He opened his mouth, then snapped it shut again. A long-drawn-out jaw-grinding sound broke the silence. "What ... what is it ...?" he stammered.

"My God, what have you done to him?" asked von Bartlitz.

"Nothing special. It won't hurt him long. A little ju-jitsu. In half an hour he'll be back to normal.... Get up!" he said to Schwanecke.

Schwanecke first looked at him blankly. Then life came back into his eyes, recognition—and fear. With a groan he bent forward. Crouched for a few moments on his hands and knees, he shook his head, and then, leaning on an overturned stool, struggled to his feet. Painfully bent, with arms hanging loose, he stood in front of his adversary, still dazed by the lightning attack.

"Now give the case back," said the young soldier quietly.

Slowly and heavily, as if he had a burden to carry far above his strength, Schwanecke dragged himself across the room and gave Deutschmann the cigarette case back.

"The cigarette too," said the soldier.

Schwanecke took one cigarette from his coat pocket and held it out. Deutschmann hesitated.

"Take it," said the soldier.

Deutschmann took it.

"Now say you're sorry," said Schwanecke.

"Righto. I'm sorry," said Schwanecke.

"Thank you, young man," said von Bartlitz. "That was just in time."

The soldier turned slowly towards him and gave the former colonel a long look. "You don't have to thank me," he said, his quiet voice now trembling slightly. "I didn't do it for *you.* If you'd been the only person concerned, I wouldn't have lifted a finger, you—officer. You are yourself to blame if you sit here and get beaten up by people like that." He pointed with his head towards Schwanecke, who had sunk on to a stool. "You yourselves helped to set up the people who sent you here, because you wouldn't do anything against them while there was still time. More than that, you actually supported them—you officers!" His voice was now icy with scorn. Von Bartlitz looked stupefied. The young soldier took a quick step towards him, bent forward and said: "Do you know why *I* am here" Because I dealt with a bastard of an officer just like I did with Schwanecke. Only he deserved it a dam' sight more. I only wanted to teach Schwanecke that I've no desire to be tyrannised over by bullyboy privates any more than officers and N.C.O.'s. *He* can be taught that way, you lot can't. You'll never learn." He brushed von Bartlitz aside, and stopped by Schwanecke. "How do you feel?" he asked in a gentle, friendly voice.

"Boy!" Schwanecke looked up with deep respect in his eyes. "How did you do that? You must teach me. No one's ever dealt with me like that before."

9

Behind Hut 2, which housed Platoons 1 and 2 of B Company, stood a crate. In the crate was a rabbit.

Sergeant Major Krull didn't notice the crate when he first passed, though really a crate had no business to be there. He was too busy thinking about the problem of Lieutenant Bevern and the prescribed slimming course. Then he did a double-take, and swing round as if stung by a hornet.

It was certainly a crate, and in it crouched a live, well-fed rabbit. "Who does this creature belong to?" he yelled.

The soldiers had finished their cleaning duties and werc standing round in the last rays of the pale autumn sun. Krull caught sight of Deutschmann. "You, Deutschmann, who does this creature belong to?"

"I don't know, sir," Deutschmann yelled back. He had learnt that in the army loudness of voice was essential—the louder the better. The more you shouted, the more you were valued by your superiors.

"Belongs to me, sir," said Schwanecke, taking two paces forward.

"Oh," said Krull.

"Yes, sir. I am an animal-lover, sir." He beamed at Krull. "I just can't live without a nice pet of some sort."

"Where does it come from?" Krull bent over the crate and looked at the rabbit, which ran away from the turnip it was nibbling and shrank into the back of the crate.

"It's a stray," said Schwancke.

Krull turned away and marched off. Outside the office he

met Obermeier, who was just about to leave the camp and only half listened to the Sergeant Major, standing stiffly to attention and reporting to him the astonishing phenomenon.

"Enjoy life in the barracks as much as you can," he told Krull, slapping him on the shoulder. "You won't have much chance once we get to Russia."

With that he left Krull on the wide square, pondering on the significance of the last remark. Krull was extremely frightened of the word "Russia". But he had the faculty of pushing out of his mind anything unpleasant to contemplate; so he returned to the immediate problem of Schwanecke and the rabbit. He rushed back to the hut.

"You pinched it," he said to Schwancke.

"Oh no, Sarge, it's a stray."

"And the crate's a stray too, is it? And the turnip? They all came sailing through the air—just like that?"

"Yes, sir."

Krull breathed in very deeply, till he looked as if he would burst. "Round the square, quick—march," he yelled. "At the double. Faster, Faster."

Schwanecke doubled away, grinning.

"And again!" cried Krull, when Schwanecke arrived back. Schwanecke trotted off once more, and eventually stopped in front of Krull, panting.

"You pinched it."

"I never, sir. It's a stray."

Krull was ready to give up. He turned away mutely and almost tripped over Lieutenant Bevern, who had come up unnoticed and observed the scene in silence. Krull wanted to make a report, but Bevern waved him aside. Slowly, whipping one boot with a thin cane, the adjutant walked up to Schwanecke.

"So you're an expert on rabbits?" he asked in an affable voice.

"Specially buck rabbits, sir."

Bevern raised his eyebrows. "Buck rabbits?"

"Yes, sir. They've taught me responsibility, you see.

"Responsibility. What do you mean?"

"Well, when this rabbit ran up to me, I wondered whether

to let it go free. Then I decided it wouldn't be right. You must never do that, must you, sir?"

"Do what?"

"Pass the buck, sir."

There was a sound of muffled laughter. "Silence!" roared Bevern, beside himself with rage. He made Schwanecke lie on his stomach and crawl round like a worm, through the dust, through the kitchen refuse, through some pools from A Company's blocked and overflowing latrine.

After he had crossed the square on his face like this for the third time, Captain Barth opened the window of his room and called out: "Stop that."

Bevern walked jauntly to the officers' hut, leaving Schwanecke on the ground.

"What do you think you're doing?" Barth demanded when Bevern came in.

"Schwanecke tried to make a fool of me. I thought I would teach him to take a worm's eye view."

"Rubbish."

Bevern stiffened.

"And you think that's the way to win the war?" Barth made a gesture signifying 'Go, clear off, get out of here.' Bevern understood and turned to go. But before he had gripped thc handle of the door, Barth's voice stopped him. "If I were you, I wouldn't make an enemy of that man. We're going to Russia. Now get the hell out of here."

Meanwhile Schwanecke stood up, swaying. His face was mud-encrusted, distorted, frightening to look at. Gasping, he leaned against the hut wall.

Deutschmann ran off and fetched a mess-tin full of water. Then he unbuttoned Schwanecke's shirt. Schwanecke looked at him with blank, uncomprehending eyes. He drank half the water and shook the rest over his head. "Bloody Bevern!" he muttered, in a choked, unnatural voice, and Deutschmann thought: I wouldn't be in Bevern's shoes after this. "Like any more water?" he asked Schwanecke.

"No, thanks, mate. That was fine. Like a cigarette?"

At that moment the quiet, couscientions Ernst Deutschmann admired the old lag, Karl Schwanecke. And the two men, doctor and social outlaw, were drawn towards each other in an attraction all the stronger from the sense that both of them, and all the rest of the men with them, had one common enemy.

Obermeier was not at all pleased when he heard what had happened. "May I point out," he said to Bevern, "that I am in command of B Company and not you. You have no authority over the troops, you are simply here as adjutant."

"But that convict ..." Bevern began. Obermeier cut him short. "Quite apart from the fact that he is in my Company, the way you treated him was a disgrace."

"Are you lecturing me on my duties and how I carry them out?" Bevern went over to the offensive. "Your Company, comrade, is a shower."

"I shall report you to the C.O. for that," said Obermeier coldly. "What's more, I refuse to be called 'comrade' by the likes of you. There is no comradeship between us, and if this were peace-time, I should be delighted to punch your stupid face."

"Lieutenant Obermeier!" Bevern went pale, With a swift movement of his arm Obermeier brushed him aside, and walked off.

Bevern went straight to his room, took out of the cupboard a thin folder with lists inside it, and made a cross against the name of Lieutenant Fritz Obermeir. I'll show you, he thought, I'll show you, you can't do that to me.

Lieutenant Bevern was in Penal Battalion 999 for a definite purpose: it was his job to report everything that happened in the unit, with special reference to the political reliability of officers and N.C.O.'s.

Krull that evening sat in his room getting drunk. He had heard that the battalion would be on the move in two days—to Russia; and that was the best possible reason for getting drunk.

Men may drink fast or slow, in small sips or big gulps. Krull was exceptional. Whether it was beer, spirits, or wine, he would put the glass or mug to his lips and down it at a single draught, without any sign of swallowing or any movement of his larynx. "Like a sponge," said Sergeant Hefe, half admiring, half envious. "He really can soak it up, it's a wonder it doesn't all run out of him at once the other end."

In the German army there are a whole lot of regulations against excessive drinking. But however much Krull lived by regulations otherwise, he did not heed the ones about drink, especially when he was angry.

This evening he was both angry and frightened. Angry with Schwanecke, with Bevern, with Obermeier, with all the men in his company and all the other companies all over the world and with the whole lousy world. He was scared of the very word Russia and very frightened of what might happen to him there. It was not only that the Russians would be shooting at him and might hit him. Even a penal battalion might have arms, and what could be simpler than for a bloke like Schwanecke to hit him instead of an advancing Russian? It was a terrifying prospect. They're all scum, he thought, they ought to be put against the nearest wall and bang, bang, bang, then we'd get some peace.

Krull went on drinking, gazing out glassily at the big dark square. He had no friends, no girl at home, only his fury and his fear, his voice and his authority, and a lot of soldiers under him who hated him. It was not enough for a man, Krull felt; so he went on boozing until he passed out.

The next morning on parade the men were told the battalion would be moving in two days. "Bet you it's Russia," Schwanecke said afterwards. "I can feel it in my bones."

"What would we do there?" said Wiedeck.

"You can just imagine," said Schwanecke, grinning.

"Russia," murmured Deutschmann, "Russia."

"Bastard of a country," said Ratface.

"Don't you worry, Professor." Schwanecke bent forward and gave Deutschmann a nudge in the ribs. "It won't be half as bad there. And I tell you"—now he whispered—"there's a heap of opportunities for the likes of us. Stick close to me."

"What do you mean by that?" asked von Bartlitz, who had heard him. Schwanecke ignored the question. "You'll see, professor. I'm an old front-line rat, I know my onions. There are a heap of opportunities. You'll be amazed how we'll manage, or my name's not Karl Schwanceke. Or do you think I'm longing to die a hero's death for Führer, compatriots and fatherland?"

10

Julia Deutschmann worked fast and feverishly, but with all necessary care. She forced herself to keep all her thoughts on her task: this was the only way in which she would be able to repeat Ernst's months of work in the shortest possible time. She worked at night and slept by day, till eventually there were no longer nights and days for her: she worked till her mind wandered from sheer weariness and her head sank on to the flap of the desk. She ate hastily, when the feeling of hunger became too strong to resist.

One evening while she was chewing her vile-tasting bread and margarine and drinking weak peppermint tea, the alert sounded, followed a few minutes later by the sirens announcing the raid itself.

She sat alone in the cellar of their house, amidst an inferno of exploding bombs, anti-aircraft fire and shaking walls, with dry dust-filled air which choked her and made her cough. But even now she remained calm, as if she had received assurance from someone or something stronger than the bombs, that nothing would happen to her.

Nothing did. Some houses quite close were destroyed, and the reflections of nearby fires brought a reddish glow into the rooms. She closed the window and pulled down the black-out curtains. Some panes were shattered.

While she was sweeping up the broken glass, the telephone rang. It was Dr. Kukill. "I wanted to ask whether everything was all right with you," he asked. His voice sounded breathless, abrupt, rather unsure.

"Why do you want to know that?" Julia asked. She noted with surprise that the voice was almost soothing to her. It was simply a human voice speaking to her in this eerie silence punctuated by distant thuds and bangs. No matter who the voice belonged to. It was only gradually she realised that the man who was speaking to her was the one who had destroyed her happiness, whose fault it was that she had been thrown into this nightmarish, hopeless state.

"After that raid—well, I'm glad nothing happened to you, Doctor." Now he resumed his light, chatty tone. The most astonishing thing about that, was that he found it so easy to use it with *her* as well, as if he were talking to an old friend.

"I'm all right, only a few windows broken."

"That's not too serious. I'll send someone tomorrow to put new panes in. But I do think it would be better if you went to a safe air-raid shelter when there's an alert."

"I'm all right here."

"May I come and see how you are tomorrow?"

"There would be no point."

"May I?"

"Please don't. I'm very busy."

"What are you busy on? You're not . . . ?"

"Yes, I am. I told you I was going to, didn't I?"

"Now please, please don't do anything silly, anything rash. You know how dangerous it is. How can I stop you?"

"It's quite useless your trying to stop me." Julia could not help smiling a little to herself. This conversation was unreal and absurd, but somehow rather amusing. The man she could only think of with hatred in her heart, the man whose judgement was responsible for Ernst going into the penal battalion, was pleading with her to be careful, to stop her work, and only to—why *was* he doing it, come to that? Might it be . . . ?

Disregarding the agitated voice still speaking to her, she hung up, and went back to the lab. Luckily the windows here had remained intact. She lit a candle and sat down at the desk. There was a long night's work ahead, and after the raid she hoped it might be a quiet one. But in other districts of Berlin the fires were raging fiercely. . . .

11

Deutschmann was walking at a slow leisurely pace across the barrack square to the cookhouse, where he had been sent to peel potatoes, when suddenly, without any warning, he collapsed. Bright circles and spots began to dance before his eyes; he opened his eyes convulsively, a crippling weakness crept upwards from his legs, and he was wondering in surprise what this meant—when the square in front of him and the huts and trees behind him surged up and buried him beneath them.

He could not have lost consciousness for long. When, in the darkness that surrounded him, the circles and spots began to dance, getting brighter and brighter, and when he opened his eyes in amazement, he saw a puddle quite close in front of him. At the same time he felt wet coldness on his face. He still did not understand. Surprised, but also a bit indifferent, he wondered where he was and how he had landed here. How did he come to be lying with his cheek in a puddle, and why wasn't he able to get up?

He tried to pull his legs up, but in vain; a long shudder ran over his body.

Then he heard heavy steps approaching fast.

Erich Wiedeck bent over the motionless Deutschmann. "Ernst!" he said, shocked. "What's the matter?" He turned his friend over and unbottoned his coat. Deutschmann stared at him from glassy, uncomprehending eyes, and opened his mouth as if trying to say something, but only small babbling sounds came out.

After a moment's hesitation, Wiedeck lifted his friend on to his shoulder, and was astonished that the tall burly man felt so light. He quickly carried him into the part of the camp where the sick-bay was, a little away from the rest of the complex.

It was nothing serious. A simple fainting fit. About noon Deutschmann could stand up again. Still rather weak and shaky on his legs, he walked down the long narrow passage to the toilet. On his way back he saw the door of the sick-bay open, and two soldiers came gasping in, carrying a stretcher. Behind them, like a startled hen, ran Kronenberg, the medical orderly.

Deutschmann pressed himself against the wall to let the group pass. On the stretcher lay a soldier whose face was a frightening purple, his mouth opening wide for air, his hands going constantly over his chest to his neck and down again, his body rearing at short intervals, as if he wanted to get up and run away in his anguish and suffocation.

"And the M.O.'s not here, what do I do, the M.O.'s not here," wailed Kronenberg desperately.

"You're a medic, you should know," panted one of the soldiers whose hands were gripping the stretcher.

Deutschmann came up behind them into the treatment room. Kronenberg, normally a stern watchdog if anyone made an unsolicited entry into 'his' rooms, as he called the sick-bay, did not take any notice of the intruder, but ran around helplessly, not knowing what to do. He could scarcely be blamed: after a crash course in nursing and first aid he had become a medical orderly, and this man, whom the soldiers were now carefully and gingerly laying on the couch, was obviously likely to choke to death from asphyxia or the Lord knew what. At any rate it looked as if he might die any moment.

"Where's the M.O.?" one of the soldiers asked.

"Gone somewhere," said Kronenberg, "I don't know ... "

"Then you'd better look for him."

"Where do I look?"

"What's the trouble with him?" asked Deutschmann, coming up to the patient and bending over him.

"Do you know something about these things?" asked Kronenberg, hope dawning in his eyes.

"A little," said Deutschmann. "What's he got?"

"How should I know?"

"Man, you're supposed to be a medic, aren't you?" said one of the soldiers.

"You did give him an injection before," said the other.

"What sort of an injection?" asked Deutschmann.

"That has nothing to do with it," said Kronenberg. "He got an anti-tetanus injection. Some rusty barbed wire had ..."

"Fetch adrenalin and a syringe," ordered Deutschmann sharply. "And hurry up, or something may really happen."

Now he was again where he belonged, in a room smelling of medicines, disinfectants and sick people, by a couch on which a man was struggling with death. The weakness, uncertainty and clumsiness had fallen off him at a stroke. He was once more as he had been in the years after he had qualified, when he was working in a Berlin clinic, going from one patient to another, fighting for their lives—the clinic where he had got to know and love Julia.

Kronenberg looked at him in wide-eyed astonishment and brought what he ordered: an ampoule of adrenalin a syringe and needles from the gleaming steriliser. Deutschmann pulled up the patient's sleeve and felt for his pulse. It was very faint and irregular; sometimes it stopped for a moment in an alarming way.

"Petrol!" he said.

The two soldiers stood by watching him, the way people through the ages have watched a doctor at work, curious, shy, admiring.

He tied down the patient's upper arm so that the veins at the elbow stood out thick and blue. Then he rubbed the skin over with a wad of petrol-soaked cotton wool and stuck the needle into the vein. "Shock," he said.

"How d'you mean, shock? What ..." Kronenberg began, but Deutschmann, slowly and calmly pressing the fluid into the vein, told him in a quiet, low voice: "Not everyone can take anti-tetanus serum."

"Will he pull through? one soldier asked.

"I think so," said Deutschmann.

Long tense minutes followed. He had done everything there was to do, and now could only wait. Gradually the purple colour left the man's face. He began to breath normally again, and his pulse became regular, although it remained fairly weak.

"It's all right," said Deutschmann at last. "Nothing can happen now."

"How can you do all that so well?" Kronenberg asked him, at once amazed and grateful. He had every reason to be grateful, for it had slowly dawned on him that he would have been to blame for the man's death: he had given a double dose of serum, on the basis that it would be twice as effective.

"I should have some know-how," Deutschmann answered with a smile. "After all, I'm a doctor."

"A doctor?" Kronenberg whistled through his teeth. It was clear from his broad, heavy face that he was cogitating some plan, but he did not say anything. He never said anything before he had thoroughly weighed it up from all angles.

In the evening, when Deutschmann was again lying in bed, Kronenberg came and took him to his little room adjoining the treatment-room. "Listen," he said, after Deutschmann had sat down on the only chair. "I've got an idea. But first of all let's have a drink. Like one?"

Deutschmann nodded.

Kronenberg opened his locker and took a bottle from the very back. Deutschmann's eyes opened wide. French cognac! Kronenberg grinned at him. "From the old man, You know. The M.O. I can twist him round my little finger when I want to."

They drank.

After only a few sips Deutschmann found the world a tiny bit more tolerable, in fact almost agreeable. He forgot the Sergeant Major and the N.C.O.'s, he forgot his illness and weakness and despair, the dark hopeless time he had to go through—he and all the others, he and Julia, he and Kronenberg and Wiedeck and von Bartlitz and Schwanecke and all the rest.... He sat up comfortably on his chair and waited with some excitement to hear Kronenberg's idea.

"Look," Kronenberg began, "I know it's no joke out

there." With his thumb he gestured towards the blacked-out window. "You get my drift?"

Deutschmann nodded.

"I have a suggestion. I need a helper here, you get my idea—another orderly. Then you'll be free of the gang, Krull and the rest, nobody can do anything to you, and we'll have a good time here."

"How will you manage that?" asked Deutschmann, hesitating. The idea seemed absurd, incredible. He, Dr. Ernst Deutschmann, professor at a university medical school—a medical orderly. The scum of the medical corps. When as a doctor he would have been at least a captain after a year—if he hadn't been in a penal battalion. On the other hand, why not? If peoples were needed to carry a piano in the army, the sergeant looked for instrument-players. If the N.C.O.'s wanted to have their huts scrubbed, they chose very good swimmers who wouldn't be afraid of water. And if Kronenberg needed another orderly, why shouldn't he take a doctor?

"You leave that to me!" said Kronenberg with a grand gesture. "I told you, didn't I—the M.O. and I—you get my drift?"

"And—what would I have to do?"

"Oh, well, just empty a few pisspots, stick thermometers in bums and so on. You know about all that, don't you! And afterwards in Russia—God knows. Agreed?"

"Pisspots," said Deutschmann doubtfully.

"You're too good for that, eh? You can go back to the huts then, you're quite fit again. Krull will be waiting for you, I'm sure."

"Can I have some more schnaps?" asked Deutschmann, giving himself a little more time. Pisspots, he thought with a shudder. Thermometers in bums. But he had already decided. "All right, then" he said, after a swing of the brandy. "Let's do it."

Next morning he was already helping Kronenberg with the temperatures and then going with an armful of chamber pots to the sick-bay latrine to empty and rinse them out. And during the morning he saw with some concern that Kronenberg liked talking quite well but was not so fond of work. However, he was pleasant enough, good-natured, didn't bawl: you could get on with him. It was better to be here than being chased across the barrack square by Krull and Co.

In the evening Kronenberg talked to the M.O., Captain Bergen. He thought it best to start with a question about one of the patients. "Is the heart case in Room 3 serious, sir?"

"Why?" Captain Bergen looked up from his notes. He had the pedantic habit of writing a kind of log which no one read and which lay in thick folders in the rolltop desk. "Another attack? Give him myocardon."

"Right, sir. By the way, there is something else, sir."

"Yes? What is it?"

"Private Deutschmann is quite a bright bloke, sir. We need another man for the sick-bay. Someone to give me a bit of a hand. With all the fatigue parties, the sick-bay is so crowded that by muself I ..." He stopped and hastily amended: "That is, I can manage it myself, but it sometimes takes too long in urgent cases. And specially now when we're going to Russia ..." He wisely did not mention that Deutschmann was a doctor.

"I'll talk to the C.O. Which Company is he?"

"B Company, sir."

"Right. Now leave me in peace, Kronenberg." Captain Bergen buried himself in his log, and Jakob Kronenberg left him with a smart about-turn and a flashing salute—but not before seeing that the Captain had noted: Ask For Pte Deutschmann, B Coy, as Medical Orderly.

"You have to know how to handle people," Kronenberg told Deutschmann later. They were sitting at the window, and the medicine man was initiating his apprentice into the secrets of 'stick' and 'twist'. "This Deutschmann comes to us or else I quit, sir I told the M.O." Kronenberg looked at his new assistant to make sure his words were having their effect. Deutschmann dutifully expressed his admiration. "And of course after that he said Yes."

Kronenberg banged the cards down. "Vingt-et-un. Right, your deal."

It was a good evening.

12

Obermeier was studying the marching orders. Wernher, C.O. of A Company, stood at his side.

"First to Warsaw," said Obermeier, spanning his finger over the map, "then on to Bialystok and Baranowicze. Two days' stop there and on to a train. Then to Minsk and Borisov."

"Borisov on the Beresina," mused Wernher. "On 26th November 1812 Napoleon crossed the Beresina. I was always good at history."

"And on 10th November 1943 Penal Battalion 999 crossed it. You can use that one day for your memoirs as a landmark in your life. In the tracks of Napoleon."

"Hope we don't suffer the same fate as he did," said Wernher with a sigh.

Obermeier bent over the map and train timetable again. "From Borisov we go on to Orsha. There we finally detrain."

"Hope we get that far."

"I think we'll do that all right. Apparently there are Bulgarian troops in bunkers to give us security. The trouble will start when we're the other side of Orsha. There are Russians continually slipping through our positions and reinforcing the partisans. Round Gorki, they say, there's a complete battalion of partisans in the woods with all the arms they need. By the way, have you any idea what secret mission we're to be given there?"

"Not a clue. Barth is keeping his mouth tight shut. Actually I doubt whether he knows himself." Wernher straightened up and adjusted his close-fitting elegant tunic: he looked every inch the gallant German officer of tradition. "Put off facing the horror so long as you can," he quoted. "When do we move off?"

"Latest orders, tomorrow morning 07.00 hours." Obermeier smiled. "I'd advise you to ride off to your widow at once. Or have you said goodbye already?"

"Half and half. She's the last woman I'll see for a long time," lamented Wernher. But he stayed and called the roll of A Company. The men regarded this as a final proof that things were growing really serious.

Sergeant Major Krull had B Company on parade at 20.00 hours precisely. He had slung on his 0.08 pistol, the steel helmet was clamped on his broad head, and he wore his own riding breeches, stuck into long, black, gleaming boots. He looked a fine warrior.

The Company stood ready to march: with packed kitbags, rolled blankets and groundsheets. Spades were the only weapon or tool they carried. They had no epaulettes or collar patches. They were a grey mass of men drawn up in three ranks. On the command "Eyes—Left", They jerked their heads to one side.

"B Company, twenty-four N.C.O.'s and one hundred and fifty-seven men present and correct, six men in sick-bay, three men detached." Krull's voice rang loud over the square. Obermeier moved up and inspected his Company.

Von Bartlitz in the front rank was pale, his face calm and impassive as ever. Behind him was the ex-major—what was his name?—a daredevil type who had risen fast to his former rank. Most of the men were experienced old soldiers who had no illusions about where they were going or their chances of survival; only they still kept that remnant of hope which is deep in everyone's heart so long as he lives: perhaps I'll come through.

At the end of the Company, like a rearlight, so to speak, stood Deutschmann, slightly bent forward, with his Red Cross armband and his first-aid kit. A doctor acting as a medical orderly. And when Lieutenant Obermeier thought of it, just before he began his brief address to his Company, the absurdity of the thing shot through his mind: high-ranking veteran officers, who knew more about warfare than the present lot who presumed they could lead armies and win the war, stood here about to go to the front as cannon fodder. Specialists who were in such demand, criminals who belonged to no army in the world. A doctor as a medical orderly, when everyone moaned about the shortage of doctors....

Obermeier pulled himself together. "Men!" he said. "You know you are going to Russia, I need say no more. We shall do our duty at all times wherever we are. We move off tomorrow morning at 07.00 hours. Column three is to move first, and will have the wagons ready on the goods platform by the time the rest of the Company arrives. I need two more men for the kitchen truck. Bartlitz and Vetterling two paces forward—march."

Captain Barth, who had been watching through the office window, stepped back. Wernher was making the same speech to A Company. Elegant and wiry, he stood in front of the three columns and admonished his men in fine commanding voice. That's the stuff, thought Barth. Obermeier thinks too much. What on earth is he at, putting von Bartlitz and Vetterling in the kitchen truck? As if they could stay alive there. Stupid, he thought, dam' stupid.

The first lorries moved off over the parade-ground taking the batallion to the station.

13

Sometimes a whisper would go through the woods near Gorki and Bolshoi Sharipy. It flew from cave to cave, from one buried hut to another. Then, when the night came, shadows would move through the undergrowth like huge armed ants—to the edge of the wood, to the road to Babinitchi, to the river Gorodnia. Lights would flare up in the darkness, all over the place, baneful, strewing death round them, rending the silence of the woods. Human voices would cry out, then die away in groans; shrill commands, searchlights extinguished by shots, shadows dashing through the snow and perishing in the forest as if they had never been. Then more snow would fall, till the flakes covered all sign of the night's affray. The next few days the sun would shine on nothing but small hillocks, from which a hand might be sticking out, or a yellowed face, or a leg in a coarse boot. Or it would show a man crawling slowly and painfully across the snow, dragging his legs behind him, screaming for help.

"There's a new battalion come, Annashka," said Misha Starobin, shaking his fur. "Does the lieutenant know?"

Anna Petrovna Nikitevna crept out of the cave and shovelled snow into a battered saucepan. "Sergei is already in Orsha," she said.

"I hope to God the Germans don't catch him." Misha got up and put on his fur.

"He's living at Tanya's, his sweetheart." Anna laughed.

"The new lot have no numbers." Misha watched Anna hanging the pan over the fire. The snow was slowly melting.

Into the snow-water went a small piece of meat and the wings and breast of a crow. "God protect Sergei; the new lot look bastards."

Anna laughed at his saying "God". When he spoke of God, was he afraid? A big strong man like Misha Starobin. How can he be afraid, she thought, as she stirred the snow. No German will go into the woods of Gorki. Anywhere that wolves live, man is usually safe too.

Through the thicket crawled a short bandy-legged man in a long, ancient sheepskin. His fur cap with the ear-flaps was encrusted with snow. When he saw Misha and Anna, he waved, and worked his way through the knee-high snow to the cave.

"Little brother Piotr! and how's the collective? Occupied by the Germans, eh?" Misha chuckled, held out his hand to the little man and pulled him up.

Piotr Sabayev Tartuchin blinked his small cunning eyes. The yellow skin over the round face was like wrinkled parchment, the nose a button with two holes. His shoulders were surprisingly broad.

"There are Germans running round out there!" He walked towards Anna's pan, overturned it, and with his boot pushed snow on to the fire. The flame went out with a hiss. "The smoke can be seen, you blockheads. Eat your *kapusta* cold."

Anna picked the pan out of the snow and threw it into the cave. "They won't dare come into the wood. Are there many of them?"

"No, but if they see the smoke, they'll know where we're hiding." Piotr wiped his eyes and his yellow face stiff with cold. "The lieutenant says there's a meeting tonight."

"Blast you!" said Misha, thinking of the lost meal, and then: "Tonight, eh?"

"We have to capture a man from the new lot. They have no numbers, not even epaulettes. Perhaps it's a special detachment to catch *us*."

"Rubbish. Who's going to catch *us*?"

"They've come fresh from Germany, young and old. Sergei says they're a strange collection. They hardly have any arms."

"And yet they hope to catch *us*?" Misha laughed scornfully.

"They've probably got secret weapons, you donkey!" Those will come on afterwards, Sergie says." Tartuchin blew into his hands, then thrust his fur collar higher against his face. "Where are the others?"

"Where do you think?" Misha described a circle in the air. "In the wood, of course. You'll find them, little brother."

Cursing, Tartuchin stamped on through the snow and vanished again in the thicket.

"Tonight, Annashaka," said Misha quietly, as if afraid his voice might disturb the deep silence, "If we're lucky, we'll get some tinned meat and rusks."

14

At Orsha, Lieutenant Sergei Petrovich Denkov sat at the stove glancing through the papers Tanya had given him. Of medium height, slim, brown as a Caucasian, he wore the threadbare and much patched clothes of a poor peasant on a collective farm who had let the Germans take him over and now eked out a meagre living. Tanya Sossnovskaya, at his side, looked like a picture by a traditional icon-painter. Her gleaming black hair lay close to her head, her slightly protruding cheek-bones gave the narrow face with its big eyes an oriental magic and mystery. She wore a woollen blouse, tightly stretched over the round breasts, and thick, quilted trousers thrust into Russian leather boots.

Sergei had been looking at her for some while. "You're beautiful, Tanuschka."

"Read the papers, Seryoshka." She blew into the fire of the stove and listened to the hum of the water in the kettle."I'll make some good strong tea." She looked up from the fire, her face flushed by the flames. "When do you have to leave?"

"In two hours." Sergei put his narrow hands on to the papers. "Where did you get them?"

"From their HQ. I was engaged as charwoman. A sergeant took me to his room, then went off to fetch wine and spirits. He was gone a long time—and I copied the papers and hid them here." She pointed to her bust and smiled. "I'd left before he came back. Are the papers valuable?"

"I don't know yet. The new troops are called 999. But why don't they wear epaulettes with numbers like the rest? They don't have any epaulettes at all. Strange." He rose and went over to Tanya. "You must find that out, my girl, but without your sergeant!"

"Are you staying here tonight, Seryoshka?" She asked softly.

"I can't. They're waiting for me in the wood."

An hour more, and he would be going through the German supply bases, a poor, ragged peasant plodding through the snow to his hut somewhere in the vast expanses. The German sentry on the Dnieper, at the wooden bridge he had to cross, would stop him. "Where are you going, scum?" And he would humbly say "Damoi, little brother, damoi." Going home. The sentry would nod and let him cross the bridge—as usual. He was just a simple peasant in an old sheepskin coat with a high fur cap. Behind Orsha there was a sledge. Fedya would be waiting there with two horses. They would fly over the snowfields like ghosts, past Babinitchi, circling round Gorki. The land was wide, and the Germans couldn't be everywhere. Then came the wood, the dark well which stretched from horizon to horizon. "The wolves' home" the peasants of Gorki and Bolshoi Sharipy called it. Now it was inhabited by men—Stalin's wolves, the Second Company of Partisans under Lieutenant Denkov.

Tanya moved, and he came out of his reverie. "Tea," she said quietly. She poured out a jug-ful. The samovar stood in the corner, it would have taken too long to get it going. Tanya sat at his side and watched him drinking the hot greenish tea from a saucer.

"They want to have me as interpreter because I know a little German," she said. "Shall I, Seryoshka?"

Sergei nodded several times. "Of course. You'll learn all the more."

"Will you come oftener then?"

"Perhaps." He looked into her big dark eyes. Her narrow face floated in the dusk of the room. "You're beautiful," he said. "You'll have to be on your guard with them."

"I hate them, Seryoshka."

"But they don't hate you."

"They'll never get that far, never!"

She looked at the stove. Sergei followed her eyes. Behind

the fireplace, in a recess of the wall, lay a loaded and unlocked Russian army pistol.

"Within six months we'll have won back Vitebsk and Orsha," said Sergei. His voice was hoarse with excitement. "Then we'll get married Tanyushka. Only six months more. We'll hold out."

She nodded bravely, wiped her big eyes, and smiled at him. "Are you going now?"

"Yes." He kissed her. Her lips were cold.

"God protect you!" she whispered.

He left the house quickly and ran across the yard in the darkness. God, he thought, where does she get God from? He was a Bolshevik, he did not have any god and did not want to have any. His god was the Party, it was Russia, and an infinite hatred for the German invaders.

15

Captain Barth reported to the Garrison Commander at Orsha. The old Major, a reservist, who obviously felt quite out of his element in the Russian solitudes, regarded the papers which Barth had presented to him. With watery eyes he looked over his spectacles. "999. What regiment, what division?"

"Battalion 999 is an independent penal battalion, sir."

"Penal battalion?"

"Yes, sir."

"Hm." The Major inspected Barth suspiciously from head to foot. Bet he used to be in the cavalry, thought Barth. That's the way you look at a horse that's going lame. Can't blame him. He must see me as a superior concentration camp overseer.

"You are in command?"

"Yes, sir. My battalion has come to Orsha to hold the line."

"To hold the line. Of course." The Major again looked critically at Barth. "You are responsible to me. Or have you special orders?"

"We have, sir. My battalion is to be engaged within the framework of the defence with special responsibilities for duties outside the scope of other units," Barth said with a note of irony in his voice.

"I understand." The old Major did not try to hide his almost physical discomfort at this conversation. He looked at Barth's ribbons and thrust his lower lip forward. "You've already been at the front?"

"From the beginning. Poland, France, and the advance into Russia till 1943. I was with the tank spearhead which saw the towers of Moscow."

"And now 999?"

"Yes, sir. I volunteered."

"You volunteered?" The Major fussed about putting the papers in a folder, as if trying to hide his surprise and bafflement. "I'd be glad to have a talk to you one evening soon, Captain. Over a glass of schnaps."

"Many thanks, Major." Barth smiled slightly. The bait was fixed, and the old boy had nibbled at it.

While Barth was reporting to the Major, Deutschmann sat in his billet, a ruined farm-house, and wrote to Julia. The small room was sparsely lit by two candles; their two weak, flickering lights threatened to go out whenever anyone came through the door and the draught blew icily through the room. Big shadows, now blurred, now sharply outlined, danced on the smoke-blackened walls and flitted over the paper as Deutschmann wrote:

"My own darling Julia,

You won't have got a letter from me for ages, sweetheart. Or isn't it such ages after all? To me anyhow it seems an eternity since I wrote to you from our old camp. We are now somewhere in Russia, and then we were in Europe. I know that where we are now is marked on the map as being in Europe, but it is such a completely different world we've entered, so strange and unfamiliar, that I sometimes wonder if I'm really here or whether it's only a dream. What it was like before doesn't seem to exist any more: the pictures that come to mind when I think of past days have become pale and shapeless—except for you, my dearest. You are as strong in me as ever, stronger and more vivid than ever before, in fact. So much so that I feel I can hear your voice and feel your breath on my cheek. . . ."

Deutschmann stopped and looked in irritation at the door as it opened noisily. Sergeant Hefe charged into the room. "Wiedeck, Schwanecke, Hugo, out, at once. We've got to go on a work party."

"I'll stick," Schwanecke announced, still engaged on the round of Vingt-un he was playing with Wiedeck and Count Hugo von Siemsburg-Welljausen, known to everyone as Hugo. Then he condescended to notice Hefe. "What's up?" he asked, slowly looking up. "What work party?"

"Mend a fault on the line," said Hefe. "It's gone dead."

"Here we are again," said Schwanecke, standing up with a sigh. "The line's always going dead in this bastard of a country."

It was Krull who had discovered that the telephone connection to A Company at Babinitchi had been broken off. "What cretin laid the cables?" he shouted through the low room of a fairly well-preserved farmhouse where the office had been established, with candles all over the place stuck into tin or cardboard boxes. "The morons, they can't even lay a telephone line. Shut the door, you clown!" he cried, as an ice-cold draught came on to the back of his sweating neck. Then, turning round, he shot to his feet, for the "clown" was Lieutenant Obermeier. "Oh, sorry, sir. Telephone connection to A Company broken off, sir," he reported. "A fine start!"

He had already noted that it was "a fine start" at their first stop, Baranovitchi, when the whole Company had to move from one goods train to another, because most of the wagons were needed for the transport of artillery ammunition. The Company were crammed into a few wagons, about forty men to each. Also, after a change of trains, Schwanecke had appeared with three tins of tuna fish and a small sack of biscuits.

Krull had given up shouting "Where'd you get it?" every time it happened. Schwanecke's answers were always so stupid that the whole company grinned. So this time he had only said: "If there's a single report that the stuff's been pinched, I'll have you tied to the buffer and make you run behind the train." There was no report, of course. As Schwanecke told his mates with a grin, "Who'd report that" They obviously pinched the stuff too."

Obermeier tried the telephone himself, turning the crank-handle and listening. Nothing. The line was dead. "Have you been able to reach the battalion?"

"Not them either, sir."

"Oh well, nothing for it but a work party to find the fault and repair it."

Krull gave a sigh of satisfaction. A work party was something for him to get his teeth into.

So Hefe set off with six men on the snow-covered road from Gorki to Babinitchi.

Schwanecke, the strongest, had the cable coil on his back. Wiedeck carried the control telephone, and Lingmann the two heavy boxes of tools. Lingmann was a former sergeant who was too fond of drink and when drunk said rude things about the whole world including his superiors and even the rulers of the Reich. At the end of the small column trudging through the snow was Hugo—Count von Siemsburg-Wellhausen—a quiet, unobtrusive, amiable character who bore his lot with equanimity. In the battalion's files it was recorded that he had been convicted of planning treason and inciting acts of sabotage against army property. The facts were that early in 1943, when the 6th Army had been senselessly sacrificed at Stalingrad, he had gathered round him a small circle of officers, with the objective of organising resistance to the regime and if possible concluding an armistice while there was still time. But the group were soon betrayed. He was not condemned to death because his brother, who lived in Spain and worked for the German intelligence services, had good connections with important circles in New York and could have divulged various interesting items of information if Hugo had been killed.

Ahead of the column went Sergeant Hefe, carrying a sub-machine-gun.

The night was icy and dark. The two men checking the wire jumped up and down periodically to keep their legs warm. At various places the road was blocked by snow. Only isolated masts considerable distances apart showed its direction.

Misha Starobin and Piotr Tartuchin were standing by a cluster of bushes. They had built a snow-shelter of interwoven branches. They chewed sunflower seeds and stared into the white night.

"Are you sure you cut the connection properly?" Tartuchin whispered. "They should have been here ages ago. A German company without a phone is like a babe without its mother."

"Sh," hissed Misha. "Can you hear?"

They listened hard. The wind blew, softly singing, whistling and rustling, through the bush and across the open steppe. Misha spat out his sunflower seed and straightened up. A sound which did not belong here suddenly came out of the night; it was the rattle of the cable coil on Schwanecke's back, at first soft and scarcely audible, gradually becoming louder, and suddenly a muffled cry. Misha reached behind him for the sub-machine-gun. "Are they coming from Gorki or Babinitchi?"

"I can't see yet."

"Can you hear them?"

"Yes. Now keep quiet." Tartuchin slid into the snow and lay there like a bundle of rags. Misha pushed a second sub-machine-gun over to him.

"There!" whispered Tartuchin. "From Gorki!"

"How many are there?"

"I can't see them yet, I can't see them yet," muttered Tartuchin, as if talking to himself, as if he had forgotten Starobin and the cold and wind and snow, as if there were nothing else in the world except himself and the sounds coming from men he hated more than he had ever hated anyone before. He was there on his own with them and with his sub-machine-gun and his hatred and the overwhelming desire to kill them, to shoot them down like dogs.

By now they could distinguish voices. They heard the man in front calling behind him: "Everything in order?", and the man in the rear reporting: "All clear."

A distorted smile came over Tartuchin's frozen face. The Germans were now quite near the place where the cable was cut. Misha slowly and carefully pushed his sub-machine-gun on to the small hillock of coagulated snow, pressed the butt to his cheek and took aim at the small group which had stopped on the road.

"Break discovered!" One of the searchers held up his hand. Schwanecke levered the coil off his shoulder and wiped his face. Despite the biting snow he was sweating.

"Broken?"

"Looks like it."

Lingmann put down the box of tools. Wiedeck kneeled to attach the control telephone.

"Quick as you can, it's cold," said Hugo.

"My fingers are numb, man," said Wiedeck.

"Come on, get a move on," said Hefe.

Schwanecke sniffed the air like a suspicious animal. There was something wrong, he felt uneasy. "What's the matter with the wire?" he asked.

"Damaged," said Wiedeck. He had now attached the control telephone. He wound the handle and listened. Then he nodded in satisfaction. Krull's voice could be heard at the other end. "Found it, have you? Taken you a bloody long time, you cretins. What was it, then?"

"The wire got damaged somehow," said Wiedeck.

Krull's loud, nagging voice could be heard over the receiver. With a grin Hefe took it out of Wiedeck's hand.

Tartuchin and Misha looked at them briefly, and Tartuchin whispered: "You take them left to right, I'll go right to left. Then we'll have them under double fire." He pressed the butt of the sub-machine-gun against his shoulder. "Right in the middle, into their bellies!" he whispered. "I'll say when." He voice was almost tender.

Schwanecke kneeled down at Wiedeck's side, lifted the wire to eye level, and felt over it slowly and searchingly with his finger-tips. Suddenly he shot round, threw his arms up, jumped into a hollow of drifted snow, and cried: "Take cover!"

The next moment, as if by a magic spell, the others were all lying on the road. At the same moment they heard the rattle of sub-machine-guns. Shots and whistling bullets came out of the night. Where from, Hugo wondered. Oh yes, from the bushes quite near the road. As he dropped to the ground, he felt a dull blow on his body and his left shoulder went dead. He wondered what had happened. There was no pain. Then he noticed something warm and wet running down his back, and realised he had been hit. "They've got me," he groaned, a note of surprise evident in his voice.

Wiedeck was lying at his side, head pressed into the snow. "Where?"

"In the shoulder."

"Bloody hell—we can't shoot back," muttered Wiedeck despairingly. "What do we do, we can't shoot back?'

They had only the one-sub-machine-gun, with which Hefe was banging away into the night, in the direction from which the shots had come. He combed the area with his own shots.

The two partisans lay behind their show-heap, flat as a piece of snow-covered earth. The bullets whistled through the air far away from them and high above their heads. They began to shoot again themselves.

Schwanecke crawled over with snake-like movements to Hefe. His face was distorted. "The wire was cut through," he said.

"We'd all have had it but for you." Hefe raised his head and at once pressed it back into the snow. A bullet hissed just above him and directly afterwards a second made the snow whirl up in front of them. Without aiming he pulled the trigger and sent a long volley of shots over the bushes.

"Here, man, give it to me, that's hopeless," Schwanecke said angrily. He had been in Russia before and knew his enemy well.

Hefe gave him the sub-machine-gun, and seemed happy to be rid of it. When Schwanecke touched the cold metal, a sudden change came over him. He became one with the weapon, as if it had grown into an extended dangerous arm which he could use like a part of his body—as if he had been born with a sub-machine-gun in his hand. While the others collected in the middle, Wiedeck pulling the wounded Hugo behind him, Schwanecke rolled into his snow-drift and burrowed like a snowgoose scenting danger. Without taking careful airm, he directed fire at each bush, changed the magazine, fired again. Like Tartuchin and Misha he was in his element. His senses reacted with the instinct of an animal, like lightning and with complete certainty. He had no thought for the danger threatened by the enemy. His only concern was to kill.

Soon he stopped shooting. There was no point when he couldn't see his target. The snow-covered road in the wide

Russian steppe lay utterly still as if nothing had happened. On the horizon, like a dark wall, threatening and mysterious, was the wood.

They waited, unmoving: the two partisans behind their snow-heap, Schwanecke in his drift. They listened, hardly breathing. Tartuchin's yellow face was stiff. He turned his head towards Misha. The bullets had whipped just over their head, coming uncannily close, and thudded into the snow in front of him. That had made him careful. It was not the same man who had shot first. "He's met us before," he whispered. "They'll get reinforcements, let's go back."

The tension had become almost unbearable, but the spell was broken by the telephone ringing shrilly through the silence of the night: a sound from another world. Tartuchin raised his head and peered in the direction of the burring sound. Wiedeck, who was lying near the phone, stretched out an arm and took the receiver off. "Shh!" he hissed into the mouthpiece.

From the receiver came Krull's furious voice. "You morons, where's the connection to A Company gone?"

"For Christ's sake—they're shooting at us. Partisans! Private Siemsburg—wounded."

Tartuchin's gun banged off. He shot in the direction the ringing had come from. Wiedeck put the receiver into the snow and pressed into his hollow as deep as possible.

At the other end of the line Krull sat on his tin box aghast: at first he could not take the fact in. But in gradually dawned on him that he was now beyond doubt in this bastard of a country which scared him worse than hell. It was a realisation that up to now he had thrust away from him. He had refused to believe it, so as not to become a quivering, terrified wreck. "They're shooting!" he stuttered. He could hear the bullets clearly, then there was a crash on the line, and the connection was broken. "They've hit it!" Krull dropped the receiver as if a bullet might whizz down the line to his ear. "The partisans are shooting at them ... Siemburg's wounded...."

"That's war, Sergeant Major." Obermeier beckoned to Corporal Kentrop. "Up there with twelve men, Kentrop, and get there fast. But be careful—no unnecessary casualties. Take hand grenades—and Deutschmann as first-aid man."

"The bastards!" said Schwanecke furiously. "The damn bastards." He was kneeling in a drift shooting at the two small dark figures running zigzag, then vanishing in the dim light into the bushes, then emerging again for a few seconds, and finally disappearing into the darkness for good.

Misha panted behind the swift, supple Tartuchin. The periodical fierce rattle of the German sub-machine-gun had frightened him. He hurled himself through the bush, tore his face on the hard, frozen branches, and lay down in the snow, breathing heavily.

"Mother God of Kasan!" he gasped. "That was the devil himself!"

The little Asiatic was silent. He tore off a field-dressing with his teeth.

Misha stared at him. "Did he hit you?"

Tartuchin still said nothing. His eyes were full of burning hate. He put the dressing on his hand and felt the pain going right up his arm. Hate glowed in him like a fever. "I'll kill him," he growled at last. "He's the only man who's ever hit me, there'll be no peace between us—until one of us is dead. Him or me."

16

Dr. Kukill said: "I don't believe you've even been out of the house for ages. Or have you?"

"No," said Julia.

"Oh, I'm sure you'll enjoy this. I think you'll find it a pleasant evening. Do you know the 'Bosnian Cellar'?"

"No."

"It's smallish but rather nice," Kukill went on chattily as he drove through the sparse traffic. "I've ordered a table there because I thought you wouldn't want to go to one of those splendid places swarming with uniforms. I'm right there too, am I not?"

Julia nodded.

"I know the owner quite well. You might even say we're friends, as far as one can be friends with a hotelier, you know. He seems to have good connections, so that you get things there that you don't even get at the places where our lords and masters go. Only for his friends, of course. You'll see—the man's quite a character..." The words flowed lightly from his lips, just loud enough to be audible without strain through the noise of the engine. Now and then he turned his head and smiled at Julia. The meagre blue light from the lampposts were reflected in his glasses.

Julia sat pressed into the corner, scarcely listening. His words ripped past her ears, only half penetrating into her consciousness, like the murmur of a brook when one has been sitting by it for a long time. During the last few days Kukill had often rung her up, sometimes twice a day—and she had always dashed to the phone. Not for his sake. Whenever the shrill ringing pierced the silence in the house, she thought, now! now!—and behind that 'now' lay an expectation of something that must come, that would surely come, a communication from Ernst or somebody with a message from him. Or even, best of all, perhaps he would be at the phone himself. She knew that this hope was vain and quite unrealistic. But nothing is too vain and unrealistic for a person to lose the last glimmer of hope.

She lived in constant expectation. Something must happen, a redeeming word must be spoken, she could no longer endure this permanent tension in which she lived.

But nobody except Kukill had rung up. It seemed as if the people who in the past, before Ernst's conviction, used to be in and out of their house, had never existed. Friends: when she throught of this word, a brief, bitter smile would pass over her face. Friends: she thought how true it was that someone who has fallen on bad times—or worse, has suddenly come on to the list of enemies of the almighty regime—has ceased to have any friends. Till now she refused to believe it could be like that; perhaps because she, like Ernst, was ready, whatever happened, to stand by people she was bound to in friendship. But now she saw that their 'friends' thought otherwise, and this filled her with bitterness and sadness.

Dr. Kukill had kept on pressing her to go out with him. "You really must have a change of scene, Frau Deutschmann," he would say on the phone. "You really shouldn't stay within your four walls or keep thinking of things you can't change. It's not good for you, believe me."

In the end she had agreed. True, Dr. Kukill was the last man she would ordinarily have gone out with if she had wanted to 'escape from her four walls'. But she told herself that in this case she must set aside her antipathy and hostility. He was the man who despite everything could achieve a revision of the trial and Ernst's rehabilitation. He and no one else. So she must not offend him—or not too badly. But how far should she go? His presence was repulsive from the start, he filled her with a feeling of physical dicomfort. Yet she caught herself recently almost looking forward to his telephone calls. Not that anything had changed in her attitude towards him. On the contrary: besides revulsion she now felt fear, for she saw that it was no unselfish sympathy that made Dr. Kukill want to help her. He desired her. She was too much a woman not to sense that, and some time the moment was bound to come when he would tell her so.

He parked the car outside an unpretentious building in a road off the Kurfürstendamm. Colourless, care-worn figures hurried along the pavement—Berlin after four years of war. It seemed as if the lively, bustling capital had ceased to exist.

The woman who took their coats evidently knew Dr. Kukill. She was very conscientious and friendly, qualities not very common in those days. It was the same with the old waiter who received them in the dimly-lit ante-room, escorted them through the door at the back and took them down a long passage and into a back room which was evidently reserved for friends of the house.

The room was quite small, with soft lighting, colourful tapestries on the walls; the tables were small, mostly for two people, with snow-white table cloths. And there were even table-napkins.

"Let's first do something for our appetite," said Dr. Kukill cheerfully, and nodded to the waiter who was to serve them here. Without asking, the waiter brought two balloon glasses filled with golden slivovitz. He evidently knew just what Dr. Kukill wanted.

"This is no ordinary brandy, dear lady," said the doctor, moving the glass lingeringly beneath his nostrils. "The Balkan peasants who distil it somehow seem to capture and preserve the sun and the smell of warm earth, grass and plums. Don't know how they do it." He face had lost its austerity and puckered sharpness.

I've got her sitting here and drinking brandy with me, he thought. I've got her to stop thinking of me as a monster. I'll get her further than that. I'll make her forget Deutschmann. She's beautiful although she's grown so thin. But perhaps that has made her even more beautiful, because her face and her smile are sad. He thought what more he would do, and said: "Try to forget, at least for a short time. And don't get the idea I want to talk you out of anything you have in mind."

"But that's what you try to do the whole time."

"I've stopped trying," said Kukill. "I only want to say that you'll work all the better if you forget the whole thing at least for a few hours. Try to switch off. It will make you stronger."

"You may be right, perhaps I really should try," said Julia, responding in just the way he hoped.

"That's right. So drink up, I'm sure you'll like the taste. Then we'll choose our meal without ration cards and rubbish like that. We'll eat what we feel like; and then—shall we go dancing?"

"Dancing? What do you mean? I thought ..."

"Yes, it's still possible, although officially banned. Shall we?"

"No, I don't think so."

"Your health! Perhaps you'll change your mind ..."

17

Private Hugo Siemsburg was taken to a field hospital at Orsha. He was the battalion's first casualty. His left shoulder blade had been shattered by the shot, and he would have a shoulder askew, making him incapable of carrying a kitbag. "Nice get-you-home shot," commented Sergeant Major Krull, when Siemburg reported for transport to the hospital. "Hardly put his nose outside the camp, and blow me down, he's back home."

"Next time you can come with us," said Hefe pointedly "I can fix you with a shot like that any day." Russia seemed to have somewhat relaxed the stiff, inhuman discipline in the battalion. But that was the case with all the other units in the German army who were having to fight in the expanses of Russia. Discipline often gave way to a deep and strong feeling of attachment and comradeship such as only long-lasting mortal danger can produce. But this feeling was also often displaced by a hostile selfishness, in which everyone thought only of himself and how he could survive these terrible days.

Deutschmann's first-aid kit came into its own that night for the first time. Krull watched him suspiciously as he cleaned up Hugo's wound—on the road he had merely covered it with an emergency dressing. When he had finished, he put four bandages neatly round the shoulder and under the armpit, and fastened them with a safety-pin. Krull screwed up his mouth. At this moment he felt small and unimportant beside Deutschmann.

"Four bandages" Isn't that wasteful?"

"When it's your turn, I'll only use two," said Deutschmann coldly, while pushing an anti-tetanus injection into Hugo's buttock.

Krull went away, grumbling to himself. In these two first days life in B Company just behind the front was more than improvised. They were put here in the snowy solitudes on the edge of Gorki, and didn't know what they were supposed to do. The front itself ran four or five miles east at the beginning of the wood. At this time it was quiet there too, as if the men, and with them the war, had been petrified by the cold. Now and then some ammunition sledges passed. The commander of the infantry battalion forward of them looked in briefly and had a very friendly greeting for Obermeier, until he learnt that this was a penal battalion company. Then he became very formal and soon departed. "As if we had scabies," commented Kentrop.

The word seemed to have got around that there was a penal battalion in the sector. First occasionally, and then more and more often, officers, paymasters, sergeants, and once even a colonel appeared—the Divisional Commander of the 26th Infantry Division, who was passing through Orsha—to cast an eye on the activity being pursued in such a death's-head unit. They were disappointed. Just like A Company in Babinitchi—where Lieutenant Wernher sat around gloomily thinking of his lady friend at Murovana—B Company enjoyed a strange calm. They carryed out their duties, which consisted in keeping billets clean and clearing roads and tracks of snow, and otherwise merely loafed about. The Battalion was expecting orders. They had obviously not been sent to the Dnieper to take their ease; there was something in the wind. "This lull is a con," Schwanecke remarked to Deutschmann. "Things are brewing up somewhere, and when the ballon goes up, we'll be right in it, you bet your life. It's time we did something."

Hugo Siemsburg was taken to Orsha by supply sledge. Deutschmann had to go with him and was also detailed to fetch some important papers from Captain Barth. It should have been Sergeant Hefe's job, but as Deutschmann was going to Orsha anyhow, Barth said on the phone: "Why not use our medical orderly as a postman too?"

The journey in the motor-sledge went without incident. Here and there they saw muffled-up, ragged Russian peasants. "Poor devils," said the corporal driving the sledge. "They're trying to save their farms, as if there was anything left to save. They've all been screened and are glad they don't have to work in collectives any more. A lot of them are collaborators for us and see to our supplies. Partisans look different."

As they drove through Babinitchi, one of these ragged characters was standing on the road and waved to the sledge. His hollow face under the high woollen cap was yellowish brown.

"'Morning, little father," the corporal shouted down to him.

Sergei Denkov gave him a wide grin. "Morning, little brother," he called back, and waved again.

At Orsha Captain Barth gave the waiting Deutschmann a thick envelope. "Operational orders, take good care of them," he said.

Deutschmann saluted and left. He trudged slowly through the dirty straggling village. He was free till the evening. At the battalion HQ he had learnt that the next sledge would not be leaving till night-fall. So he went off to visit Hugo in the field hospital, one of the few solid brick buildings in the place; it had once been a school. Hugo had meanwhile had a new dressing put on and was to go by the next train to Borisov. There was no X-ray equipment in Orsha.

"If I'm lucky," he said with a faint smile, "they'll be able to mend my shoulder-blade. Just depends which surgeon gets his hands on me. They say there's a fantastic man at Sokolov, medical superintendent of a university hospital. But I don't suppose anyone from Battalion 999 will get to *him*."

"Not even if he's a Count?" asked Deutschmann.

Hugo yawned. He had been given an injection, the pain had eased, and he was feeling sleepy. "The days of counts are over," he murmured. "But tell me, you're a doctor: do you think they'll be able to get me more or less patched up?"

"To the best of my knowledge," said Deutschmann," and

remember I'm not a surgeon. I'd imagine they can work it so that afterwards you won't even know you've been wounded."

"Hope so, hope so," murmured Hugo drowsily. "Do you have to go? Pity. It's been good knowing you, Ernst. Maybe we'll meet again somewhere, some time."

Deutschmann wandered along the roads, on which the snow was frozen hard, down to the Dnieper, and stopped near the wooden bridge where he was later to meet the corporal with the motor-sledge. Ice drifted on the sluggish waves and broke on big iron spikes with which the Pioneer Corps had protected the bridges. A girl was plodding along with a big basket of logs, putting it down on the snow now and then, wiping her face, and then picking the basket up again. She was making her way towards a farmhouse on the Dnieper half covered in snow.

Deutschmann watched the girl for a while, then walked slowly down to the bank to help her. He stopped behind her. Her hair gleamed in the sun like black paint. She had not heard him come. With a sigh she bent down to pick up the basket which she was again resting. At that point he put his hand on her arm.

She swung round, her eyes full of terror. A brief pale flush came over the cheekbones slightly protruding from the narrow face. She pressed her hands against her bust and her big dark eyes looked at Deutschmann apprehensively.

"Are you frightened?" he asked. "Look, the basket is far too heavy. I'll carry it home for you."

"Niet!" She shook her head. The fear in her eyes melted, and the hint of a smile flitted over her face. "I can carry."

"You speak German?"

She nodded. "A little," she said. "A little bit." She looked at the shoulder of his tunic and saw it had no epaulettes. What was that Sergei had said? They must be trying out a secret weapon. She thought feverishly. What to do? She must question him, hold on to him, she must … no soldier in the world goes about without epaulettes. "Have you been a long time in Orsha?" she asked.

Deutschmann bent down and picked up the basket. "You go first, I'll carry this home for you."

"Thank you, soldier." She walked on in her quilted

trousers and Russian leather boots. Her body swayed a little as she walked; she was thin, and incredibly slim at the waist. Deutschmann had till now had a different and more conventional idea of Russian girls: he had thought, as most people did, that they were all short, fat and round. But this girl here …

"Very heavy?" she turned to ask him.

"Not very."

She laughed, showing teeth white as the snow all round. "Not for a man."

A brief sharp picture of Julia shot through Deutschmann's head—all of a sudden he saw her very clearly standing before him—and then he forgot it again. The basket was heavy and pressed on his shoulder. He was not used to carrying heavy loads.

The girl pushed open the door of the hut. Deutschmann dragged the basket in, and with a sigh of relief put it down by the stone stove near a fire that was blazing cheerfully.

"Not look round," she said quietly. "It is war, and war is dirty." Deutschmann listened in delight to the sound of her soft melodious voice, which the strong Slav accent made even more attractive. He had heard a lot about how good it sounds when Russian girls speak German; now he was hearing it for the first time himself. He sat down on the chair and looked at an icon hanging on the wall near the stove. It had become smoky and dark with age.

"The Holy Mother of Kasan," he said.

"You know her, soldier?"

Deutschmann smiled. "How old are you?" he asked in Russian.

She swung round and stared at him, frightened again. "Twenty," she said, also in Russian.

"Very young—and very pretty," he said. A strange, quite unfamiliar light-heartedness came over him, making him feel relaxed and cheerful and curious at the outcome of this adventure.

"You speak Russian?" she asked.

"As much as you speak German," The weak light from the open fire played over Deutschmann's face. "Who are you?" he asked. "What's your name?"

"Tanya," she said.

"Tanya. Very pretty. And what do you do here? Are you living all alone?"

"Yes."

"Aren't you afraid—of the war, of us?"

"Yes. I am afraid, of the war—and of you." She went back into German. "Why have you carried the basket?"

"To help you. It was too heavy for you." He rose. "Well, Tanya—Tanyuska, as you Russians say—I must go now."

"Where?"

"Where? To my comrades."

"Near the Gorki woods?"

Deutschmann gave a start and looked at her suspiciously. But she smiled at him like an innocent child. Her face was mild and gentle, the reflection of the fire gave her hair reddish tints. "How do you know that?" he asked.

"Everyone knows that. All troops who pass here go to Babinitschi and Gorki."

"You are not from Orsha."

"Why?"

"Your face is different. Where do you come from?"

"From the Volga. You know it?"

"No."

"You would never forget the Volga. It is beautiful, wonderful. It is. . . ."

"*You* are wonderful," Deutschmann broke in quietly.

She laughed. It sounded light, silvery and free. "You like to eat?" she asked.

"But you haven't anything yourself. I am not hungry."

"It is a Russian custom, you are in Russia, you are my guest."

Deutschmann nodded, incapable of speech. It seemed like a dream and he was afraid of waking up. Tanya took a quick small step towards him and stroked his face with the tips of her fingers. He took her hand and kissed her. The hand was small and slim and did not fit here in this dilapidated hut—any more than the girl did herself. He was living through a miracle. The girl was a miracle, and her hand was one, and her fingers, which now stroked his lips.

"What is your name?" she asked.

"Deutschmann...."

"Oh, not nice name. Horrible name. I will forget it. You are Michael, the great shining hero, Michael."

"Yes," he said, trembling. A weakness had come over him against which he fought in vain. Her magic had captured him, and he knew he would never overcome the weakness and the magic. "You are beautiful," he whispered. "You are lovely."

He ate meat and bread and eggs. Tanya served him; she stood at the stove and fried the eggs in a large copper pan. Outside evening fell over the Dnieper. Ice crashed against the pier. Dull explosions from blasting rolled through the dusk.

Tanya sat down near Deutschmann and stared out through the window and over the river. He had put his arm round her shoulder. She nestled up to him, as if seeking protection from this tall, strange foreigner so different from Sergei and the other men she had met till then, so different too from the German soldiers she saw every day. She had laid her head with its smooth black hair against his cheek.

"I must go," he said at last. His voice shattered the magical silence. She nodded and lifted her face. "Kiss me," she said, in a very low voice.

He kissed her. Her lips were soft and cool.

"Tanya," he whispered, and kept repeating: "Tanya.... Tanya...." What had happened to him? How was this possible? He was sitting here in the heart of Russia and holding in his arms a warm, supple, slightly trembling girl's body, sinking into a soft, tender, twilight stillness in which there were only the two of them and nothing else ...

Headlights probed from the bridge. A motor convoy thundered over the wooden boards with engines howling ... He had to go. He must tear himself away from her. It was just no good ... Julia. He stood up with a jerk. "Goodbye," he said hoarsely.

"Auf wiedersehen, Michael."

Her eyes followed him till he disappeared in the dusk. She was apprehensive and sad.

The motor-sledge was already waiting for him. In silence he squatted down by a grumbling corporal on the uncomfortable seat. He scarcely heard what the man said. He stared into the snowy night, his mind elsewhere. He did not feel the icy cold or the bumps from the unsprung sledge. He thought of Tanya and Julia and then Tanya again.

Between Gorki and Babinitchi they passed a shaky old farm-sledge. The small shaggy horses drawing it trotted through the snow as if this were all they knew: snow-storms and solitude. Sergei Denkov gave a polite friendly wave to the motor-sledge.

But Deutschmann scarcely noticed him either. He saw Tanya's eyes and heard her soft, lilting voice. Did the south wind have that lilt when it blew over the Volga?

18

Lieutenant Obermeier read the orders Deutschmann had brought from Orsha. He read them a second and third time before going to the telephone and having himself connected with the battalion through A Company at Orsha. Before doing so, however, he ordered Sergeant Major Krull out of the room. “Go and see what they’re concocting at the cookhouse. And don’t come back for half an hour.”

Krull left the office, deeply offended.

“Hullo, Obermeier,” said Barth in an amiable voice. “What can I do for you?”

Obermeier cleared his throat. He did not know whether Barth was really feeling amiable or was only putting it on, you could never be quite sure with Barth. “I have just read the orders, sir.” The papers in his hand quivered.

“That’s fine. And are you happy with them?”

“Happy with them? Did you think I would be, sir? What does it mean, construct a trench system between Gorki and Babinitchi according to attached plan? That’s an impossible bit of digging. And anyhow you said there was something else we. . . .”

“All superseded, Obermeier. Nothing stays the same, New every morning is the plan, left hand doesn’t know what right hand’s doing, et cetera, et cetera. Like any more proverbs?”

“When do we start?”

“Tomorrow.”

“The ground is frozen solid to at least three feet, with about two and a half feet of snow on top.”

"What has that to do with impossible digging? There are picks, and if necessary, you can do some blasting."

"Another thing is that we're under enemy observation for over a mile of the road behind Gorki. Are we to dig our trenches under enemy observation?"

"Listen, Obermeier." Barth's voice became dry and hard. "You think too much. When it says in the orders, construct a trench system between Gorki and Babinitchi, then that applies to the sector under enemy observation as well. The work will either be done at night or in the early morning. High Command is expecting that after the thaw, that's to say towards the end of February, the Russians will start a major counter-offensive to squeeze the German wedge at Smolensk. Vitebsk is in danger. There's hardly any snow there, the mud roads are frozen, an ideal runway for the Russian tanks. In the south, near Kiev, the Russians are pushing forward over the big Dnieper bend and trying to break our flanks. The whole front stinks, Obermeier. A rallying position is to be built here, and quite a lot depends on it. You can judge how much from the fact that it's being constructed so near the first front line. It's because of the runway, my dear Obermeier. And the troops being pressed back from Smolensk are supposed to find new prepared positions here. That's why we have to get on with our impossible dig, even under enemy observation."

Obermeier put the papers down by the telephone. "We'll lose half the Company on this job," he said.

"Make it two thirds. There are battalions at the front with only a young lieutenant and twenty to thirty men. Anyhow, you still don't seem to have grasped the idea of the thing."

"A superior death sentence, in fact." Obermeier meant his voice to sound ironical, but it came out as shocked and desperate.

"Death sentence? You're really too romantic. Better forget these big words. You have clear operational orders, that's all there is to it. Don't imagine Wernher is any better off. He and his company have to build three walls to hold up the snow-drifts. Every night the partisans destroy what they've built up by day. Last night they were under fire. He's suffered fourteen dead and thirty-three wounded. A complete partisan unit, brilliantly led, by the way, engaged him in a proper small battle with machine-guns and hand-grenades. Anything else you want to know, Obermeier?"

"No, sir." Obermeier hung up. He sat in the half-dark hut, staring at the candles stuck on the tin boxes.

Outside, Krull was bawling around. He had caught Schwanecke, Wiedeck, and Deutschmann making some soup from cubes over a small wood-fire. "From my girl friend's parcel, don't you recognise it?" asked Schwanecke, knowing as well as Krull that he had not received any parcel. He had stolen the cubes from a Red Cross food depot during the two-hour stop at Orsha.

"What a shower!" cried Krull furiously. "A fine lot of heroes to die for the country."

Obermeier stepped out of the hut and beckoned Krull over to him. "Twenty-five men to drive to Babinitchi tonight and fetch implements. Three sledges will be enough. From tomorrow morning we'll be digging."

"Digging?" Krull's voice was dull and uncomprehending. He looked across the expanses of snow and screwed up his mouth. "Here?"

"Where else?"

Krull could not restrain a "Christ!"

Obermeier regarded him with distaste. "Keep your religious fervour to yourself, Sergeant Major. As far as I am aware, you haven't lifted a finger on any work party, so I don't suppose you will now."

That night a party of twenty-five men set off with three sledges, under Corporals Kentrop and Bortke, to Babinitchi to collect the implements which had been taken there by a transport unit in Orsha.

Schwanecke crouched on the first sledge behind a machine-gun, his alert, frowning eyes scanning the snow-fields and bushes for any movement. They drove past Lieutenant Sergei Denkov who sat deep in a patch of bush, invisible even to Schwanecke's sharp eyes. Tartuchin crouched at his side, his heavily bandaged hand in a sling.

The sledges reached Babinitchi unimpeded. A Company

was like a forestry camp. Felled trees with all their branches lay in piles on the roadside and were being dragged through the snow by motor sledges. Five to eight men then lifted them up and planted them into the snow, in holes which had been made beforehand with picks in the iron-hard ground. Fir on fir, with trees in between stacked diagonally across: a green wall against snow-storms and drifts.

Lieutenant Wernher, The C.O. of A Company, sat glumly in his heated farmhouse compiling the list of losses from the previous night. He even wrote personally to some of the next of kin. Among the dead were a former major, two well-known lawyers and an author. It was only when he was writing "fallen for Greater Germany" that Wernher hesitated, feeling how idiotic it was. "They did their duty to the end," he wrote, and "their death was merciful. Let that be a consolation." It was true enough, he thought, a consolation: they've finished with it all.

The collection of digging implements and explosives was carried out without incident. Then the sledges travelled along the road back to Gorki. They rattled like ghosts with long snow-trails past Sergei and Tartuchin crouching in their scrub.

"Now!" said Tartuchin, with a hard grin on his mouth.

They stared at one place on the road. The first sledge, The second.... "Damn!" hissed Tartuchin. Sergei ground his teeth, the muscles stood out on the sunken cheeks. The third sledge. Nothing!

Tartuchin banged his fist into the snow, his yellow face distorted with fury.

There! Quite a way behind the third sledge a glaring flame hissed out of the snow, a crashing detonation shattered the night, part of the road shot up to the sky and rattled down again in dirty cascades. "Delayed ignition," said Sergei, shaking his head, and spat angrily.

After the moment when a volcano seemed to have erupted, the landscape returned to its deep, drowsy peace, as if the snow and frost had swallowed every sound. The last sledge, which had Kentrop in it, collected a few lumps of earth pelting down, and shot forward abruptly.

Like scurrying shadows the men jumped out of their

sledges. Twenty-five soldiers lay flat in the snow to give the invisible enemy less of a target. Corporal Bortke crawled over to Schwanecke with the machine gun, and pushed back the steel helmet, which had fallen over his face when he dropped to the ground. "A mine," he said.

"Yes, some mine."

They scanned the region. The bushes, the isolated copses, the hollows, stretching all the way to the woods of Gorki.

"Wait." Schwanecke cast his eye thoughtfully over the clusters of bushes. He scented danger like a hunted animal. Something told him that the men who had laid the mine were still quite near. Slowly he drew the butt of the gun to his shoulder and shot a quick, rattling fire over the bushes, then went lower, combing the branches just above the ground. The sharp, fierce rattle of the gun was a relief. Here and there a dark head emerged from the snow, and crawling bodies moved together into groups.

Tartuchin and Sergei lay burrowed in the snow. Schwanecke's bullets whistled a few inches above their heads. The Mongolian screwed up his slanting eyes. "That's him again, I'm dead sure."he said, his voice hoarse with hatred. "He's the only man who can shoot like that." The bullets hummed above them, breaking off branches and shaking ice splinters over their bodies.

"No good," said Bortke. "I always said they'd gone."

Dark figures climbed out of the snow and ran to the sledges. A few moments later the chug of engines shattered the night. Kentrop and Schwanecke walked back to where the mine had exploded, Schwanecke with the gun slung round his neck, ready to shoot from the hip. They stood by the crater, which had torn a yawning black hole over the whole width of the road. "That would have done its work," said Kentrop. "We were lucky again."

Tartuchin stared at the man with the machine gun. A shudder went through his squat, broad-shouldered body. Sergei sensed it and put a hand on his shoulder. "Steady there, calm down!"

"That's him, Lieutenant."

"We'll get him, Piotr, you can bet your boots on that."

They watched the sledges drive on. Then the noise of the engines died away in the distance.

"I'm going back to Orsha," said Sergei. "Tell the comrades in the wood to have a rest. In three days I'll be back with orders. I'll be talking to the Comrade General."

"And where can we reach you before that?"

"At Tanya's."

Tartuchin grinned and smacked his lips. Sergei looked at him furiously but said nothing. He crept out of the bush, stretched himself in the icy cold and slapped his chest all over to warm up.

Dawn began to break over the wood: pale grey, full of snow-clouds, only a slight touch of colour in the night sky.

Sergei crossed the road. He stopped a moment near the big mine-crater, looked into it and shrugged his shoulders. "Nichevo. Another time!" Then he ran on—to Babinitchi.

A small sledge came up over the plains. Fedya waved to him—Sergeant Fedya, in the guise of a poor peasant.

"Anything new?" Sergei climbed into the sledge.

"No, Lieutenant."

"To Orsha. Drive round Babinitchi."

They reached the Dnieper without seeing a single German soldier. Sergei smiled quietly. "The steppe is death to them," he said slowly. "How can a ship sailing over a sea think the sea belongs to her?"

Wernher could hardly believe his eyes when Bevern suddenly turned up in Babinitchi and trudged into his farmhouse like an apparition from another world. Wernher was in bed.

"Morning, Wernher," said Bevern.

Wernher looked at his watch and found it was four a.m. "Hullo there," he said, wishing the damned snooper to the devil. What was he wanting here in the middle of the night? Wernher slipped on his tunic and put his hands through his hair.

"I am here representing the Commanding officer," said Bevern stiffly. "I would like to inspect your sector."

"Would you indeed?" Wernher got up. "You've chosen just

the right morning. Up to one o'clock we had three dead and seven wounded. How many there are now, I don't know."

"Partisans?"

"No, not this time. If it had been partisans, I would hardly...." Wernher looked across at his bed with a grin, raised his tea-cup and blew on the steaming tea. "This time it was regular troops. My men are digging and building over an area seven-and-a-half miles wide covered by the enemy. Now and then this bunch of Russkis bang a few shots off at us, just to say, Don't forget, we're still here."

"Not pleasant," Bevern sat down and looked round. "Have you no map" Surely you must have a map of your sector?"

"Yes, of course I have, But what do we need a map for? Let's go out and look at the whole position ourselves. It'll soon be light—well, it never gets completely dark here."

"Under enemy observation?" asked Bevern, hesitating.

"Why not? If my men have to work there, we can safely take a look, eh?"

"Don't forget that these people have all been convicted by law."

"And we are officers who are supposed to set them an example," said Wernher.

Bevern looked at his hands. "All right, Let's go."

19

A week after the battalion reached Orsha, the hospital arrived. Jokob Kronenberg with four men formed the advance section and went into Orsha to look for Ernst Deutschmann, until he heard that Deutschmann was with B Company near Gorki. Kronenberg reported to Captain Barth, who immediately gave him a shock by saying: "Good thing our medics are here. The hospital goes to Barssdovka on the Dnieper. There it can take the wounded from the Battalion's whole sector. So far we've had seventeen dead and thirty six wounded."

Kronenberg left HQ in a fairly gloomy mood. He found it disturbing go be told that a very exposed spot had been chosen for the Battalion's hospital. Of course he had expected something like this—after all, it *was* a penal battalion—but as usual he had a nasty feeling in his stomach when faced by the actual fact. He at once passed on his anxieties to Captain Bergen when the M.O. got to Orsha in the early morning on a makeshift hospital train.

Captain Bergen had been given an assistant, a young surgeon with no previous front-line experience, who had till then been at a Warsaw base hospital. He looked insignificant, narrow-chested, with slender arms and legs, almost effeminate. The long eye lashes and his shy manner increased the impression of helplessness he made on Bergen. Very unobtrusively he had worked himself into the hospital routine, and had only once stepped out of his grey anonymity. During the drive up to the front they had stopped a day at Borisov, and there was an accident at a crossroads when a munitions truck collided with a small command-car. A young lieutenant had been dragged out of the pile of scrap, his left leg hanging by only a few shreds above the knee: the blood was pumping out of a torn vein in rhythmical bursts. On the road itself, right by the wreck of the command-car, Bergen's assistant had amputated the leg. From that day Bergen had felt a quiet respect for his unimposing young assistant, Lieutenant Hansen.

After looking for the lorries, Kronenberg returned to Orsha station. The makeshift hospital was still in a siding. Hansen had established a casualty station in a cattle truck and was treating some casualties on the railway yards. Bergen, meanwhile, was trying to find the transport officer in charge. In contrast to his usual placidity, he had made up his mind to assert his rights energetically. After all, they were at the front now.

"Got the trucks?" asked Hansen, as he bandaged a crushed hand. He looked down at Kronenberg, who was standing near the track. He had his lambskin coat open, but even so was sweating.

"They're arriving at night-fall, sir. The C.O. says it's impossible to drive through these few miles in Ivan's sights—even with the Red Cross. They shoot at anything that moves over the snow." Kronenberg sat down on an empty barrel and wiped his face. "What a dump!" he said disdainfully.

A smile came over Hansen's delicate, slightly girlish features. "And I thought you'd feel fine when we were in Russia, Kronenberg."

"Why, sir?"

"Oh, well, aren't you what's called a front-line rat? How often have you been in Russia?"

"This is my fourth time, sir."

"I've always heard that the German soldier who's once been at the front doesn't feel happy at base, and perks up again at the sound of enemy fire. Do you reckon that's right?"

Kronenberg lit a cigarette. He looked at a soldier from a construction battalion who was trotting over the track, now that his hand was bandaged, returning to the columns who were changing lines smashed by grenades, and repairing sidings. "I don't know," he said. "Anyone would get in a funk at the idea of going back to Russia. But then, when you're here again, you somehow feel you're at home. Sounds crazy, doesn't it! Russia and home!"

"Why not?"

"Oh well, it's such a miserable country, and then the people—hauling our ammunition on to lorries by day and at night blowing those same lorries to pieces."

"But they can't all be partisans."

"Not all but plenty. More than we think." Kronenberg spoke with the cigarette in his mouth and chewed round on it. "We're going to Barssdovka, the C.O. said. That's on the Dnieper, the most miserable hole you can imagine." He flipped away the cigarette-butt and got up from the barrel. The sharp snow-wind blew over the plains in a long gust. He buttoned up his lambskin coat. "You come from Warsaw, sir. You don't know what it's like yet. Oh well, you'll find out soon enough. To me our men are like clay-pigeons on which the Russians are learning to shoot. There'll be a heap of work for *us*."

"But we're doing some shooting too, aren't we, Kronenberg?"

Kronenberg looked at him in surprise. "Oh yes, of course. That's war, isn't it! We try to destroy the Bolsheviks, and the Bolsheviks try to destroy the National Socialists. And both claim they have right on their side."

"And who *have* got right on their side?"

Kronenberg spat and said firmly. "Us, of course, sir. Who do you think?"

Captain Bergen climbed over a heap of rail and trudged back to the hospital train. Hansen jumped out of the wagon and went towards him. "Have you had any joy, sir?"

Bergen shook his head grimly. "I have merely established that we've got a model peace-time bureaucracy here, with nobody accepting responsibility. A mass of officers and offices ..." He made a weary dismissive gesture with his hand.

"It seems Captain Barth has promised lorries for nightfall, sir." Hansen pulled down his ear-flap. "A sharp wind," he said. "If all goes well, we'll be ready to open the day after tomorrow."

They waited till nightfall. As the sky turned grey and then dark, a few lorries rattled over the railway terrain and stopped outside the hospital train. A sergeant major reported to Bergen, who looked in dismay at the lorries. "You're going to use these wrecks?"

"Why not? We've carried all sorts of other things in rattle-traps like these."

Kronenberg took the sergeant major aside. "This is his first time in Russia, so keep your cool and do what you think best. In the end he'll be surprised how well we land up at Barssdovka."

"If they don't catch us."

"The partisans?"

"Who else? All hell's let loose at Gorki." The sergeant major beckoned the trucks on to a ramp, on which crates with dressings, drugs, surgical equipment and folding beds were now stacked. "How long do you mean to stay in Barssdovka?"

Kronenberg grinned. "Till final victory."

At Barssdovka they waited for Deutschmann and some men from B. Company. The road through the shot-up village was swept clear of snow, the telephone lines were already laid, and a patched-up farmhouse had been cleared to serve as a medical post. When the small convoy drove out of the night into the village and swung rattling past the first destroyed houses, a short, broad-shouldered, bandy-legged Russian appeared in front of the first truck and waved at them with a cheerful grin. He ran in front of the convoy and pointed out the way to where Deutschmann was lighting up the barn as best he could with torches and battery headlights.

Frozen to the bone, Kronenberg clambered out of his truck and did some knee-bends to get the blood circulating through his stiff limbs. The little Russian raised his hand in a friendly way and say: "Good evening."

Kronenberg nodded. "Come here, bandy-legs. You a collab?"

"Da."

"Then go behind to the Captain and help him unload. Understand?"

"Da."

"Off you go, then."

Piotr Tartuchin departed, smiling, and plodded over in his thick fur boots to Captain Bergen, who was directing the lorries to the barn.

Deutschmann and Kronenberg enjoyed a laugh of recognition and slapped each other on the shoulder. Deutschmann had not shaved for two days, his stubbly face was crusted over with ice and flushed by the cold.

"Not had any more black-outs, have you?" asked Kronenberg solicitously, reaching in his shaggy fur coat and bringing out the obligatory bottle of schnaps.

"No, I haven't. The Russian air seems to suit me well."

"How is it suiting that bastard Krull?" asked Kronenberg.

"Hardly creeps out of his hole. He's in a blue funk now we've got up here."

"How about the rest of you?"

"Bartlitz in the cookhouse has become a great chef! Most of the Company seem to be putting up with this blasted digging better than might have been expected."

"How's Obermeier?"

"Fine chap," said Deutschmann with enthusiasm. "Always out in the road with the diggers. He usually manages to have some schnaps to share out too—even though it's forbidden. I don't know how we'd get on if anything happens to him."

On the dark road Captain Bergen shouted for Kronenberg, who made a gesture with his thumb in the direction from which the shout had come, grinned, and swallowed some more schnaps. "Hear that? If I'm not there, the old man is helpless as a baby."

Bergen was standing by a crate which Tartuchin had dropped.

"Heavy," said the little Mongolian, humping his shoulders apologetically. His slit-eyes contemplated the field dressings which had rolled into the snow from the burst crate.

Bandages, cotton wool, dressings, plaster … and a heap of things in the other crates, you could be sure—things which would be bery useful in Gorki wood, where they had to use scraps of old shirts for dressings and the injured screamed with pain from wounds turned septic.

When Kronenberg arrived, he chased Tartuchin away. "Clear off, that's not for you," he said, and to the others: "The crates in the farmhouse, the beds and palliasses in the barn. Take care with the second truck, there's glass in it."

The lorries were unloaded by torchlight, and a makeshift theatre was established in the farmhouse. Lieutenant Hansen set up the operating table, helped put together an instrument cabinet, and arranged the room so that major operations could be performed. A big lamp was fixed to the ceiling: its beam enveloped the operating table in dazzling light. The room's two windows had, therefore, to be blacked out with blankets, so that no target was presented to Russian light bombers, the so-called 'sewing machines'.

When the trucks had been fully unloaded and the soldiers had almost completed the interior installations, they heard a loud droning on the Gorki road. Kronenberg, who was standing with Deutschmann and Tartuchin outside the entrance to the barn, lit a cigarette in the hollow of his hand. "What's that?" he said. "A sledge?"

Deutschmann nodded. "From C Company. Wood to make cupboards and stretchers here."

The outlines of a big motor-sledge emerged from the night. Like a huge spider it crept through the snow, turned in a curve round the trucks and stopped with a squeal outside the barn. A muffled figure jumped out of the cab, brandishing a sub-machine-gun, and ran up to Kronenberg. "Hullo, my old ugly mug," he shouted.

"Well, strike a light—Karl!" Kronenberg gave a delighted laugh. "You're still in the land of the living, then?"

Schwanecke grinned. "Nobody finishes me off that easy."

Tartuchin stood apart, leaning against the barn wall. His body was racked with long shivers. His broad yellow face suddenly appeared dead and motionless, as if carved out of stone. He hid his wounded left hand in the wide fur sleeve of his coat. He had ground his teeth so hard that his jaw ached;

but he did not notice it. At that moment he would scarcely have noticed if a knife had been cutting into his flesh.

Schwanecke reported to Bergen and Hansen, and helped with the setting up of the hospital. A pale dawn was rising, the tops of the trees became lighter and appeared out of the blackness of the night. During the day it was quite impossible to drive back to Gorki; a stretch of five miles was under continual enemy observation, and anything that moved above the white snowfield attracted immediate attention from the Russian artillery, who were excellent marksmen. So Schwanecke stayed all day in the new hospital, strolled round with Kronenberg in the war-torn village, examined the farmhouses for things he might be able to use—and came to the place where Piotr Tartuchin lived.

It was a small log-cabin with a barn and a draw-well, the hoister of which was half rotted away. Schwanecke kicked the door in, and suddenly found himself facing Tartuchin, who was sitting crouched on a bench near the stove and smoking a cigarette. He did not move when Schwanecke lumbered into the low room—the ceiling almost touched his fur cap. It was as if the Mongolian had been expecting the German. With glinting eyes he looked towards Schwanecke, who stopped in the middle of the room, sniffing the cigarette smoke.

"Makhorka?" he asked.

"Da."

"Good shag in your paper. Is it Pravda?"

"Niet, no Pravda. This here German paper. Pravda better."

With the heel of his boot Schwanecke kicked the door shut, not taking his eyes off Tartuchin. "German paper no good, eh? German all no good, eh? Germans kick you in behind, eh?" He suited the action to the word.

Tartuchin raised his hand and smiled.

He still grins, thought Schwanecke, he still grins although I've booted him in the behind. How can he? Then he suddenly saw the gleam of deadly hatred in Tartuchin's eyes. It was not just the hate of a Russian soldier for a German, or of a down-trodden man who loved his home for a man belonging to the army which had invaded his country. It seemed more than that—a quiet personal hatred, deadly and merciless, which would not be resolved until either he, this yellow Mongolian, or he Schwanecke....

Involuntarily Schwanecke took a step back, then drew in his arms and bent forward as if about to charge.

"You understand?" asked Tartuchin.

"Yes," said Schwanecke.

Silence.

"All right," growled Schwanecke. "I know what you want."

"Now—you will kill me."

"Right first time," said Schwanecke.

Tartuchin smiled. The smile stayed on his face even afterwards, as if it were carved into his features. "Why, little brother?" he asked quietly. "I am poor, I am tired, I am nothing."

"One mistake," said Schwanecke. "You're poor, you're tired, but you're something, something that...."

Tartuchin got up from his bench. With short, almost tripping steps he walked across the room.

Schwanecke lowered his sub-machine-gun. Now, he thought, now I can put him away. If anyone asks me, I can say he tried to attack me. He jumped up from his bench and leapt at me, it was self-defence—but nobody will ask any questions, no one will know about it. One fewer, one of these damned partisans, I'm dead sure he *is* one. People will say, Good for you, Karl, Nice work, Schwanecke, kill some more of those bastards, Schwanecke.

Tartuchin had come up to the table, He had a tobacco pouch in his hand, and held it out to Schwanecke. "Why do you not shoot?" he asked.

Schwanecke said nothing.

"Tobacco?" asked Tartuchin.

"Give it here." Carefully, not taking his eyes off the Mongolian, he rolled himself a cigarette. He licked the piece of paper, unravelled it with his teeth and stuck it together. Then he threw the pouch back to Tartuchin and waited till the man had also rolled himself a new cigarette. The table stood between them like a barricade.

They smoked. In silence. Dry, pungent smoke and the smell of burnt newspaper filled the dark, dirty hut. Why don't I shoot, why don't I shoot, thought Schwanecke. If I don't do it now, then he'll do it one day, and he looks as if he could score a hit. Why don't I shoot the son of a bitch?

And yet, although he knew that the man facing him was his deadly enemy, with no other point of contact except a fight to the death; although he knew that from now on he would not have a moment's peace, at least not here, in these parts, so long as this small, broad-shouldered, slit-eyed Mongolian was alive; despite all this, he did not shoot. Something inexplicable, which he did not understand himself, stopped him doing it. The man looked so indifferent or perhaps he was just putting it on? Was it this that prevented him, Karl Schwanecke, from pulling the trigger and riddling the Russian partisan with bullets? The man was so calm as he waited for the next minute which might see him dead or dying. It would have been so easy to shoot, but Schwanecke found he couln't do it. In fact he suddenly noticed that his hand, which held the cigarette, was trembling. Furious with himself, at this strange paralysis of the will, he pressed the cigarette together and hurled the mixture of shredded paper and glowing shag into a corner of the stove, making the sparks fly up. "Get going," he said harshly to Tartuchin.

"Going? Where?"

"How the hell should I know? Disappear where you came from, to your lot."

"My lot?"

"Don't be stupid," said Schwanecke angrily. "Do you think I don't know who you are and what you belong to?"

"You know!" Tartuchin confirmed. "So why do you not kill me?"

"I will, by Christ, I will. But not here." Like lighting Schwanecke reached over the table, gripped Tartuchin by the chest, with tremendous strength pulled him across the table and slung him against the door. "Get going!" he yelled. "Do you hear? We'll meet again. Now get the hell out of here."

The Mongolian fell on to the mud floor near the door. Mutely he picked himself up, and without looking at Schwanecke opened the door and stepped out into the snow. A rush of cold air came into the room and chilled Schwanecke, who stood leaning against the table, Watching

Tartuchin strap snow-shoes on to his fur boots. Then he heard the crunching steps quickly moving off.

It was Kronenberg who awoke Schwanecke from his reverie. He came lumbering into the log-cabin, dragging after him a sack of potatoes which he had found hidden under straw in one of the farmhouses.

"Karl, what's up, man?"

Schwanecke started and stared at him absently.

"Whatever did you do to the Ivan? The bloke dashed past me as if he'd seen a ghost and is now toddling over the steppe as if he meant to foot it all the way to Moscow." He put the sack down near the door and came into the low room. The smell of the makhorka cigarettes was still strong and pungent, and made Kronenberg cough. He sniffed the air. "Been smoking together, have you? Pipe of peace, was it?"

Schwanecke pushed away from the table, went past Kronenberg without a word, kicked aside the sack of potatoes, which was blocking the entrance, and then stood in the cold, low afternoon sun. The snow was dazzling. If you shut your eyes, opened the lids only a small crack, and looked across the shimmering snow through the lashes, it was almost blue. In the village the lorries had been driven behind the barns; across the snow-field outside the village a small motor-sledge came sweeping towards it. Probably casualties for the hospital.

Kronenberg trailed his sack of potatoes behind him and panted along on Schwanecke's heels. "What's got into you?" he asked. "You shell-shocked or something?"

Without speaking Schwanecke turned round; and he disappeared behind a cottage.

There he stood in the snow, gazing across at the small black dot of a man slowly creeping over the snow-field towards the woods on the horizon, which were already beginning to sink into the dusk. The dot became smaller and smaller and eventually disappeared in a hollow, as if it had been sucked out of the world. Schwanecke spat, turned round and trudged back to the village. It was time to think of leaving.

Outside the farmhouse where the operating theatre had been set up, he came on Deutschmann, leaning against the door, pale, lean, in a dream, his mouth clamped tight. Although he was not wearing a great-coat, he did not seem to notice the cold.

"Time we got going," said Schwanecke.

Deutschmann nodded, but did not move.

"Has something happened?"

"No."

"You think too much, mate," said Schwanecke, grinning. "Much too much. That doesn't do you any good. Switch off, I tell you."

"Three dead and two whose legs we had to amputate," said Deutschmann.

"I'll tell you something. This is the first time you've been at the front, and that's why it's hit you, although you're a doctor and must be used to things like that. But it's different here at the front from somewhere in a proper hospital—I can understand that. Only believe me, if I started thinking, I'd shoot myself in the mouth on the spot. I had a dose of it a few minutes ago. It was worse than the worst running fire. I made up my mind never to think again, mate. Come on, get yourself dressed, we want to be on our way, on our way home, you might say."

Grinning, he crossed the road to his sledge, broad and sturdy, looking even more massive in his fur. Deutschmann gazed after him, and a small wry smile flitted over his face. On our way home, he thought. When I was going to see Julia, I would say: I'm going home. Now I'm going home—to Krull. Think too much, do I? Switch off? How can one? How will those men live without legs? How can you live when you can't walk any more? On my way home, to Julia, to Krull. Rubbish.

He turned round and went into the house to get ready for the journey 'home'.

20

Krull was on the war-path.

On the table in front of him lay precise sectional plans of the trenches to be dug, and he was entering in red ink those that had been completed. He had drawn the map to a scale of 1:2000, and after lengthy calculations had worked out that B Company had dug over fifty yards too little. The target had not been achieved, despite picks, blastings, and ten-hour working days. For Krull this signified a serious military failure, which would be laid at *his* door. Fifty yards short! He made his calculations again, but the fifty yards did not become any fewer. Presumably Lieutenant Obermeier was still in ignorance of the fact. Krull pondered how he was going to break the news of the debacle to the company commander.

First thing to do was to call his N.C.O.'s into the office. He had decided also to take action against the growing negligence and lack of discipline, so he reverted to barracks routine: the N.C.O.'s had to appear in full service dress, wearing their steel helmets.

Sergeant Hefe tapped his forehead before going in with Corporals Kentrop and Bortke. "Screw loose, I'm afraid, boys." On entering, they saluted and looked at Krull, who was squatting behind his improvised desk, the sectional plans clearly visible in front of him.

"Aha," said Kentrop out loud.

Krull looked up abruptly. "Yes, my lad. Aha it bloody well is. B Company strikes me as a home for aged criminals.

Slow-...-coaches. The Russians will just have to wait till our fine gentlemen are ready. Here!" He banged his fist down on the table. "I've worked it out that we are fifty yards short of our target."

"Are you sure you've worked it out right?" Bortke asked gently.

"Are you suggesting, Bortke ..." Krull went red.

"Oh, listen, Sergeant Major." Hefe took off his steel helmet, sat down on a crate, and took the plans from the desk. "This is the stretch where you can only dig by night. In daylight we're under enemy observation, they see every mouse that creeps out of the snow."

"What about it?" Krull tore the plans out of Hefe's hands. "There are others in the front line constantly under enemy observation."

"They're down under ground. We have to stand and dig." Bortke followed Hefe's example, and took off his helmet. "How about your coming out with us and seeing for yourself? Good idea, don't you think?"

"Oh now it's the squad leaders who are responsible." Krull began to retract a little, Bortke's proposal did not appeal to him. "I'm just saying that if it's reported that the digging's going too slowly, there'll be hell to pay."

"Then they should come and have a look for themselves," said Bortke.

"Which battalion HQ ever did that?" demanded Kentrop. "But have you any suggestions, Sergeant Major?" He was very correct as usual. He had kept his helmet on, and was the only one still standing. Krull respected Kentrop, but always felt rather uneasy in face of his calm and composure. Now, too, he only gave a glance at Kentrop before turning back to Hefe.

"We must try to dig by day as well. We *must* make up the missing fifty yards. If our men up in front stick their necks out, we can't play hide-and-seek here."

"Quite right, Sergeant Major." Obermeier had come in through the second door, which formed a connection to the ruined parts of the building. When the sitting N.C.O.s began to jump to their feet, he waved them back to their benches, walked over to the table and picked up the drawings. "Neat work, Sergeant major."

"Exactly to scale, sir, so that we can check the work's progress every day."

"Can you really do that?"

"Yes, sir."

"Here from your desk?" Obermeier put the plans down in front of him. "You haven't drawn the sectional map on the spot. How can you be sure that your fifty yards isn't due to a mistake in drawing or calculation. The best thing, Sergeant Major, would be for you to verify your calculations on the ground tomorrow. Go out with the Company and measure the trenches with a tape-measure. Then check with your plans. The places under enemy observation will be of special interest, of course."

Krull did not dare answer. This was something he handn't expected. His heart began to throb violently. He felt he must be looking very pale, and the three N.C.O.s were all staring at him with shameless grins on their faces.

"All clear, Sergeant Major?"

"Yes, sir." Krull breathed deeply. The fear in his bones could not dispel his adherence to discipline.

"Tomorrow morning, then. When does your squad move off, Hefe?"

"At half-past-five, sir."

"You will take the Sergeant Major with you."

"With pleasure, sir."

Obermeier turned on him. "Don't make damn' stupid remarks. War is not pleasure and never was. Suppose you're under fire and something happens to the Sergeant Major. Or can you guarantee that nothing will?"

"No, sir."

"Well then." Obermeier turned to the telephone. Krull had listened to this exchange as if from a great distance, not really taking it in. A dull weakness had crept up his legs. He held on to the edge of the table and stared at the plans without seeing anything. Then he heard Kentrop's voice: "You can be sure, sir, that we shall all risk our lives to get the Sergeant Major out again if anything does happen. If we don't succeed at once, he'll only have to wait till nightfall at worse."

Obermeier did not answer. He looked at the wall, cranked the handle of the telephone and rang A Company.

Krull slowly looked up, into the maliciously grinning faces of his N.C.O.s. "Right," he said painfully. "I go out with you tonight. Then I'll be at the trenches in the morning and can measure them by daylight. And ..." Now his voice grew more assured—"Heaven help the lot of you if it turns out that they really are fifty yards short." He turned and quickly left the office. Hefe looked at the two others in amazement. They said nothing; they were equally staggered. For the first time Krull had fought a battle with himself before their eyes—and won.

Obermeier turned round. "Why are you still standing here? There's new wood for lining the bunkers just coming in from Babinitchi."

Sheepishly and somewhat chastened, the three N.C.O.s left the room. Outside the house they stopped and looked at Krull, who was yelling at some men unloading sledges too slowly for his liking.

"Quite his old self again," said Hefe.

"Who'd have thought it of him?" said Bortke.

"Don't kid yourselves," said Kentrop. "Or are you going to tell me you aren't scared yourselves?"

"No one could pretend that," Hefe growled. "Which of us hasn't sometimes trembled with terror? Only with Krull it's been worse than with anybody else. Till now anyhow. We'll soon see if there's really been any change."

21

To strengthen the defence system, the trenches were interspersed with small bunkers every fifty yards. These were dug out by night, and the men dragged boards through the snow, with which the bunkers would be lined in the early morning just before dawn. Wiedeck and Katzorki—'Ratface'—were crawling round fixing this lining, when Deutschmann ducked into the trench, breathing heavily. He leaned up against the wall, which was frozen hard.

"Look who we've got here. Visit from a high-up," said Ratface, a crooked grin exposing his black stumps of teeth.

"Anything the matter?" asked Wiedeck.

Deutschmann shrugged his shoulders. "Nothing. I have to wait till there *is* something."

"Then you won't have to wait long," said Ratface.

Only a third of the Company at a time stayed in the trenches; the rest moved off at daybreak. Periodically the earth shot up and shook the men to bits. At brief intervals the whine of shells came through the icy air: the organ notes got lower and lower, like a humming-top just before it stops. Then the men would throw themselves against the trench wall, stick their head in the snow, and listen, their faces distorted by fear, for the crashes to come. Twice, five times, seven, ten, twelve times they heard the thunder around them, the blast pressed them against the ground or almost lifted them off it. Fountains of stones, ice and earth spurted up and then pelted down on their backs. And in between they heard the shrill, whirring whistle of the glowing shrapnel that went hissing into the snow.

"Damned near," said Wiedeck.

"Yes, quite near enough for my liking," said Deutschmann.

After the end of the barrage they got up and with their heads down raced to the next bunker. Breathlessly they stumbled down the steps and sat on the stacked boards. Wiedeck lit himself a cigarette and offered one to Deutschmann. Ratface did not smoke; he bartered the few cigarettes he collected for bread, margarine and sausage meat.

"If things go on like this," said Wiedeck, "the new defence positions will be smashed before they're even finished."

Deutschmann leaned against the cold earth wall. "The positions should be established further west," he said. His unshaven face had become still leaner and sharper. He no longer wore a Red Cross armband. It was not the custom in Russia, and when anybody did wear one, that usually had no influence upon the enemy: medical personnel were fired on by both sides, with or without armbands. "What use is a trench system little more than half a mile behind the frontline? When the offensive gets going, half a mile won't mean a thing."

"They should have made you a general," said Ratface.

Wiedeck took quick puffs at his cigarette. Since the birth of the child he had not heard from his wife. His letters remained unanswered, he didn't even know whether they were sent on after censorship. Of course everybody knew the Battalion had no rights. No rights to send mail, no rights to receive mail, or parcels, no rights to normal military rations. They were outlaws, criminals, in grey, worn and patched uniforms, consigned to hard labour until they became worthless. There was nothing anybody could do to alter that, not even Lieutenant Obermeier or Captain Barth. Obermeier had, in fact, once rung up Barth and asked about mail. "Mail?" enquired Barth in surprise. "Are you expecting any mail?"

"Not just for me. My men have no idea at all what's happening at home. It's worst for the married men, of course."

"They're dead lucky, Obermeier. Tell your men that they

can be happy if they don't know what's happening at home. Anyhow mail goes through the depot battalion in Posnan. There's a Major Kratzer there in charge of supply. I hear he possesses the golden party badge, and he's been a teacher at a national socialist educational institution. At the moment it's pretty cold in Posnan. If Kratzner puts the letters in the stove, they'll help him to keep his hands warm."

So 'wait' was all that Wiedeck or anyone else could get out of Obermeier. Gradually Wiedeck, like the rest, relapsed into a sort of apathetic fatalism which nothing could shake. Artilery fire? What about it? Death? That's war. Work? I'm used to it. Life? It's lousy. Now he said: "Who cares if it's half a mile or five miles? We still have to dig."

"Right," said Ratface.

"And we'll all be dead soon anyhow."

"Not necessarily," said Deutschmann.

"Do you really believe that? Do you think we'll be given a pardon and sent back to a base job? Might just happen to Schwanecke or Ratface here. After all they're ordinary criminals."

"Hey, listen," protested Ratface.

"They might be pardoned so they can be hanged some day later on. I suppose I may have a chance of coming through myself. After all, I'm only a simple farmer. But you or Bartlitz and the other politicals—you won't be pardoned till you're under the ground."

"I'll soon be out of all this," declared Ratface.

"No one's out of it," said Wiedeck.

"Bloody pessimists," said Ratface, standing up and going to the bunker entrance. "I tell you I.ll be back in Berlin in a month or two. When I'm drinking the best coffee at Kranzler's, I'll send you a card." He grinned back over his shoulder and climbed into the trench.

Deutschmann looked out of the bunker on to the small piece of snow wall visible at the entrance. Outside, the light artillery was probing the field, some machine guns were rattling; periodically they could hear the discharges of light trench mortars and the dull explosions of rifle grenades.

"Off we go again," said Wiedeck. "Still, if you're really tired, you can sleep through it."

There was a brief, shrill whine through the air, and then some shells from the Russian artillery exploded near the bunker. Deutschmann found himself lying on the ground; some lumps of earth from the bunker ceiling peppered his back. And through the humming and ringing in his ears he suddenly heard a human voice outside. It sounded familiar, but he couldn't place its owner. Then it stopped being a human voice. There were sounds that an animal might make, an animal that had somehow found human speech in its mortal terror and could scream out its agony for all to understand. "Jesus Christ!" the voice whimpered, sobbed and shrieked. "Jesus Christ" A long groan, and then again: "Jesus Christ. . . ."

"Ratface!" cried Wiedeck, jumped over Deutschmann and crawled out of the bunker. Deutschmann pulled himself up, sprang to the exit, dropped to his knees and crawled out. His first aid bag was in his way, it hung between his legs and trailed on the ground. With a short frenzied movement he slung it on his back, then he was outside, and the whimpering was quite near.

Katzorki was leaning against the trench wall. His face had gone grey; the nose stuck out, sharp and yellow. The lips were drawn back convulsively from the black stumps of teeth, and without the lips moving the choked whimpering sounds came out of his mouth: "Jesus Christ, what's . . . Jesus Christ . . ." His eyes stared at something bloody that lay in front of him.

It was only now Deutschmann saw that Katzorki's arm, on the far side, had been torn off. Blood was splashing from the huge lacerating wound, it ran down his uniform, painted the dirty snow red, and formed a small but rapidly growing puddle in the frozen grass round Katzorki's boots. Katzorki's knees gave way, he slid down the trench wall and stayed sitting on the ground, in the middle of the pool of blood. He still gazed at the torn-off arm lying before him with the palm turned downwards and fingers crooked. He lifted his right arm as if wanting to reach for something or looking for a hand-hold; but the arm sank helplessly, and he tipped over to the side, still repeating endlessly: "Jesus Christ, Jesus Christ . . ."

Wiedeck was deathly pale and frozen in horror. Deutschmann thrust him aside and bent over Katzorki. With flying hands he opened the first-aid bag and began rummaging around in it, not taking his eyes off Katzorki. But then he stopped abruptly. It was no good. He saw death spreading over the wounded man's face.

Werner Katzorki, Ratface to his mates, was buried behind a cottage near Company Headquarters. His grave was a little way away from the two rows of crooked snow-covered birch crosses. For on the day he died a stray shell had come down between them and torn a flat hollow in the stone-hard ground: a welcome piece of assistance for the two Russian collaborators who had to dig the graves.

The burial attracted little attention. It was night, and the Company were working on their excavations up front. A few of the men who were outside by day stood rather helplessly round the flat hollow which was to be Katzorki's grave. The dead man was already stiff: with mouth wide open and grinning he lay on a tarpaulin near the hole. On his stomach was the torn-off arm; the enormous wound brought a shimmer of pink through the white hoar frost which had settled on it.

The two Russians were standing by impassively. "Right, you two, go ahead," said Wiedeck.

The two men took hold of one side of the tarpaulin, lifted it and rolled the stiff body into the grave. Burying the dead with tarpaulins had been forbidden. Tarpaulins were rare; the living could make good use of them, the dead didn't need them.

Up on the front the noise of battle continued ceaselessly. The rumble of artillery fire rolled across the plains, and in between the furious rattle of German machine guns could be heard, along with the more cautious tack-tack of the Russian guns. One of the grave-diggers climbed into the hole and laid Katzorki straight on his back so that his face was turned to the sky. Then they quickly began to cover him with earth.

There was no funeral address; and before the body had been completely covered, the soldiers left the grave. Deutschmann had done the only thing that could be done for the dead man: on a rough board nailed to the birch cross he had written in copying ink:

PRIVATE WERNER KATZORKI
1912-1943

And underneath, in smaller letters:
"Perhaps he's better off now."

22

Lieutenant Bevern turned up again in Babinitchi. Wernher had no idea what he wanted there, nor did Obermeier, whom Wernher quickly rang up as Bevern climbed out of his sledge, took the salute from the corporal on guard, gave him a passing reprimand for not wearing his steel helmet, and gazed after Wanda, Wernher's interpreter, who had just passed him. Despite the shapeless thick coat and the felt boots she wore, it was impossible not to notice that she was extremely pretty.

"Disgusting!" Bevern grunted, and at once thought of a lecture he would give at the next training evening: The Undermining of the German Soldier's Morale by the Russian Woman.

Wernher put down the receiver, regarded Bevern from the window and grinned. "I think Wanda might be some temptation even for our worthy adjutant," he remarked to his sergeant.

"Blood out of a stone, sir, do you think?" the sergeant permitted himself to say, knowing Wernher's opinion of Bevern. He left the room as Bevern came in.

"Hullo, Wernher, I'm back. Are you surprised?"

Wernher shrugged his shoulders. "Surprised? No—why should I be? In war you have to expect unpleasant surprises."

"Thank you very much," said Bevern, stiffening. But he decided he must control himself and take the first step to a reconciliation or at least a good understanding. The officer corps must stick together through thick and thin, through good times and bad, especially the bad, well, difficult times.

"Why do you have to be so hostile?" he asked pleadingly. "You make it sound as if I'd been sent here just to annoy *you*. But we must stick together, mustn't we? After all, we're all in the same boat."

"Only you're rowing in the opposite direction," said Wernher harshly.

"You are unfair. I only do my duty."

Wernher sat down. "Ah," he said. "Just your duty. I see, I see. Three days ago, for instance, you collected the men on leave from the field hospital at Barssdovka and took them out on a march. That was your—duty, eh, Bevern? Wounded men who, in any normal unit would be sent home for six weeks. I know, I know"—he brushed aside an objection before Bevern could open his mouth—"we aren't a normal unit, and there's no leave for the likes of us. All we can hope for is a rest at base, at Orsha. Not much of a holiday resort is it! And there, in the make-do convalescent area, you collect men who still have half-open wounds, and take them out on a march. One two, one two, sing up, my lads, and all that bull. You make them hobble through the countryside, you organise parades and barrack square drill and night manoeuvres—and all that with men who can hardly stand on their feet."

Bevern looked out of the window. His youthful face was proud and stubborn. "Toughening up," he said eventually. "The army can't go in for mollycoddling. And a little exercise never hurt anyone."

"Try asking a doctor about that."

"Oh, come off it," said Bevern contemptuously.

"One might call that sort of thing pure sadism, Bevern,"

"Call it what you like. There's nothing anywhere to say that convalescent soldiers should be given civilian-type treatment. Sick or well, they're still soldiers. Which is what we need, Wernher, don't you understand? Real men, hard and merciless to themselves. That's the only way they can become hard and merciless towards our enemies. After all, you're an officer, you *must* understand that. Look, Wernher, we've got a bloody hard battle to fight, it may still be quite a long way to final victory ..."

"Oh, cut it out. When I hear that, I think of a record that's got stuck in a groove. Hard ... hard ... hard ... final victory ... final victory...."

Bevern stiffened, ready to pounce. His face and tense figure expressed a single thought: now I've got you. "And do you by any chance not believe in such a thing?" he asked, in a quiet voice. His intention was all too obvious and Wernher was surprised at its naiveté.

"What do you mean?" he asked ingenuously.

"Your remark just then, when you said ..."

"Listen, Bevern, I could have you in front of the C.O. for this. You're trying to put words into my mouth I wouldn't dream of saying. You are a bad national socialist. I am not a Party member, and yet I would never allow myself to do the things you do. You disgust me. The way you've treated men who ought at least to have a few days' rest because they've been wounded, because they've given their blood for Germany, even though they're in a penal battalion, is absolutely nauseating, to put it mildly. I'm ashamed to wear the same officer's uniform as you. You're not only a bad national socialist, you're a sadistic swine."

Bevern left the farmhouse without a word. Deadly pale and looking stunned, he stopped a few moments on the road. Then he walked slowly and despondently to his sledge. "Back to the Battalion," he told his driver in a peremptory tone.

Wernher quickly rang up Obermeier and gave him the gist of the conversation. Obermeier was silent for a few seconds, then his voice came through the wire thin and distorted. "You're mad, Paul."

"I've had enough, Fritz."

"But listen, I—we—must keep our heads above water. We mustn't let ourselves be carried away. What will happen to our men if we suddenly—if we land up somewhere as privates in a penal battalion just like them?"

"One can't always be thinking of that," said Wernher.

"One must try."

"I had to use plenty of self-restraint not to smash his face in."

"I can just imagine. Still, go on using it ... Are you coming over here today?"

"I'll try."

"Right—see you then. We must find some way. It oughtn't be too difficult to get the bastard put where he can't do any harm."

Wernher put down the receiver and looked thoughtfully out of the window towards the sledge, now gliding far out over the steppe.

23

Another sledge rumbled through the night.

It was snowing. The snow swirled out of the grey-black of the sky in thick snowy flakes. Silently it covered the land. The new snow whirled up in clouds before the sledge's runners and scattered its dust over the muffled figure in the driving seat.

Schwanecke held on with both hands. Now and then he swore. The sledge bounded over frozen snow humps. He kept on being bounced off the seat and shaken to bits. The sub-machine-gun which he had slung round his neck hit him in the pit of the stomach. The small engine under the seat made a shrill whining noise. Would it stand up to this continual overloading?

Suddenly he saw on the road a figure emerging from the drifting snow. A small shaggy figure in a thick fur, just as muffled up as he was himself. Alone and forelorn, the figure stood in the midst of the greyish white expanses. When the sledge rattled up, it raised an arm, without moving from the middle of the road.

Schwanecke stepped on the brakes. The sledge swerved a little, skidded, then stopped. He turned off the engine and climbed down from his seat. He lifted the sling of the gun over his head and took a grip on the trigger. Slowly he went over to the mutely waiting figure.

Then he recognised him, stopped as if rooted, bent forward and raised the muzzle of the gun.

Tartuchin put up both hands to indicate that he carried no

weapons. Knitting his eyes together, so that their pupils could no longer be seen at all, he stared at Schwanecke. For a long time he said nothing, but finally he opened his mouth, to say with stiff lips: "So it's you."

A cold shiver ran over Schwanecke's back. His eyes left Tartuchin and traversed the snow-covered steppe in a quick precautionary glance.

Tartuchin smiled faintly. "We are quite alone, little brother." He made a sweeping gesture to include the wide expanses round them and above them. "No one can see us."

Schwanecke nodded. "Good." His own voice was strange to him. He knew he must fight and he wanted to fight. "Right then, let's have you!" he said, and in his voice there was the hint of a small, mirthless, triumphant laugh.

Tartuchin felt in the pocket of his fur and held out towards Schwanecke two short, slightly curved daggers. Even in the darkness Schwanecke could see that their handles were richly decorated.

"Beautiful. Are you selling 'em?"

"You or me." said Tartuchin.

"Can't you make it cheaper?"

Tartuchin's smile froze. "Choose one, they are same."

Schwanecke pulled off his glove and felt the edge of one of the daggers with the tip of his forefinger. It was sharp as a razor. "Not bad."

Tartuchin nodded. "Has to go through fur."

Schwanecke picked up a dagger, weighed it in his hand, threw it up in the air, adroitly caught it again, and then took two steps back.

"Why fur?" he said, unbuttoning his thick lambskin coat and throwing it down in the snow behind him. "We don't need any fur in hell, so let's get on with it."

Tartuchin hesitated for a moment, then he too peeled off his shaggy fur and threw it into the snow. To the east, over the misty woods, the sky turned pale, grey, streaky.

"Ready, get set," hissed Schwanecke, crouching and stretching out the hand with the dagger slightly in front of him.

Tartuchin bent his knees ready to attack. The blade of his dagger shimmered faintly.

For seconds they stood facing each other. Both had stopped thinking. Suddenly, with a sound like a groan, Tartuchin shot forward in a lightning thrust at his adversary. But Schwanecke easily parried, and brought his knee hard into Tartuchin's groin.

The Mongolian howled like a wounded wolf, and doubled up in pain. But he kept his face turned upwards. Schwanecke charged forward and stabbed at that face.

Tartuchin parried the blow. He turned on his axis, and lunged when Schwanecke fell past him in the path of his own stroke.

Schwanecke could not parry, in fact he did not even see the Mongolian's lightning thrust. A hot, stabbing pain coursed through his right hip, and almost simultaneously he felt something warm flowing over his thigh. "You ... bastard!" he gasped, and tried to jump aside, but stumbled. Thc right leg had gone dead, he couldn't put any weight on it.

Tartuchin circled round him. He threw a short quick glance at the edge of his dagger, saw that it was bloody, and began to grin. A wild intoxication came over him. Blood! Blood! *His* blood! "I'll kill you," he panted. And again: "I'll kill you—I'll kill you!"

Schwanecke was silent. His right thigh was burning like fire. He had stopped hating the other man. In him was a cold, icy will to kill. He was calm. He saw the distorted face circle round him, and moved with it, the dagger in his extended fist. Then suddenly, like an arrow from a bow, he hurled himself on to the Mongolian's small crouched figure. The attack came so suddenly, silently and unexpectedly, with a cold calculating ferocity, that Tartuchin could not escape it. All he could do was to drop in the snow and thrust the dagger upwards. But he did not manage to hit Schwanecke. He saw Schwanecke's face above him, quite close, each hair of the beard distinct: a cold impassive face, which did not even move when he made a wide stabbing stroke from the ground and hit his enemy in the back.

Tartuchin felt the short dagger-blade pierce his body once and then again, and he began to yell shrilly, thrashing around him. In his voice was fear and desperation, terror at the death hovering over him, and a longing for life. With a desperate howl he hurled Schwanecke aside and jumped up at the same time as Schwanecke did. Then he saw the German's hand with the dagger jerk forward again.

At this moment Tartuchin lost control.

He turned and ran screaming along the road. With a bleeding face, and burning body full of wounds, he staggered on. He was crying with pain, and did not even notice that he had fallen into the snow and was creeping on all fours towards the wood. Behind him he trailed a red streak like a thin string unravelled from his own body. He thought: let me die, let me die, he's robbed me of my power and my courage. But he crawled on, picked himself up and staggered to the wood. With his hand he scooped up some snow and pressed it on the burning wounds on his face.

When Tartuchin disappeared behind the curtain of snow, Schwanecke dropped to his knees. At first he was still smiling, but the smile soon disappeared. The triumph had gone out of it and given place to desperation at the raging pain. His right side felt dead, and the wound in his back burned as if someone had sprinkled salt into it. His head sank into the snow, and he felt the icy cold gratefully on his brow. But he must not, could not give up. On his knees he slid across the road, pulled himself up, groaning, on to the sledge seat and dropped over the steering-wheel. He had to drive it. Every minute lost brought him near to death, and he didn't want to die. He must drive it, drive it. He felt for the ignition key, turned it, opened the throttle, and the engine started: rattling, juddering. The seat shook. Then the sledge shot howling down the road at top speed to Barssdovka.

Schwanecke lay over the wheel. He drove through a cloudy dream-world, in which only his pain existed. And so there arrived in Barssdovka a howling sledge tacking drunkenly from one side of the road to the other, skidding to a stop in a high snow drift outside the field hospital.

Slowly, as if he didn't want to give in even now, Schwanecke fell on to his side, tried to get a grip on himself, then curled up and rolled into the snow.

Soon afterwards Kronenberg found him lying there unconscious.

24

Wiedeck was sitting in a half-finished, shored-up bunker, smoking a cigarette, the last of his ration, when the narrow entrance darkened and a broad figure made its way into the bunker. Wiedeck's cigarette was left suspended in mid-air half way to his mouth. At first he thought it was an illusion, but no—the figure was Krull. "I'm going mad," he muttered, as he slowly stood up.

"Hey there, you ruddy slackers, knocked off already, have you? Oh, I see, there's only one of you in here. Where are the others?"

"What others?" asked Wiedeck.

"The rest of your squad, man. Or are you building a bunker on your own?"

"I still had something to do," said Wiedeck, not very convincingly. He had hidden in this bunker half an hour before relief time, just to have a rest. He was dog-tired and it was fairly warm here. Anyhow it was warmer than outside, where that bloody wind whistled over the plains and the snow crystals stabbed your face like needles.

"Well, I don't know," grumbled Krull. "Seems to be quite cosy here. Fine to be a soldier, eh? Now I know why there are fifty yards of trench missing. Instead of digging, you shower sit around here. It was high time I had a look for myself at what was going on."

Wiedeck stubbed the cigarette out carefully, put the fag-end away in his coat pocket and sat down again. Krull stared at him in amazement for a moment, then shouted:

"Off your arse at once. Out of this bunker and get moving with that pick."

"Not me," said Wiedeck. "The relief's due now. I've been here all night. And the whole time I've had nothing to eat and no rest-break. Slackers, are we?"

"Rest-break? Is the German army some sort of rest-home?" yelled Krull, who was feeling very strong. With Hefe and Kentrop he had driven from Gorki with four sledges to the digging sites, under enemy observation, without the Russians firing on them. This made Krull suspect that all the reports about enemy fire were grossly exaggerated and only served as an excuse for dereliction of duty. Of course it was rather mysterious that there were so many dead and wounded. Perhaps some were self-inflected wounds, By God he'd have to keep a sharp look-out for that sort of thing.

Directly he reached the trenches that had been dug, he decided to make a tour of inspection. Instead of men hard at work he found tired figures sitting in the bunkers or on the trench floor—waiting for their reliefs to come. Eventually he reached the small advance bunker where Wicdeck was having his rest.

It didn't look at all bad in such a bunker. Hard earth, lined with wooden boarding, thick beams shoring up the roof, a few recesses where bunk beds with palliases could be put up. Really comfortable. But he had plenty of time, he could look round later. First, though, he must chase the recalcitrant Wiedeck out of here. He was opening his mouth to give the man a thorough bawling out, when he was stopped by a distant thunder. Directly afterwards there was a whine through the air, followed by four, six, eight crashes; the ground and the bunker walls vibrated slightly. Krull held on to a beam and pulled his head well in. His fat face had gone pale, and despite the icy cold there were suddenly beads of sweat on his brow. "What … what was that?" he asked, when the attack seemed over.

"Russians," said Wiedenk tersely. He had not stirred from his stack of planks. Sunk into himself, elbows propped on his knees, he sat there and looked at Krull.

"Russians. Was that …"

"Artillery. I thought you'd know that. Or haven't you ever been in the front line?"

"Shut your trap!" Krull bellowed. Wiedeck had touched one of his closest secrets. According to his papers he had seen front line service—1939 in Poland and 1940 in France. In fact his unit had been kept consistently in reserve, marching miles behind the advancing troops, hearing the thunder of guns only from a distance and otherwise living in style with chickens, eggs, wine and other spoils of an advancing army. But this was something nobody was obliged to know. Afterwards he served at a base camp where he had to train recruits, and then the soldiers of the penal battalion, how to behave under enemy fire. The shells of the Russian light artillery round the bunker were the first he had experienced at close range in his long military career. "Is it often like this?" he asked, in a subdued tone.

"The Russians saw you coming, and now they won't let you go," said Wiedeck. "Did you come with the relief?"

"Of course, what do you think?"

"Oh, hell, then I must get a move on." Wiedeck rose, strapped his water-bottle to his belt and put on his helmet. As he pulled the hood of his combat-kit over the helmet and pulled the zip under the chin, he peered across at Krull, who was still clutching the post. "Are you staying on here, Sergeant Major?"

"Yes, of course." But Krull's voice was no longer so resolute. He had forgotten that Wiedeck had just now behaved with a gross lack of discipline, for which he, the sergeant major, had intended to take him to task in no uncertain terms. Now he envied the man who was being relieved, and searched for a possibility of joining him. But how? The company commander had ordered him to measure the trenches, and he himself had said in broad daylight that he would do it. I'm a bloody fool, he thought, how could I have, now could I? But I don't want to stay here alone. Nobody could expect that of me. I'll go back with Wiedeck, to the others, and after that—we'll see what happens. But I can't stay here alone! An isolated shell whined away high over the bunker and crashed somewhere behind. Oh, I can't stay here alone ...

"Where are you off to, Wiedeck?" he asked hoarsely.

"To the collecting point. They're waiting for me." He stepped out of the bunker and Krull followed him.

"I'm late, too, hope they haven't gone without me," Wiedeck muttered, afraid he might have dozed through his relief: he would have to hurry, or he could well be stuck here all day—you couldn't cross the snow-field in daylight.

Then it came: roaring, whistling, whining through the air. A flashing black wall of fire rose from the ground where the German front line was.

Wiedeck looked over the edge of the trench, then turned to the cowering Krull and cried: "Come on, at once, if you're coming with me. We can still make it now, but soon it'll be hopeless. The Russians will put up a barrage and we shan't be able to move."

It was the usual surprise attack by the heavy Russian artillery, preceding a dawn offensive by tanks and infantry. It was the sort of softening-up attack that was taking place in hundreds of places along the Eastern Front at this period; just at this time of morning; introducing a day full of death and agony and mortal fear, like countless days before it and countless days to follow.

It wasn't a particularly strong barrage; or at any rate it didn't have the furious, overwhelming destructive power of other such attacks which were usually a prelude to major offensives. But for the soldiers who had to endure it and could do nothing else but claw into the frozen earth and wait for the blow that would wipe them out, it was hellish enough.

Hell for the infantry-men in the front line; a foretaste of the hell that would soon come for the soldiers of the penal battalion just behind them. And a hell for Krull, who suddenly found himself facing a situation which still now he could not imagine. Death for him had had something glamorous about it, and was also painless: a brave, splendid soldier's death; and one that he also assumed would never some to *him*. What was happening now was quite different, the thing now looming huge before his eyes bore no relation to the soldier's death read about in books. It was a pitiful, anonymous, impersonal, terrified croaking. It was bursting up him, it threatened to bury him under it, and it turned him into a pathetic fear-tormented wretch who had no other wish than the mere desire to go on living.

And when a salvo of Russian shells landed just short of the trench in which he and Wiedeck were crouching, and when he saw that Wiedeck really meant to run away, the only man beside himself in these terrible spaces shattered by exploding shells, he lost the last spark of self-control. He wouldn't, he couldn't go on, and still less could he stay alone. So he clutched Wiedeck's arm, crying: "You'll stay … you're not going, are you?"

"Let me go, blast you!" Wiedeck shouted back, and tried to shake him off. But Krull clung to him like a leech and pulled him down. "Let go!" yelled Wiedeck.

"I can't stay here alone … not alone."

"Then come with me, for Christ's sake."

"Wiedeck … " gasped Krull. "We're mates, man. Stay here and help me with the measuring—do you hear?"

"I'm not mad."

"Wiedeck—Erich! … "

He tore himself loose, but Krull did not give up. He jumped on him from behind and pulled him back. Pressed tight against each other, they stayed crouching by the trench wall.

"I tell you for the last time: let me go. You'd better let me go, or I'll break your skull in," said Wiedeck coldly, controlling himself with difficulty. He knew he would be unable to control himself much longer. It was not the first time he had seen a man go to pieces. But all the ones before Krull had been his mates, his comrades. This bastard here, this big-mouthed bully—he had to get shot of him, or else….

"You just can't leave a comrade alone….!" stuttered Krull, his face grey and hollow, saliva running over his chin, the picture of repulsive cowardice. And Krull had said the one thing he should not have said. Anyone else could have said it, but not him. Wiedeck clenched his fist, and punched the sergeant major in the face with all his power, and then again and a third time. Krull doubled up, but Wiedeck lifted his head and struck again and again at that repulsive, distorted face. "Comrade!" he spat. "You're a bloody fine comrade. I'll smash you to bits."

Suddenly disgust overcame rage, and he could not be bothered any more. He gave one further parting punch, which made Krull's head bang against the wall. Then he drew his head in, raced across the trench, threw himself to the ground when a shell whined and landed about thirty yards in front of him, jumped to his feet again and dashed on, to the collecting point.

When he came whizzing round the corner of the trench system, he found the place empty. The snow had been trodden by many boots, there was a solitary spade leaning against the trench wall. In the distance he could hear digging: that would be the relief shift who worked during the day. Now and then he saw a shovel blade flash over the edge of the trench, or the brief gleam of a pick being swung. Heaps of earth and snow burst out of the ground, as if some gigantic mole were in action.

The Russian artillery were now putting up a barrage behind the German front line. Quite soon the fire would be returned—and he would be in the middle of it.

Wiedeck wiped the sweat from his brow. The others had left. He was stuck here for the whole day. And he had to hurry. The best bunker was really the one he had just come from. Even if Krull were there.

He ran back. He found Krull where he had left him. Doubled up, covered with earth and mud, he was sitting on the trench floor. He looked up nervously and gratefully when Wiedeck kicked him with the tip of his boot. "Are you back again?" he asked, in a small, broken voice, as if he could not believe that he wasn't alone any more in this terrible trench, in the middle of a terrible, threatening world which seemed to be bent on exterminating him.

"The others had cleared off, I got there too late because you kept me back. Now we have to stick around here all day. Come on, let's get into the bunker now."

Wiedeck had ceased to feel any hatred for Krull. His fury had abated, leaving only indifference and a trace of scornful pity.

"All day," muttered Krull as he crawled behind Wiedeck into the bunker. He knew he had put up a miserable show, but he no longer cared. Heroism couldn't be acquired by order and he was not a hero, why should he conceal the fact? With trembling hand he got a packet of cigarettes out of his pocket, opened it, and held it out to Wiedeck.

Wiedeck took a cigarette, without looking at Krull. He could hardly bear such a pitiful spectacle. "Shouldn't you be measuring the trenches?" he asked mockingly. "There are fifty yards missing, Hefe told me, and you discovered that. You worked it out very carefully, didn't you? I tell you what: when the Ivans have quietened down, we'll go out and measure. You do the measuring and I'll write down the results. That's if we haven't had our chips by then."

"What d'you mean?"

"Can't you hear that the Russians are attacking, you stupid idiot? Clean out your ears."

From up there in the front line they could hear quite distinctly the furious rattle of machine guns, the drone of the mortars, and then three or four times in quick succession the shrill, dry crack of hand-grenades. And behind that was another noise; the hum of heavy engines, most of the time just audible but occasionally with a louder drone.

"Tanks," said Wiedeck. "Hope they don't break through."

Krull looked at him with wide, shocked eyes. There was now something childish in them, an uncomprehending amazement which gave his grey, bloated face an appearance of almost touching helplessness. But Wiedeck didn't see this; and if he had, it would have made no impression on him. "Let's hope our blokes up front hold the line," he said. "Then we can go and measure. Those were Obermeier's orders, weren't they?"

"Obermeier can stuff himself," said Krull.

"Well I never!" Wiedeck said with irony. "Now who was bleating all the time about discipline? It was you, wasn't it, not me?"

Crump. Something landed quite close to them.

"That was a near one," said Wiedeck calmly.

Krull crouched on the ground. His mouth was full of bile; it burnt in his throat. He could not stand it any more in here. He couldn't sit here any more waiting for the end which was coming to him with deadly certainty. He must do something, make some move, get out of here as far as possible, only to be out of this rat-trap. He suddenly jumped up and staggered to the entrance.

"Stop! Where are you going?" Wiedeck managed to grip him by his coat. "Where are you off to, you stupid fool?"

"Let me go!" cried Krull. "Let me go. I want to get out!" With clenched fists he thrashed around him; his face had lost its helpless childishness and was threatening and distorted. "I want to get away from here!" he yelled. "The tanks.... I want to get away!"

It was not easy to master him. Wiedeck was breathing very heavily when he at last had Krull lying on a stack of boards and only whimpering softly.

"Pull yourself together, for Christ's sake," he said coldly.

"I want to get out of here, I want to get out!" Krull whimpered, and then Wiedeck saw him fumble with his pistol holster. But before he could pull the pistol out, Wiedeck knocked him down with a few hard punches, and took the pistol away from him.

Outside, there was a loud, piercing whine through the air, and then a crash on the ground like continuous thunder; many explosions that sounded like only one.

Wiedeck checked that there was a bullet in the pistol. Then he secured it again. "Where's the ammunition?"

"Why?" asked Krull obstinately.

"Come on, let's have it."

Krull gave him four rounds. That was better than nothing. If the Russians did break through, Wiedeck at least wanted to go down with one gun blazing.

He thrust the pistol into his belt. "Come on, Krull, we'll go out now."

"Where to?"

"Into the fresh air. Here goes."

Wiedeck ran ahead through a barrage of explosions. He did not need to look round, he knew Krull would be following him like a shadow. In long bounds he made it to the hollow where the trench system ended. Krull panted after him. He had lost his helmet. He hurled himself down when Wiedeck threw himself into the snow, and jumped up when Wiedeck bounded through the shells like a hunted rabbit.

In those minutes of their flight to the rear, Sergeant Major

Krull came through his baptism of fire. He experienced a change like millions of soldiers before him. Not that he became a different person; he remained the same unfeeling and obtuse sergeant major he had always been. But the pitiful animal terror gradually fell away from him. He regained his self-confidence, and the world round him returned to its usual dimensions. Certainly there was still some fear left in him; but it was the normal fear of any soldier who has to hold out in his trench and fight off the attack. So after long years of wearing uniform Krull at last became a soldier—who suddenly understood that it is just the terrible panic fear of death which makes many men run blindly to their destruction. Like just now in the bunker when he wanted to run out and Wiedeck had had to knock him down so that he didn't really do it and run into the Russian shells as they landed. So strictly speaking, Wiedeck had saved his life. But Krull didn't get too excited about that. Wiedeck had only done what he, Krull, would do in the future—for anyone who wore the same uniform and was, so to speak, in the same boat as himself. From an arrogant, self-seeking loner, Krull now became a man who retained all these qualities but had discovered a sense of comradeship known only to men who for a long time have shared a common bond with life and death.

In a well-built bunker further back they waited for the end of the Russian surprise attack. The German front line had once again withstood the Russian offensive. And when it was over, Krull went out to measure the trenches in accordance with Obermeier's orders; he told Wiedeck to stay in the bunker. Half an hour later, when a man appeared with hot coffee, a chunk of bread and some spirits, and gave it to Wiedeck, saying that Sergeant Major Krull had sent it, Wiedeck wondered what had come over the sergeant major. But while he drank the thin, dark brew and munched the bread, he began to understand. He was an old front-line soldier and had often had similar experiences.

Hope Krull doesn't go all out to win the Iron Cross now, he thought. He'd probably be in a state to do the deeds you read about in the papers, as performed by 'heroic German soldiers'. In which case, thought Wiedeck, the new Krull would be even more dangerous than the old.

25

The sledge shook and rattled through the night. Deutschmann sat by the driver fighting against sleep. Captain Bergen had sent him to Orsha to fetch medical stores. Kronenberg and the other medical orderlies in the battalion were deemed indispensable—there were too many wounded who had to be treated before being sent back to their units—and another orderly was engaged during Deutschmann's absence, a man to organise the transport of the wounded. "You understand something about it, all the drugs and stuff we need," Bergen had said to Deutschmann. "Here's a list for you, have a go at the supply people at base. And don't be fobbed off until you've got everything on the list. I know very well that the stores are full."

Deutschmann was afraid of this assignment. He was afraid of going to Orsha, because he did not know whether he would be strong enough to avoid a meeting with Tanya; strong enough not to go to the small log cabin near the bridge over the Dnieper. He longed for this meeting, he longed for Tanya, for her slim, soft face, her fine-limbed body, for the look in her grey-green eyes, for the warmth and devotion she radiated.

The road was bumpy and icy. The sledge rattled over the bumps like a mad thing. Deutschmann clung to the seat and stuck his boot up against the dashboard. The driver at his side, an old Service Corps corporal, smoked a long curved pipe which he had filled with Russian shag. It stank, and the smoke made Deutschmann's eyes smart. He turned his head away, and stared across the snow-field, through which the ice-covered Dnieper flowed.

The corporal gave him a nudge with his elbow. "Hey, you."

"Yes?"

"You're from 999, aren't you. Bloody shower, eh?"

"I suppose you could call it that," said Deutschmann.

"Do you get anything to eat?"

"It's all right."

"But not enough to fill your bellies?"

"Do *you* ever get enough for that?"

"No, you're right there. Is it true you've all been condemned to death and then reprieved? Or is that all a lot of cock?"

"Some of us were."

"Were you one of them?"

"Yes."

The corporal was silent. He puffed hastily at his pipe and blew the pungent smoke in front of him. "What did you do?" he asked after a while.

"That's not very important."

"Well, anybody can be curious." The corporal seemed a bit huffy, and it was quite a time before he started again: "A cousin of mine is in a mob like that," he said. "He opened his mouth once when he'd have done better to keep it shut."

"Then you know the form."

The corporal left it at that, and spat into the snow. There was the Dnieper. The outline of the town emerged before them. On the river, behind the big wooded bridge, lay Tanya's hut. There was thin smoke coming out over the roof. Deutschmann's heart beat slowly and heavily. He could get out now and go down there, she was at home, he would knock at the door and walk in, or perhaps he wouldn't even knock, but go quietly down the steep path and just go in, she would be standing at the stove and wouldn't hear him come, and he would put his hands over her eyes and say nothing. Of course he mustn't say anything, or she would know at once who he was, and then she would turn round, and he would squeeze her very tight....

"We're nearly there now," said the corporal.

"When do we start back?" asked Deutschmann.

"Tomorrow morning."

"We can't go back tonight?"

"I'd like to see the idiot who'd drive through the partisan area by night."

Not till tomorrow morning, thought Deutschmann. So I'm staying in the whole night here. I could go to her and stay in her house. I could....

They were driving between the mean, dark houses on the outskirts of the town. "Is it far?" asked Deutschmann.

"No—five or six blocks more, and then we're there."

It was some hours before Deutschmann was through with all the formalities and the loading of the sledge. The penal battalion didn't seem to be on the quartermaster's and dispenser's lists. It was not till Deutschmann had spoken to Captain Barth's clerk and the clerk had spoken to the captain himself, and the captain had finally let out a few mild oaths over the phone, that everything clicked.

"I'm going to the Army Hostel," said the corporal when they had finished the work. "Coming with me?"

"I don't think so," said Deutschmann.

"Oh, come on. Why not come along too? There are some very nice birds there, and they've got beer too."

"Thanks all the same," said Deutschmann. "We'll have a beer together another time." He had decided. Or rather, he didn't need to decide. He knew from the very beginning that his longing for Tanya was greater than his fear of a meeting with her. He wanted to go to her, and as he walked faster and faster through the dark deserted streets of Orsha towards the Dnieper bridge, his longing became greater and greater, more and more passionate, until in the end he was almost running.

It was just after eleven at night before he was at last standing outside the wooden door of Tanya's. Thin smoke was still curling out of the chimney, the fire in the hut never went out. It was cold. The cold stabbed Deutschmann in the face, crept under his great-coat, pierced his feet.

He hesitated. The hut was dark, and Tanya would certainly be asleep. The river bank was quite deserted. The ice on the river had closed up. In the morning the Pioneers would have to blast it again. Eventually he pressed against the door. It was not locked; for a moment he thought about how you seldom found locked doors in Russia, and how this hardly squared with the ideas one had at home, in Germany, about this vast country.

The door moved with a creak in the darkness tinted red from the firelight. Thick logs glowed and crackled in the open fire, sometimes a small flame licked upwards, lit the room briefly, and then sank back into the embers. The door to Tanya's room was open.

He closed the door behind him, and breathing deeply, stopped in the warm reddish twilight. Then suddenly, through the soft crackles of the fire, he heard Tanya's breathing.

The boards creaked under his feet as he slowly moved across the room towards the dark opening from which the sleeping girl's quiet deep breathing came. Then he stopped, took off his coat, cap and gloves and put them down, without taking his eyes off the open door into her bedroom. The warmth in the house softly enveloped him.

He stopped in front of Tanya's bed. Slowly, as if afraid to wake her, to disturb the deep rhythm of her breathing and bring consciousness into her peaceful face, scarcely visible in the warm darkness, he squatted down on his knees and brought his face quite close to hers. Her mouth was slightly open, her hair lay black and silky on the pillow.

She stirred and woke.

"Tanya," he whispered.

Her eyes were wide open, big and dark. A slight smile played round her lips, just the hint of a smile. Or was he mistaken? Did he only imagine that he could read happiness that he had come? But then he heard her voice and knew he had not been mistaken. "Michael," she whispered back, her bare arms came out from under the blanket and drew his body down to her.

When Deutschmann woke, he looked at his watch. It was nearly six. "I must go soon," he said.

"When?" she asked.

"In an hour."

"Must you really?"

"Of course. Did you think I would stay here? They'd very soon pick me up."

"You *could* stay here ... I would hide you ... You could stay here for ever, and one day there will be peace." She clung to him as if afraid she would lose him irretrievably if she only let go of him for a moment. "I love you, I love you so much. I love you more than Russia, more than my mother, more than my father, more than everything, everything. I don't know how it has happened, I don't know at all, but I love you so very much!" And then after a while, in which Deutschmann was silent, both moved and shaken by the passionate outburst, she spoke as if she were dreaming and were already in a future for the two of them that did not exist and could not exist, as he knew all too well. "When the war is dead," she said, "we shall go on living, Michael, I will go with you wherever you go. I love my country, but you will be my country, anywhere, everywhere...."

As Deutschmann got dressed, a feeling of unreality came over him. All this was impossible. How did he come into this hut? What had happened? How could it be possible that this beautiful girl loved him? God, how could that all happen? It was an illusion, the real existence was the uniform, the penal battalion, Lieutenant Obermeier and Sergeant Major Krull, his new mates, Wiedeck and Schwanecke, the bleeding, shattered bodies and the constant fear of death. Everything else was a dream, one of those dreams one dreams as a soldier somewhere in a cold filthy hole or a dark stinking bunker, while death prowls outside. And reality was also the thought of Julia and their shared past, although sometimes this too sank into unreal remoteness, as if it had never really existed, any more than last night really existed.

Tanya made some tea. They had breakfast in silence, both lost in their own thoughts. Yet Deutschmann felt—and knew at once that Tanya felt the same—that they were as close as two human beings can be.

They did not hear Sergei Denkov's steps as he pushed open the door and walked into the hut. His cap, his fur, his eyebrows were covered with frost. He pushed the door shut with his heel and looked silently at the two of them. His eyes were wide open and strangely empty. Without looking away from them, he took off his high fur cap and threw it on a chair. Then he smiled, and a cold shudder ran down Deutschmann's spine. It was the tight, menacing smile of a man who does not feel like smiling and wants to hide something behind the smile.

"Good morning," said Deutschmann hesitantly.

"Good morning," Sergei answered. His voice was quiet and hoarse. His eye went down from Deutschmann's face to his uniform. No stripes, no epaulettes, no arms. When the new unit had arrived in Orsha, he had sent a radio message to Moscow about this and received the answer that it was a penal battalion. Sergei knew the penal battalions in the Russian army. Rogues, murderers, criminals, enemies of socialism. In peace-time they worked in mines or logging in the virgin forests of Siberia. In wartime they had to do other things, if they were strong enough to survive the hardship that faced them before they died.

Then he looked at Tanya. Her eyes were shining in that pale face. He understood what they were saying. He saw the black shadows beneath them, and his smile stiffened to a threatening mask. He did not need to ask. He knew what had happened. He knew exactly....

Tanya got up. "This is Sergei," she said. "A farmer from Babinitchi." And then, loud and clear, turning to Sergei: "This is Michael."

Sergei looked at her in silence for a second or two, and then, not knowing that Deutschmann understood Russian, spoke two words in that language. He said them in quite an ordinary voice, which made them sound all the more contemptuous: "You bitch." Then he turned and began walking to the door.

Deutschmann jumped to his feet. The paralysis which had come over his at the sight of the young Russian fell away. "Stop!" he said. Now he bore little resemblance to the soft, irresolute and helpless-looking Deutschmann of his first days in the battalion. Slowly he walked round the table and planted himself in front of Sergei, who had turned round and was regarding him coldly.

"Why?"

"Who are you?" asked Deutschmann.

A brief smile crossed Sergei's face. "Why?" he asked again.

"Where do you live?"

"In the wood," said Sergei slowly.

"I knew it," murmured Deutschmann.

"What?"

"You are ...?"

"What?"

They looked at each other for a few seconds in silence. Then Sergei nodded. "Da. A partisan."

Deutschmann heard Tanya give a slight cry behind him. But he did not turn round. He looked into Sergei's hard eyes, and thought: how can this Russian not be afraid of telling me, a German soldier, that he is a partisan? What game are they playing here, right in the middle of the German lines, or have I missed something, fallen into a trap? Are there more of his sort outside waiting for a sign? But that was completely impossible, he decided. He could hear the Pioneers blasting away on the Dnieper. It was nearly daylight, life was stirring on the streets and on the bridge. Supply columns rumbled over the wooden boards, and German soldiers were swarming everywhere. Yet a partisan was standing here, openly admitting he *was* one.

"An officer," said Sergei. And then, after a while, when Deutschmann did not answer, he went on in almost faultless German: "I wanted to visit Tanya, my fiancée. But the pure virgin I knew has become a whore. She has got mixed up with an enemy bastard while I'm fighting." His voice was expressionless, as if he were telling some trivial story. Then he turned again to Tanya and spat out, but now in Russian: "Tart."

Afterwards Deutschmann could not explain to himself what had made him do it. He had never done it before, not even as a boy. But now he raised his hand and hit Sergei in the face. With the flat of his hand, a wide swinging slap. Sergei did not flinch, or move at all. He just took the blows, and the terrible thing was that he counted them, in a harsh dispassionate voice: "One ... two ... three ... four ... five ..."

"Six" cried Deutschmann, and hit him once more.

Sergei nodded. "Six. One German soldier for each blow."

Deutschmann stepped back and was again overcome by the feeling of unreality. Tanya stood near the wall. She had pressed her face against it, and her slender back twitched. She was crying. Deutschmann looked again at Sergei, who slowly began to speak:

"I hate her. She is no good for anything. She now carries foreign blood in her, and you—you will let me go. I know just what you're thinking, but you won't do it. You won't hand me over to the military police. You are afraid to. What are you doing here with a Russian girl, a partisan? You are a man from the penal battalion, what are you doing here? You are a traitor too."

Then he turned on his heels, took his cap, and went.

"I must go now," said Deutschmann a little while later, trying to free himself from Tanya's embrace. "I'll come back," he whispered. "I will come back."

"I'm frightened!"

"I know. What can I do?"

"You can't do anything."

"I'll come back," said Deutschmann, feeling completely wretched. It was true he couldn't do anything for her, and yet she was now defenceless, exposed to the vengeance of her compatriots. "It will all be all right," he whispered, and knew he was lying. It would not be all right. Nothing would be all right for them again. The night that had just passed had opened an abyss before them, in which lurked desperation and hopelessness in face of the coming days.

He went.

At first slowly, then faster and faster, he crunched up the slope to the town, where the driver was waiting for him with the loaded sledge. He was late. The sentries at the bridge were stamping to and fro, an M.P. sergeant was having a shouting match with a truck-driver who had stopped in the middle of the road with a broken axle and was holding up the whole supply column. Deutschmann ran through the narrow streets, which were now full of life. He had left Tanya and Sergei behind. He had another day in the penal battalion ahead of him.

The driver of the sledge, who had been waiting half an hour in the bitter cold, swore at him as he clambered in; but Deutschmann scarcely heard him. His thoughts were elsewhere.

Sergei waited behind a paling till Deutschmann had gone. Then he walked slowly to Tanya's hut.

She was still standing in the middle of the room. When she saw Sergei, she put her hands up to her mouth in terror, and took a quick step towards the fireplace—towards the recess in which she had hidden the pistol.

"Leave it there," he said. "I would have to kill you if you took it out."

"What do you want?" whispered Tanya.

"You can still ask that?"

"What are you going to do? Go! Go!" She screamed the last words in mortal fear of the tall man wrapped in his shapeless fur, studying her with cold contempt.

"I'm going," he said. "I shan't come back—till we have chased the Germans out. But then, when we have chased them out, I will come back and kill you. This is what I wanted to tell you. You won't escape me. Don't try to run away. It wouldn't do you any good. We shall keep watch. And when I have killed you, I shall bring them all and tell them: Look, this is Tanya Sossnovskaia. Or rather, it was her. Now she is only a corpse. Once she was one of us. But then she made up to a German. She betrayed us. This is what will happen to anyone who betrays us."

Tanya leaned against the mud wall. She felt her neck with her hand. Her hand trembled. "Go!" she groaned. "You are a devil."

"I'm that, am I? Am I really? a devil and a whore, how well they got together! Don't they go bloody well together?" As he spoke, he slowly came nearer, gripped her under the chin with his hand, and lifted up her face. "Look at me, you whore, come on, look at me! What have you done? Have you forgotten everything? have you forgotten us all?"

"I love him," she whispered.

"Bitch!" he cried, full of fury and pain. He took a step

back and hit her. Silently, grimly, one blow after another. She dropped to her knees on the floor near the stove. He bent over and went on hitting her. She had put her hands over her head as protection, but she did not defend herself or cry out. With her eyes shut she endured the blows, till all went black before her eyes.

Sergei straightened up, turned her on to her back with his boot, and waited patiently, unmoving, until she recovered consciousness and opened her eyes. When he was sure she could see him and recognise him, he said: "I'll come back. I'll kill you."

Then he left the house, closing the door carefully behind him, and giving a friendly nod to some Pioneers with iron bars who were freeing the river bank of chunks of floating ice cleared by blasting. Extending a humble greeting on all sides, he walked along the embankment, to disappear in the maze of half-destroyed houses and barns on the outskirts of the town.

He reached one of the cottages that had remained intact, and the air of humility fell away from him, like the fur which he took off and threw into a corner. For a moment he stood there as if turned to stone; but then he could bear it no longer. He beat his fists and his brow against the wall, and terrible heart-rending sobs burst out of him. "Give me the strength to bear it!" he cried. "Oh, God, don't let me go mad, don't let me go mad!"

It was the first time in his life that he had called on God. But he didn't notice it. There was nothing else in him but a terrible, burning, unbearable pain.

26

At about the same time that Deutschmann was climbing into the sledge, the men in B Company who were in the advanced section of trenches were amazed to see a thickly muffled but still stylish-looking figure turn up: Lieutenant Bevern. He had come across from A Company to check B Company's digging work.

The first soldier Bevern came upon was Wiedeck, who had been vainly battling with his pick against the stone-hard ground. He leaned the pick carefully against the trench wall, gave a casual salute, and reported: "Private Wiedeck; digging operations. No special incidents."

"Which company?" snorted Bevern. "Call that a report? Are you digging latrines by any chance?"

"Yessir."

Bevern gaped at him. "What is that supposed to mean?"

"Yessir."

Bevern felt baffled by this dumb insolence. He realised that he would probably get the same "yessir" to any further questions he might ask. There was nothing he could do, at least not here in the trench. So he contented himself with saying: "We'll talk about this later, Wiedeck, we'll talk about it later."

He tramped on along the trenches, past some soldiers who saluted stiffly and bawled out their reports so loudly that the next lot and the ones after that were forewarned before Bevern appeared in their midst.

The rest of B Company lay in the half-finished bunkers in

exhausted sleep. They had worked all night, now they had the right to rest during the day. Orders had been received that the work was to be completed at a quicker rate, so for two days they had had to stay in their positions. They were quite glad about this, because some Russians snipers had trickled through the lines and were shooting from the nearby wood at anything that moved in the trenches. These snipers were so well camouflaged that they couldn't be picked out. A German platoon which had been given the task of detecting and liquidating them, had returned empty-handed. There was nothing to be done. The wood was large and dense, a place where a battalion or even a regiment, let alone single individuals, could hide indefinitely. Besides, it was not the thinly held front line that was threatened by these snipers, but only the men of the penal battalion; and the front line units certainly couldn't be reduced in numbers any further to carry out a search operation. Obermeier had asked Barth, who had asked his superiors, to arm a platoon of the battalion, or better still, a whole company, and send them into the wood; but this request had so far remained unanswered. So in three days six men from B Company and five from A Company had had their heads shot off.

To give some security at least for the continuation of the work, Obermeier and Wernher had posted advance sentries near the wood, who were to fire their machine guns at any suspicious movement. These outposts, of course, were all too likely to get shot themselves: and on the first day this measure was tried, the relief found two dead behind their guns. Just above their eyes the steel helmets showed a small round hole.

"What a shower!" muttered Bevern, when he had inspected several bunkers. "Snoozing away like hedgehogs. Do they know there's a war on?" With his head well down—he too knew the danger threatened by the snipers, of course, though he really didn't believe in it too much—he went through a communication trench further back to check on one of the sentries. He had to crawl on all fours the last bit of the way, till he came to a hole in which a soldier squatted—asleep.

No, there was no mistake: the sentry was asleep. He had

pulled up the wide collar of his lambskin coat so that only the top part of the steel helmet peeped out. His face was covered by the fur, and in his regular snores the thin shreds of frost which had formed round it quivered. He had stuck his hands into the sleeves and drawn his booted feet under the coat.

This was about the worst thing Bevern could imagine: a sleeping sentry! And when, kneeling and motionless, he looked down at the sleeper, he was filled with almost triumphant satisfaction: he had really caught one here. For a moment he regretted that he had no witnesses. But that would not be necessary. His word as an officer would be enough at the courtmartial, and the exemplary punishment, which could only be a firing squad, would have a very salutary effect on everyone else in this miserable mob.

His eyes went slowly up towards the sandbags piled in a semi-circle round the machine gun post for protection against the partisans in the wood. In the middle of the sandbags was a narrow gap, and in front of that stood the machine gun. When he woke the man up, he did not want to do it kneeling, which he felt would put him in a slightly ridiculous position, but standing erect, looking down on the culprit, as was fitting. Slowly, avoiding any unnecessary noise, he slipped into the hole and straightened up, still looking at the sandbags. Did they offer enough protection? But of course, he told himself, no bullet can go through that. And besides no one could see him unless he stuck his head out.

With his eyes on the sandbags, however, he had failed to notice that the motionless figure of the sentry had stirred, When he looked down again, his mouth already open to start shouting, he met the mocking eyes—of Schwanecke.

Schwanecke's injuries from the duel with Tartuchin had been painful but not dangerous. After Kronenberg had found him and the wounds had been dressed, he stayed a few days in hospital. Then Bevern had ferreted him out. "After all, the man isn't sick," he told Kronenberg. "The times are too serious for lead-swinging. See to it that Schwanecke reports for duty again tomorrow morning." Schwanecke had seethed with rage, and had uttered dire threats of what he would one day do to Bevern.

"Wake up!" yelled Bevern now.

"What do you mean? I'm already awake," remarked Schwanecke calmly.

Bevern ignored this. His only thought was: now I've got him, none of his tricks will help him now. The man was already as good as dead. And that was as it should be. It was the best thing that could have happened, that it was Schwanecke of all people he had caught. "Stand up!" he ordered.

Schwanecke slowly stood up and stretched himself. Then he yawned. "You always come at the wrong moment," he said, giving a second yawn. "I was just ..."

"You were asleep."

"Yes, that's what I was going to tell you. I was just dreaming I was in Hamburg with such a lovely blonde. You can't imagine what fantastic hips she had. And now you come ..."

"You were asleep—and you admit it?"

"Well, of course," said Schwanecke. "Although I heard you at the third bend from here. You didn't pay attention at the Military College, Lieutenant. That's not the way a man should go stalking at the front." There was a grin on his face, and mockery in his voice, but his eyes were cold, lifeless as two glass balls.

"You know what this means?" gloated Bevern.

"I dunno. What does it?"

Bevern said with emphasis; "Sleeping on sentry duty in direct vicinity of the enemy...."

"Oh, I see. That's what you mean, is it? and how does it go on?"

"Courtmartial," said Bevern quietly. "And that will take place up here directly. Collect your things together, you are coming with me." He felt very calm; Schwanecke's insolent answers bounced off him without effect. Why should he get worked up about them? The man's fate was settled anyhow.

"Oh, I can't go until my relief comes," said Schwanecke. "Will you keep me company till then, sir? We could—we could talk things out, sir. What do you say? *You* know, man to man, like. We're all on our own here, all by ourselves, and we'll be staying by ourselves for quite a time. It *is* an opportunity, isn't it—for a man-to-man talk ..."

Bevern's cold superior calm did not fall away from him at once. It was only gradually that Schwanecke's words penetrated into his consciousness; and then he understood. Shivers went down his spine, and he took a step back, as if he wanted to escape into the communication trench. But Schwanecke quite slowly extended his arm, caught him by the lapels of his tunic, and pulled him forward. In the process Schwanecke turned round so that he was blocking Bevern's retreat.

Bevern found himself incapable of resistance. What was now happening was incredible, it just couldn't be true. But when he looked into Schwanecke's face, the reality flooded over him: it *was* true. He saw Schwanecke's grinning mouth open, and the words that slowly came out of it pressed into him like the injection of a drug and took possession of him, till every cell in his body was penetrated by them.

"Courtmartial, you say? Firing squad, you say? Pff pff—and Schwanecke's gone, you think? That would make you very happy, wouldn't it? No more Schwanecke, and bastard Bevern chuffed as hell."

"Let me pass!" hissed Bevern.

"Steady there, we've all the time in the world. I said we'd have a man-to-man talk, you bastard—remember? We've lots of things to talk about. Oh no, not the pistol, what would you do with that? Do I have to smack your paws? Naughty, naughty, paws down."

Bevern dropped his hands from the pistol holster. "What do you think you're… Do you know what this means? Obstruction of an officer in…."

"Shut your trap!" Schwanecke wiped his eyes. Small pieces of ice were sticking to the lashes. He had stopped grinning now, and Bevern suddenly had the feeling that Schwanecke was somewhere far away, like a man trying desperately to think of something. Then he returned, and continued speaking.

"You're a filthy bastard, and I'm going to settle your hash now. Just think how happy everyone will be to know you're a corpse. The whole battalion will celebrate, it will be as good as a week's leave. Courtmartial, you reckoned, did you? It's you, Lieutenant Bloody Bevern, not me, that's going to get it in the neck. Yes, that's well put, isn't it—get it in the neck!"

"You—you—" Bevern cried in a shrill falsetto quite unlike his normal voice. His face was distorted, and his eyes showed panic and fear. Then he called for help, but his voice was lost in the white expanses all round, and he knew that nobody would hear him. It was hopeless, the man in front of him signified death, and Bevern knew there was no help. But he went on calling for it, not for the help of other soldiers, but for the woman so many mortally wounded men scream for in the midst of their agony when they feel their life's blood running out of them. "Help! Mother!" he cried—the quiet modest woman he had despised because she thought nothing of his faith and his ideals. And he meant not only the particular woman who *was* his mother, but all the worlds that lie hidden behind this word and spring from their bosom, and all the mothers who put their hands protectively round weeping children: the last appeal of the helpless and the dying.

In the middle of this cry Schwanecke struck; and Bevern sank to the ground, stunned.

Now Schwanecke acted swiftly and surely, as if he had practised the manoeuvre a hundred times.

Without taking his eye off Bevern, he fired three burst into the wood from the machine gun. There were certainly at least three snipers lurking there quite near. Then with the edge of his hand he chopped Bevern's carotid, and gripped him under the arms. Then, breathing heavily, he lifted the heavy slack body, carried it behind the machine gun and pushed it slowly upwards.

He didn't have long to wait. After two or three minutes he heard and felt a dull blow against Bevern's body, and immediately afterwards he heard the sound of the shot from over in the wood.

He let the body drop, and bent over it.

The face looked slightly astonished and a little distorted. There was a small, round, clean bullet hole at the root of the nose. The steel helmet showed a jagged hole behind. A smooth shot right through. War can be some use at times, thought Schwanecke grimly, and the little brothers are pretty good marksmen....

He straightened up, turned and fired a whole series of long furious bursts into the wood. He pressed the trigger again and again until the belt was empty. Then he put a new one in and fired this too. A wild, dark triumph filled him as he felt the rattling recoils of the gun in his shoulder and the sheafs of bullets whipped the snow off the branches in the wood opposite. His eyes were full of flaring madness.

"There," he said, when the second belt was empty. "That will do."

Lieutenant Bevern's death was no great sensation. It was registered, put on the lists, entered in army records. "He was a misguided youngster," Barth said on the phone to Obermeier. "There are a whole lot of them about." And Wernher, who saw his problems with Bevern so suddenly and simply solved, said: "Poor sod, I bet he died without ever having loved a girl." Only Krull was a bit thoughtful. That no one shed a tear for Bevern, that it looked, on the contrary, as if the whole battalion had breathed a sigh of relief, made him apprehensive or at least gave him food for thought. He knew he was as much hated as Bevern had been. True, he had become a little tamer since the incident in the trench, and he also felt rather more fellowship with the men than before. But he was still not too sure of them, especially as he was convinced it was the special function of a sergeant major in a penal battalion to make life unpleasant for those under him.

For Schwanecke, however, Bevern's burial behind the houses of Babinitchi was not the end of the business.

Sergeant Hefe had been the first to question him, while they were still in the trench.

"Bevern's been picked off by the snipers!" Schwanecke had related, gasping, taking care like a good actor to make his voice sound duly shattered.

"Where?"

"With me, right up front."

"Oh ...?" Hefe squinted at Schwanecke. "The bugger

couldn't have had a better death, could he? Who else was there?"

"Nobody, just me."

"So you're the only witness?"

"Right."

"And why didn't you stop the idiot sticking his head over the trench?"

"Can I give an officer orders?"

"Did you warn him?"

"Yes, of course."

It was more difficult with Obermeier, who sent for him and interrogated him in detail. "How long were you and the lieutenant together?"

Schwanecke looked at the ceiling of the hut. "Perhaps—perhaps about five minutes."

"And what did he say?"

"When he saw me, he said: Oh, it's you, you scum."

Obermeier looked at his hands. Although he too had been out of sympathy with Bevern, he felt suspicious of the hated adjutant's 'heoric death', and it was his duty as an officer, and not only as an officer, to see that this death was thoroughly investigated. In any other circumstances everyone would have believed in the unlucky chance by which Bevern had been shot, and the matter would have been closed. But he had been alone with Schwanecke of all people, and no other witnesses. That was a situation, thought Obermeier, such as Schwanecke might have dreamed of. These reflections led to speculations too devious to be pursued further, and yet... with Schwanecke one was not dealing with an ordinary soldier. He was a criminal, and you had only to look into his eyes to know that he might also be a murderer.

"How did it happen?"

"I said, Careful, sir, there are Siberian snipers over there. He says, Are you scared, you big booby? I say, No, but they shoot bloody accurately. And he says, tripe, and then there's a brmm, and he topples over. That was that. It all went very fast, sir, he always wanted to prove, you see, that he...."

Obermeier waved a hand. "All right, dismiss. Make your report to the Sergeant Major." But he still looked thoughtful as Schwanecke left him.

Breathing a sigh of relief, Schwanecke strolled across to the office, greeting a few of his mates on the way. He believed he had finished with the business for good. Bevern was dead, what can happen to me? He died a hero's death, Schwanecke thought viciously, when he was wanting to bring me before a courtmartial and get me shot, even lead the firing squad himself. But then there was a little brrm, and Bevern was gone, and not a trace left of the courtmartial …

Schwanecke entered the office without knocking, and Krull looked up. He leaned back, folded his arms negligently and nodded two or three times. "Of course. Who else would it be? The man without manners or morals. The almost perfect practitioner of rape and assault."

"You can cut out the 'almost'," grinned Schwanecke.

"And murder? Would you cut out the 'almost' there?"

Schwanecke's eyes narrowed, and his face twisted to an ugly grimace. Hot fury welled up in him, and for a moment overglowed in an uncharacteristic rashness. "It may be your turn next," he hissed.

Krull shot off his chair. "What the bloody hell do you mean by that?"

But Schwanecke had recovered his caution. "I mean that it may be your turn up here or anybody else's."

"It could mean something different. Don't take me for a fool." Krull's voice was suddenly hoarse. He was frightened of the burly, muscular man standing before him, staring at him with cold eyes.

"It could," said Schwanecke, unmoved.

Krull vented his rage in his normal parade-ground style: "I'll show you, my lad, I'll damn well show you, you can bet your boots on that …" His fat head swung to and fro as it always did when he was trying to think something out. "And when your block gets bloody chopped off, I'll put on my best uniform and go and get drunk."

Schwanecke made no answer, except to spit into the corner before he left the office.

An hour later Captain Bergen came into the house where Obermeier had established Company HQ.

"We've got medical stores for a week at least," he said wearily. "Your Deutschmann managed to organise quite a lot. I'd like him to go to Orsha again next week, if that's all right by you. They're getting some new stuff in by then. As if trouble's expected."

"Yes, I've been surprised for a long time that Ivan is so quiet. The fields are frozen hard as stone, there's not that much snow, so the Russians couldn't wish for a better runway for their tanks. It won't be long, I dare say, before the balloon goes up again."

"A gloomy forecast, Obermeier." Bergen sat down and took a quick gulp of some schnaps Obermeier had handed him in the lid of his messtin. "But that's not what I've come about. If it does go up, we'll know soon enough. I'm not an old front-line rat, but you'd have to be very thick not to feel that this is the lull before the storm. No, what I wanted to talk to you about … er, Hansen has discovered something which he only told me about today. He's written a report … It's to do with Bevern. But read it yourself, please." He handed Obermeier some sheets of paper, and took another gulp of schnaps.

After a while Obermeier said, sighing: "Pity you doctors can't write decent German."

"Well, I'll put it to you more simply. On Lieutenant Bevern's body, besides the shot in the head, a swelling at the chin was found, and more important, on the larynx at the side, with a small bruise. That means these swellings were already there before Bevern was killed by the shot through the head. Can you explain that?"

"What do you mean?"

"Look, it's possible that Bevern, on his tour of inspection through the trenches, may have slipped and fallen. That might explain the swelling on the chin. Or do you think he could have been involved in some punch-up?"

"Most unlikely," said Obermeier.

"Well, we needn't worry about the swelling on the chin. But how do you explain the one on the larynx and the bruise? These couldn't have been due to a fall. A long time ago I was a police doctor for a bit, so I've some idea about these things. Such swellings on the neck only occur when someone strikes it with a blunt object, say a thick stick or..." Bergen's outstretched hand struck swiftly through the air.

"You mean—a chop with the edge of the hand?" asked Obermeier in bewilderment.

"Could be." Bergen shrugged his shoulders. "Such blows, if delivered with great force behind them, can be fatal."

"And you think ..."

Bergen made a dismissive gesture. "Oh no. Bevern's death was clearly caused by a gunshot: in at the front, out behind. But—and this is what you've got to think about: the blow against his larynx was enough to render him unconscious, and that must have been shortly before his death. I'm no detective, and you probably aren't either. But you are Company Commander and it happened in your Company. . . ."

There was a long silence. Then Obermeier said slowly and heavily: "If I understand you aright, somebody—we'll name no names for the moment—knocked Bevern down and then shot him."

Bergen had another swing: "Hansen has established that the shot was not fired from the immediate vicinity. This is something we doctors can tell, you know. Probably it *was* a Russian sniper, after all. I wouldn't like to commit myself, but in my opinion what you said just now may have come pretty near the truth."

"So, let's put it quite bluntly: Schwanecke, it couldn't have been anyone else, first knocked Bevern out, then gave him a chop with the edge of his hand to stun him further, and finally shot him—or had him shot by a Russian sniper. Such a thing can be arranged—if one knows how."

"But could Schwanecke possibly have arranged such a thing beforehand?"

"No, that's a point. Anyhow I'm bound to pass on this report to Captain Barth." Obermeier shook his head. "I can't see that I have any option."

"That's the way it is," said Bergen, draining the rest of his schnaps. He was swilling it down deliberately to help him face what was really a very nasty business. "Even if Bevern was a swine, murder is still murder, whoever the victim may be."

"Quite," said Obermeier wearily. "I'll have Schwanecke up again for questioning."

27

Dr. Kukill had tried unsuccessfully to reach Julia Deutschmann by telephone. Since the lines were out of order after the last air-raid, he drove out to Dahlem, in the grip of anxiety and uncertainty. This turned increasingly to fear, the longer he thought about it, that she might carry out her crazy plan of repeating Deutschmann's experiment on herself.

The villa in Dahlen was locked. He rang in vain. The blinds, some torn out of their frames by the blast of the bombs, were let down as far as they would go.

After waiting a minute or two, Kukill opened the small door to the garden, and went round to the back of the house. The kitchen door, which led into the garden, was locked. Julia had obviously gone away. Strange, she had never said anything about it to him. But then he reminded himself, with a sudden surge of bitterness, that no doubt she never would tell him anything. He was the one person she wouldn't tell that she was going away, or anything else. She hated him. How could he have been such a fool as to think she would forget Deutschmann and fall in with his wishes. Where could she have gone? He knew she had no family left. Had something happened to do with Deutschmann? Perhaps she had received notification of his death in Russia.

Before returning to his car, he stood in the garden for a while and looked across to the house. He felt a tightness in his chest, it went up into his throat, it was almost a physical pain. At these moments he felt he might have given up his whole career and everything he was and represented, if the door had suddenly opened and Julia had come towards him with outstretched arms. But the door remained closed, the house was silent and deserted. So he went away again and drove off. He would return next day, and he knew even now that he would keep on returning—until he found her. He would search for her, he had to find her.

Behind a blind that hung askew, hidden at the sides by the curtain, Julia watched him from the sitting-room.

This was a different Kukill from the man she had known till now: no longer the cool, self-assured forensic specialist, the sought-after authority, a favourite of the Party and the ladies. Now she remembered the Kukill who said his nights were long and his dreams mostly nightmares. And there was something else too, an aura surrounding him, which could be seen in his manner and bearing. But she could not get to the bottom of it, and after he had driven off, she lost the wish to do so. She forced herself to stop thinking of him as she sat down at Ernst's desk. Dr. Kukill had become irrelevant.

She went into the lab and walked over to a wooden stand on which were two small phials containing slightly cloudy fluid. Without letting her hand tremble, she filled two syringes with the fluid. Her movements were neat, calm and resolute.

She opened a notebook and entered the time and date at the top of the report she intended to write on her experiment. She wrote: "11.19 a.m. First intra-muscular injection with Staphylococcus Aureus, into the musculus vastus lateralis."

Before injecting, she had cleaned with alcohol the area of the thigh to be injected. She could not help smiling at this now. How automatic her separate actions had become: fancy cleaning the place she was going to inject pus into! She was still smiling at this incongruity as she stuck the thin needle into the muscle, pressed the fluid quickly into the flesh, and then with a jerk withdrew the needle.

She injected the contents of the second syringe into the forearm. Then she entered in the notebook: "11.22 a.m. Injection No. 2 into the musculus flexor digitorum profundus. I break off the experiment here and await the effects."

She set an alarm for 9 p.m. and lay down on the old leather sofa. Ernst had often slept there for an hour or two towards morning, exhausted by a night's work. The curtains in front of the two windows were drawn, leaving a pale twilight in which all the objects around her became unreal. Near the sofa stood the telephone on a small table. By it lay a pad with the long-distance numbers of Dr.Wissek at the Charité Hospital and at his home.

She had tried to think of everything before she started the experiment. Her notes included even the smallest details. Calmly and carefully she put in order all essential points, like a tired old man conscientiusly making appropriate provisions for his death because he feels the end is near. She had even written a letter to Dr. Kukill, which, though it had not been her intention, began with bitter words: *"If as a specialist in forensic medicine you had followed your conscience or your judgment, and not the prejudices of the so-called 'hour of need', it would never have come to the point where I had to write this letter...."*

It was all complete. Calmly, like someone who has taken a mild sleeping pill, she lay down on the old sofa. Her face was very pale and her eyes closed. She thought of Ernst. She thought of the cruel Russian winter she had heard so much about, and wondered whether he had a greatcoat, whether he had received her parcel with the thick woollen gloves, socks and scarf, and the cake and two packets of cigarettes and other trifles, whether he had felt boots, or even fur boots. They were the small, fleeting, tender thoughts of a wife worrying about her husband or a mother about her son.

In the early afternoon—she looked at her watch, it was 2.16—she heard a car drawing up outside. By the sound of the engine she recognised it as Dr Kukill's. For a short time there was silence, then soft steps, crunching over the gravel, went round the house. Then there were rings at the front door, twice, three times, five times. For a moment she had to fight with all her might against the desire to get up, run to the door, open it and tell him everything, ask his help before it was too late. But she stayed on the sofa, pressed her hands to her ears and turned her head towards the wall. And again after quite a time she could just hear the car engine starting. Then the noise quickly faded out and died away: Dr. Kukill had driven off again.

The quietness of the empty house, the dim light in the lab, sent Julia to sleep. She started up when the phone shrilled near her head. But she did not lift the receiver. It would certainly be Dr. Kukill again, and she did not want to talk to him.

6.47: She looked at the injection places. A small red circle had formed round the one on the thigh. There were no symptoms showing at the forearm. She conscientiously entered these observations in the notebook, took her temperature and noted a slight sensitivity to pressure at the thigh.

About 8.30 she rang up Dr. Wissek at the Charité. She had woken before the alarm went, in the grip of an anxiety she could not master: it gave her the feeling she wasn't getting enough air.

"Hullo, my love, how are you? What can I do for you?" She heard her friend's voice as if through the roar of a wave. She felt her brow and jerked the hand back in dismay. The skin was glowing hot and wet.

"How are *you*?" she asked with an effort. "Have you a lot to do?"

"As ever. The theatre has almost become my bedroom."

"I have a favour to ask you, Wölfi ..."

"Fire away. Granted as soon as asked."

"I need a bed."

"Here in the Charité? Out of the question. But Julie, love, how do you think I could manage it?" Dr. Wissek tried to tone down the first gruffness of his refusal. "We already have patients in the air-raid shelter lying almost on top of each other. Have you also got—private patients?"

"No. I need the bed urgently, or I wouldn't be ringing you."

"What's the case, then?"

"Staphylococcus Aureus. Infection. Forearm and thigh." Julia spoke slowly, breathing heavily.

"Serious?"

"Pretty serious."

"Probably amputation, therefore. Who's the patient, then?"

"Me," said Julia.

For a moment there was silence at the other end. Then a

hissing noise came out of the receiver, as if the man there had gasped; and then she heard his voice again, but high now, altered, stupefied: "Julia—Julia—what are you doing, what's happened?"

"I have repeated Ernst's experiment." Julia forced herself to speak calmly and clearly, although the room was beginning to dance round her and she felt as if she were tipsy. "The only possibility is ... with Ernst's actinium compound ... Listen, Wölfi! You can come and collect me now. I'm lying in the lab on the sofa. On the table by it you will find the actinium and the ... instructions for use." She had to make three starts before her dry tongue, rough as sandpaper, would allow her to form the last three words. "Keep to them, or the whole thing is useless. Have I made myself clear?"

"Yes—but ..."

"I can't talk any more now. Do your stuff, Wölfi, and ..." She wanted to say "Auf wiedersehen", but didn't get the words out at once and then forgot what she wanted to say to him. Laboriously she replaced the receiver and then sank back. It's going on, she thought inconsequentially, on and on and a hundred million little creatures ... a billion....

28

Sergeant Major Krull seemed to enjoy his expedition through the finished and half-finished trenches. The surprised faces of the men before whom he suddenly appeared caused him deep satisfaction, which was greater than his fear of Russian artillery fire. Moreover, the front had been strangely quiet for several days, a quietness which the veterans found very ominous; so the hazards of his visits did not seem all that great. Possibly, too, after his first experience in the trench, he wanted to prove that this baptism of fire had made him into a fearless soldier. At any rate, he went out to the trenches one evening for the third time. But on this occasion he was fired at by partisans. It was nothing much in the way of a partisan attack, and no one would have bothered to talk about it had not Krull of all people received a palpable hit.

At the hospital in Barssdovka, Kronenberg was stupefied when the door of the barn opened and Krull came in. Kronenberg dropped the dressing he was engaged on, and pushed through the beds to the passage along which Krull was walking towards him. It was only now he saw that the Sergeant Major was supporting himself on a stick and evidently found it painful to walk. "But that's—that's impossible," he gasped.

"What is, laddie?"

"You … you surely haven't been wounded?"

"If it's any comfort to you—yes, I've stopped one. Shot in the behind!"

"Where? Where?" Kronenberg swallowed. This was one of the great moments of his life. "What did you say? In the ..."

"That's it—straight into the left cheek. I got it down a fraction of a second too late."

"And then there was an explosion?"

Krull screwed up his mouth: "Kronenberg, you stupid abortion, if you think you're going to take the piss out of me, you're bloody well mistaken. Which bed?"

"The M.O. decides about admissions, Sergeant Major. Whether you get a bed depends on how big the hole is back there ... perhaps you'll only need to have the wound dressed and then get back to the line." He walked round Krull. "I can't see anything."

"As a decent man I naturally changed my trousers."

"Again—after a year!" cried someone from the depths of the barn. Roars of laughter followed. Kronenberg grinned discreetly. "You shouldn't listen to them," He apologised. "You know, anything for a giggle."

"Cretins!" Krull snorted.

Lieutenant Hansen appeared in the doorway in his white surgeon's gown, with a long blood-spattered rubber apron over it. Krull saluted him stiffly. He was pale and obviously in some pain from his wound, but tried by his demeanour to overcome the mockery of the grinning faces all round him. Hansen felt rather sorry for him. He put a hand on his shoulder. "Come with me, Sergeant Major. I will examine you. Have you had an anti-tetanus jab already?"

"Yes, sir, from Deutschmann, the medical orderly."

Krull did not like remembering the occasion. When the attack was over, Hefe and Wiedeck had dragged him into the sledge and taken him back to Gorki. There Deutschmann sat down by him and began to count his muslin bandages. "Only 17 left," he said regretfully. "You spoke of extravagance, Sergeant Major, when I put four bandages on Private Siemsburg. I'm afraid for you now I'll have to make do with two.

"Don't be bloody stupid, Deutschmann," Krull groaned. The wound was smarting. His left leg was numb. I slowly dying, he thought in horror.

"First the jab!" Deutschmann cut open his trousers. When

he tore the blood-encrusted shreds of Krull's pants with a jerk from the wound area, Krull gave a shriek. There was not very much to see. A simple flesh wound: the small-calibre bullet of a sub-machine-gun had gone clearly through the muscle quite near the surface.

"Oh, dear, oh dear, oh dear, half your behind is gone," said Deutschmann, full of mocking sympathy.

"Shut your mouth and give me the jab!"

"Right away!" Deutschmann fetched the syringe, found a specially blunt needle, which he was actually meaning to return, drew the serum out of the ampoule, and gave Krull a paternal smack on his bare bottom. "Just be a brave boy, the kind doctor's going to give you a little prick, and it'll all be over soon."

"Ow, you!" cried Krull. Deutschmann had pressed the needle into the flesh rather more slowly than he should have, and was now pressing the serum into the muscle at the same rate. When he withrew the needle, he could hardly resist the desire to start again.

"Finished?" groaned Krull.

"Oh no, I've still got to clean up the wound and put a dressing on."

"Don't they do that at base?"

"Can be done here sometimes. As you know, this is my profession."

"Do you do it with—an anaesthetic?"

"Oh, come on, not for you. You're not that scared of a little pain, are you?"

"And then?"

"We'll see what the lieutenant says."

"When are you taking me back to Barssdovka?"

"I don't think that will be necessary. It's only serious cases that go there, you know. You were the one who insisted on that."

"But you said—it was a big wound. It might go gangrenous or something."

"And there will be a big scar, I expect. Still, you're not a belly-dancer, are you, Sergeant Major, so it won't matter too much."

The dressing was as painful for Krull as the injection had

been. Clenching his teeth, he decided to get his own back on Deutschmann whenever an opportunity presented itself. He was taken to Barssdovka that night. Everyone in the company not on duty had collected to see him hobble to the sledge and climb aboard with face screwed up in pain. When it drove off, some voices sang "Goodbyee, don't cryee ..." Krull buried himself in his thick fur. He could have wept with rage, and with the sudden realisation that he was all alone, that everyone was against him and probably wished his wound had been far worse—or even fatal....

29

About 11 p.m. Dr. Kukill appeared again outside the villa in Dahlem. He had tried several times to reach Julia by telephone, and now could not bear the uncertainty any more. He remembered some sentences she had thrown out, remarks he hadn't taken too seriously at the time, but which now took on a horrific meaning. "No one will hear of my experiment until the right moment" she said once; or "You won't be able to stop me" or: "I will prove to everyone that Ernst has suffered an injustice."

This time Kukill did not confine himself to walking round the house and looking into the windows to see whether he could find a gleam of light somewhere, the movement of a curtain, or any noise which would tell him Julia was at home. He raced round to the back of the house, knocked several times on the kitchen door, and finally broke in the window.

The kitchen had been tidied up with scrupulous precision, except for a saucepan full of bean soup standing on the hob.

"Julia!" called Kukill. "Julia—where are you? Why are you hiding from me?"

No answer. His voice rang through the silent house, and he knew suddenly that his calls were futile. The house was empty. He rushed on, through the hall, into the sitting-room to the laboratory.

When he tore open the heavy door of the lab, he remained as if rooted to the spot. The large, carefully blacked out room had all its lights burning. There was a crumpled blanket on the leather sofa in the corner. The telephone stood on a small table near the sofa, and by the telephone a white envelope: a letter.

He walked towards it, slowly, as if under a spell. The letter was addressed to him. His eyes rested on a small piece of paper pushed under the telephone: Dr. Wolfgang Wissek, Charité, it said, and then the number. Without taking his eyes off it, he tore open the envelope, and read:

"If as a specialist in forensic medicine you had followed your conscience or even your judgement, and not the prejudice of the so-called 'hour of need', it would never have come to the point where I had to write this letter.

"I shall carry out the experiment on myself. And when you read these lines, I shall either be no longer alive or have produced the proof that my husband's conviction was unjust.

"Don't think I am feeling heroic. I am terribly frightened. But it is the only way to rehabilitate Ernst so that he may continue the work we both believe in so strongly."

He made himself read through the letter again, line for line, word for word. And just because Julia did not complain but presented her case coolly and objectively, he felt his guilt all the more strongly. What she had written in the first sentence was absolutely right. But—where was she now?

Perhaps the bit of paper with the telephone number would help him? Charité—of course. She must have rung up this Dr. Wissek, probably she was there now.

He sprang into feverish action. His hands shook as he tore the telephone receiver off the hook and asked for the number written on the paper. It was quite a time before he got his connection.

He drummed impatiently on the table with his fingers, and then heard steps approaching and a man's voice: "Wissek here."

"Is Julia—is Frau Julia Deutschmann with you?" Kukill was making frantic efforts to remain calm.

"Who's speaking?"

"Kukill—Dr. Kukill. Answer me, man. Is Frau Deutschmann with you?"

"Why do you wish to know?"

"Oh, God, don't ask. What's happened?"
"It looks bad … a general infection …"
"Bad?"
"Very."

Dr. Wissek thought he heard a slight suppressed sob. But that was completely impossible, he must have imagined it. The young doctor knew Dr. Kukill, who did not?—and it seemed incredible that Dr. Kukill could weep. And yet….

"I'm coming at once!" he heard Kukill say after a while, and then the receiver at the other end was replaced. For a few seconds Wissek stood there in perplexity, then he shook his head, and hung up himself, remarking to the girl at the switchboard: "Unless I'm right off beam, it's hit someone pretty hard."

In a small private room Julia lay fighting for life. The doctors stood around helpless and despairing, and watched Professor Burger, whom Wissek had got out of bed, giving the third injection with the actinium compound developed by Dr. Deutschmann. Burger injected the serum into the arm vein so that it should take effect more quickly.

Julia lay in a coma. Her skin was grey, pale, covered with cold sweat; her finger-tips were whitish, and the nose stuck out shockingly from the sunken face.

"I don't know if there's much point in it," said Professor Burger, when he had pressed the syringe empty. "All the conventional remedies are useless with such a raging infection. And I don't have much faith in this actinium stuff. I've stopped believing in fairy-tales."

Dr. Wissek nodded, then said bluntly: "Dr. Kukill has just rung and says he's coming over here."

"What does he want here?" The white-haired consultant with the wrinkled face looked up in surprise. His blue eyes were tired.

"He was very agitated …"

"Ah yes, I see. Well, I can imagine what he wants now, After all, he was … you know the story, don't you?"

"It was disgusting." said Wissek harshly.

Burger did not answer. He pulled Julia's eyelids and looked at the eyeballs. They were stiff, glassy.

"Has she had Cardiaxol?"

"Yes."

Burger got up. "Stay with her. If anything should happen, call me."

Wissek nodded. He could not say anything now. There was a lump in his throat, and he was afraid to speak. "I don't want to see that—to see Kukill." Burger finished, and left the room.

Wissek pulled a chair up to the bed and sat down. His tense, youthful face drooped. He had been working all day. Mechanically he reached for Julia's hand and felt her pulse.

This was how Dr. Kukill found him.

It was a different man who came dashing into the room—hair dishevelled, without an overcoat, tie slipped down, face moist with sweat—from the Kukill that Wolfgang Wissek remembered, at congresses, receptions, and finally at Ernst's trial. He looked years older, his cool, mocking self-assurance seemed shattered. Without bothering about Wissek, he knelt down in front of Julia's bed.

"Why on earth did she do it?" he asked hoarsely, and Wissek had the impression he was really asking himself—or just asking, like so many people before him who had to be given the news that someone they loved was dead or dying: why did it have to be like this?

"Good evening, Dr. Kukill," said Wissek softly.

"What?" Kukill looked at him blankly, then turned to Julia again. "How much actinium have you injected?"

"Two lots of 5 cc."

"Good God—isn't that too much?"

"What further damage can it do?" said Wissek.

"And otherwise? Haven't you given anything else?" Sulphanamide?"

"We have done everything."

Kukill felt Julia's pulse, drew her eyelids up—as Burger had done—stayed on his knees for a while, then got up slowly, leaning on the bed. "And your opinion is . . . ?" he asked, not taking his eyes from Julia's face. He expected no answer, for he knew it himself. It seemed that nothing could help now. Then he turned round and went out slowly, as if every step were an effort.

Wissek looked after him, and now had no anger left for this man.

30

Lieutenant Obermeier questioned Schwanecke a second and a third time, but with equal lack of success. Schwanecke denied having had anything to do with Bevern's death. He did it very skilfully and almost persuaded Obermeier that his suspicions were without foundation. He told him once, for example: "'Course, I often wished him dead, sir—well, *you* knew, what private doesn't sometimes wish that, when an officer or sergeant is always picking on him? But to do him in, what do you take me for, sir? And you say yourself the whole thing must have been well planned and prepared. Well, blow me down, when would I have had time to do any preparing? First of all, I was in hospital, and then I had guard duty. How should I have known when the lieutenant was going on an inspection and that he would come just to me? No. it was exactly as I've told you. I said: 'There are snipers up there, sir. You'd better watch out.' And he said: 'Are you scared, you gutless funk?' and put his head up. And then they banged off at him. That's just how things went."

Obermeier sent this account of the interrogations on to Captain Barth, together with Lieutenant Hansen's report; and then talked to him on the phone, which for once was intact.

"It's all speculation," said Barth. "You can't prove anything against the man. Nobody saw anything."

"What shall I do with him? Put him under arrest?"

"No, why?"

"He could always ..."

"Run away, do you mean? Where's he to go? To the partisans? He knows very well they don't take any prisoners. And he'll hardly cross our front line. No, keep him where he's within reach. Somewhere on your staff, I reckon he could be quite useful there. And don't let him feel you're still suspicious of him, or he may take fright. Oh, yes, I meant to ask you, why are you taking such trouble to clear up this alleged murder? Unless I'm much mistaken, you could never stand Bevern."

"It's a matter of principle, sir."

"My dear boy, you'll choke on one of your principles some day. And I speak as one who should know."

So Schwanecke stayed in Barssdovka on a staff job. But everyone who had known him before found him a changed man. He had become much more sullen and bad-tempered, and his answers to inquisitive questions consisted mainly of oaths. He seemed extremely restless, and in any free time would pace around the streets of Barssdovka like a caged tiger. He wandered through the snow down the road to Babinitchi, and along the roads to Gorki and to Orsha. He was looking for the Mongolian.

He did not worry about Bevern. The matter was settled as far as he was concerned. He was not to know that between Orsha and the base-camp at Posnan, between Posnan and Frankfurt on Oder, letters, reports and telephone conversation were going to and fro concerning him, concerning him and Lieutenant Bevern. Admittedly there was no evidence of Schwanecke's guilt, but his record was known. And even if his past life had been unstained as new-fallen snow, things were still suspicious. And in those days it was not only the men of a penal battalion who were in mortal danger if they fell under suspicion.

Meanwhile Krull was also at Barssdovka, very much the centre of attention at the hospital, having heated discussions with Kronenberg when it was time for dressings to be changed, and making himself conspicuous in other ways.

31

For Deutschmann the day came again when he was sent by Captain Bergen to Orsha.

"You know the dispenser," said Bergen, pressing a long list into Deutschmann's hand. "If you only bring back a quarter of the stuff I've written down here, we'll be in luck."

The closer the sledge came to Orsha and the Dnieper the more uneasy Deutschmann became. He knew he would have enough time to see Tanya. He would surprise her in sleep like the last time. He would kneel by her bed and take her head between his hands, and then he would once more break free of the past and the present. For a time he would forget about Julia and Berlin and Dr. Ernst Deutschmann of Dahlem, and the life from which he had been torn. He would go on being nothing but Private Deutschmann of B Company in a penal battalion, a medical orderly who had to fetch bandages and drugs. Nothing beyond being one of millions in an army roll. But he would be a happy man, a man without regrets or pangs of conscience, without thought that he was being unfaithful to another woman—a woman who was so far from his present life, so unattainable, that she seemed to him like a beautiful picture he had long ago contemplated, admired and possessed.

M.P.s at the wooden Dnieper bridge checked leave passes and movement orders. While the conversations and various noises went on around him, Deutschmann looked down to the hut on the Dnieper bank. Nothing had changed. The stacks of wood were still there, the stable door hung askew in its frame, a narrow off-white path wound through the snow to the closed door of boards.

The distribution of medical stores went more quickly than the last time. The dispenser was not there, and a quiet friendly orderly collected together what Deutschmann asked for. He didn't get everything, but it was more than the quarter Bergen had anticipated. Anyhow, he wasn't much concerned about this. His thoughts and desires were in the small hut by the river.

The night was very dark. He groped his way down the hill and softly opened the door of the hut, just wide enough for him to slip in.

When he stood in the warm darkness of the room, it was as if he had stepped into a new world, which belonged to him alone, a world without Krull or Schwanecke or Bergen or Obermeier, without war. It was his world, and it was both his dream and his forgetting.

"It will never end," said Tanya, towards morning.

"What?"

"Happiness."

"We must believe in it. Then it will stay perhaps."

"It is hard to go on believing all the time."

"You can't expect it to last, Tanya."

"I would die without it, Michael."

"That's war, Tanyasha."

"Can't we conquer war—through love?"

"We two can't on our own. I'm afraid ..."

"Of what?" She raised her head a little and looked at him. He stared at the ceiling. His face was angular, narrow, alien. "You mustn't ever go away, Michael," she said, entreatingly. "You mustn't!"

"I'll have to."

"When?"

"How can I know that? Only God knows that."

"Do you believe in God?"

"Yes. And you?"

"I don't know," she said hesitantly. "I grew up with the Komsomols, you understand? I learnt there was no God, only Stalin and Lenin, the Party and Socialism. My mother—I can remember, she often spoke of God. My poor good Mamushka, she died when I was still a little girl."

"And your father?"

"He was taken away. I don't know where to, I never heard anything about him after that, and I went into the Komsomols Home." Now she looked towards the covered window, with paper stuck over the sides. Morning was near, terrible morning with the last kiss and the terrible words "Auf wiedersehen".

"What are you thinking about?" he asked, drawing her head down to him again.

"Why don't you stay with me?"

"I can't."

Outside the hut, on the Dnieper bank, engines began to hum. The supply trucks rumbled over the wooden bridge. The sound of shouting voices could be heard very faintly through the cold morning air. Further up, the ice was splitting, blasted by the Pioneers. When Deutschmann tried to get up, she held on to him. She clung to him like someone drowning. "Stay! Just an hour more, only one hour."

"It's no good. I have to go."

"I'll never seen you again!" she cried shrilly. "I know it, I know it quite certainly. You have come, and you were here. Now you're going and won't ever come back. I love you. You must never go away. Never."

He picked up the jug with the Crimean wine, which Tanya had fetched out of a hiding place the evening before when he came, and drank a long draught.

"I'll kill you if you go," said Tanya in a quiet voice.

Deutschmann was silent.

"You're staying here, Michael," she said, even more quietly, as she walked towards the stove.

He shook his head. "Be sensible, Tanya. We *must* be sensible'"

"The world is crazy, it's tearing itself apart, it's drowning, and you say 'Be sensible.' Always—sensible. You—German! Just stay here. You can live with us afterwards, I will hide you now, and when your—when there are no more German soldiers left here, I will come out in front of everyone and say: 'This is Michael, whom I love.' Stay here!"

"And your people will put us against the wall and shoot us, eh?"

"Michael!"

Deutschmann looked at her and started. She had a Russian pistol in her hand and was aiming at him.

"Don't be stupid," he said dully.

"I'll kill you if you go."

He looked at her and noticed in her eyes a frightening cold gleam. It seemed to say that she had the will to carry out her threat. He bent forward as if to reach for his boots, then charged on to her, thrust her against the wall, and pressed the knuckles of her hand so that she cried out and dropped the pistol. He kicked it towards the door and tried to defend himself against her hands and arms which were thrashing at him. "Bastard!" she cried, beating into his face with her fists. "You bastard, you bastard! I hate you! I hate you! I will kill you ... kill!"

Then she suddenly collapsed in tears. "Please leave me!" she said, and threw herself on to the bed. Deutschmann did not know what to do. It was useless trying to console her in any way. So he stood there for a while, then helplessly stroked her shoulder, and went. Before leaving the hut, he picked up the pistol and put it on the table. "Tanya!" he said.

She did not answer. She lay on the bed, and her whole body trembled. But she had stopped weeping so loudly.

"Tanya!"

"Go!" she said wearily.

"I want you to know that ... I love you, you have shown me a new world.... I will never forget you...."

"Go!"

"I'm just going. And hide that," he said, looking at the pistol. "If they catch you with that, they'll shoot you."

She did not answer, so he turned away and left the hut. He pulled the door shut behind him like a safety curtain being let down after a play which could only be performed once: he would never see it again on the stage of life.

In the small hut on the Dnieper bank Tanya lay on the blankets as if she had burnt herself out, and buried her face in the pillows—there where the small hollow of Deutschmann's head could be made out.

"Michael," she whimpered, "Oh, Michael.... I love you ... I hate everyone, everyone ..."

32

It was snowing in Berlin. Thick wet snowflakes fell from the dark sky and melted on the stones of the terrace. Dr. Kukill stood at the window and stared out into the bleak-looking garden, which merged into the long grey morning twilight. His bird-of-prey face was pale, hollow and calm. His eyes were wide open, but they were not on the garden. They were staring absently ahead of him, as if concentrating on an invisible point. Eventually he turned round, drew the heavy curtains, went with a shiver to his desk, sat down, and began to write:

Dear Dr. Deutschmann,

When you receive this letter, it will in all probability be too late. In fulfilment of a love before which one can only bow in reverence, and which is almost inconceivable to a person like myself, your wife, Julia, has repeated the experiment on herself for which you were convicted of self-mutilation. She wanted to prove that you were right and that your own experiment only failed because your antidote was too weak in its effects. It would appear that she has infected herself with too large a dose of Staphylococcus Aureus: Professor Burger, Dr. Wissek and I are of the reluctant opinion that there is no hope of saving her.

In my evidence at your trial as forensic specialist I made a judgment according to the state of present-day medicine and did not venture on to the speculative ground of possibilities; the experiment you tried on yourself, which your wife repeated on herself against my advice and despite my opposition, was so fantastic, so incredible, that sober reason refused to acknowledge its validity. It is now clear to me, however, that I was wrong. We have information from England, according to which researchers there have already succeeded in proving what you were trying to prove. But at the moment that is unimportant. I know how terribly this news of Julia will hit you, especially as you can do nothing about it yourself. Believe me, I can feel for you very deeply, I know what you have lost, for I too, I must confess, have learnt to respect and honour her very greatly.

Now that it seems as if her great love has put an end to her life, I promise you I will do all in my power to get you out of the penal battalion. I know that your work will be your only consolation, and I will support you in it with all my resources. You will hear from me again in a few days: I am convinced that it will not be too long before you are back in Berlin.

I admit my mistake and shall always feel guilt for it, please forgive me if you can. I only wish this admission could help to save your wife.

Yours very sincerely,

Anton Kukill?"

He put the letter in an envelope, wrote the address and sealed it. Then he rose, stood motionless for a few seconds, weighing the letter in his hand, and went out. He drove to the War Office and handed it in with a brief note of its urgency. His wide connections ensured that it would be dispatched towards Orsha as an important service communication.

This accomplished, he returned to the Charité about noon. Paler than ever, with stony face, he asked to speak to Professor Burger. When Burger answered, Kukill demanded tersely: "How is Julia?"

"Is that Dr. Kukill?"

"How is Julia Deutschmann? Is she ...?"

"No. She isn't. I'll give you Dr. Wissek, he was at her bedside all night."

Kukill waited. After minutes that seemed endless a weary voice answered: "Wissek here. Is that Dr. Kukill?"

"How is she?" Kukill asked again.

"A bit better. Pulse not so shallow now. The breathing is stronger, we are giving oxygen. But still a deep coma...."

"Breathing stronger?" Kukill had to prop himself on the desk. A sudden feebleness in his legs crept up over his whole body. "Stronger," he repeated, "She's better?" He almost shouted the last words.

"We can't say anything definite yet. But it looks as if the actinium had begun to work. We have injected another 5 cc...."

"As much as that?"

"We must try everything...."

"Yes, of course, of course ... we must try everything ..." Kukill echoed. He replaced the receiver and passed both hands over a sweat-covered face. "Perhaps," he muttered, "Julia ... if it works ... I'll get him out, if it ... if only it works!"

He had already put on his overcoat when he remembered the letter to Deutschmann. For a moment he stood irresolute, his hand on the door-handle, then he strode to the telephone and asked to be connected to the mail officer to whom he had handed the letter. The pallor had disappeared from his face; all his usual energy appeared again in his features. In short, jerky sentences he asked to have the letter returned.

But he was too late. It had gone half an hour before and was already on its way to Orsha.

33

When it became known that Lieutenant Obermeier had been summoned to Babinitchi to see the C.O., it started all sorts of rumours.

"There's something very nasty in the wind," said Wiedeck. "They say the QM's had a consignment of schnaps, I know what that means. When we're given schnaps, there's a real bastard coming up."

"That might go for a normal unit, I dare say." Bartlitz cut a piece of bread into small pieces, spread some cheap jam, and ate the pieces with relish—as if they were the finest delicacies. "But you don't seriously think we'll get schnaps here, do you?"

"Miracles *can* happen," observed Deutschmann.

"Who said anything about miracles?" Wiedeck demanded. "I say if we're getting schnaps, it means there'll be a real bastard of an order coming directly afterwards, the sort you can't be expected to carry out unless you're more or less tight. Suicide squad, or something like that."

"Could be," Bartlitz agreed. But nobody knew anything definite, and they had to wait for Obermeier's return. The suspense was all the greater because he was supposed to be bringing mail with him, the first mail for long weeks, which was far more important than either schnaps or a special ration of greasy bread.

The motor sledge rumbled through the white night. Obermeier was sitting dozing by the driver, a corporal who had seen long service. Suddenly the hum of the engines deepened, and the sledge slowed up. Obermeier started up from his reverie and looked at the corporal, who was peering out on to the road.

At the side of the road lay a horse. A small brown shaggy horse. Its eyes seemed almost frozen shut, the skin was crusted over with whiteness. It did not move, and from the sledge it looked as if it were half covered with snow. A Company had cleared the road the evening before, heaping the mountains of snow against the telegraph posts, which stuck out of the plains like withered fingers.

Sergei Denkov lay behind a snowdrift; on his forearm he had a sub-machine-gun with a big round magazine. He looked across at the jolting sledge emerging out of the night.

"What is it, Lohmann?" asked Obermeier.

The corporal drove slowly up to the dark heap in the snow.

"I think it's a horse, sir."

"You're dreaming, man, how could a horse get here?" But then he saw that Lohmann was right. It looked dead, or at least Obermeier thought so.

But Lohmann said: "Probably exhausted. Who could have left it lying here? May I stop?" The Westphalian farmer stirred in him, and where is the farmer who will drive past a suffering horse and leave it to its fate? Without waiting for Obermeier's answer, he brought the sledge to a stop.

Sergei pressed down the safety-catch of his gun. At the same time he pushed the barrel a bit higher. Only two, he thought. But two today and two tomorrow and two the day after.... so long as there are Germans in the world. He bit his lip, his forefinger curled round the trigger.

"Go and see," said Obermeier.

The corporal climbed out of the sledge and walked towards the horse—directly in Sergei's line of fire.

Now Obermeier too began climbing out—when the horse reared up with a sudden wild leap, as if startled by the scent of strange men, and bounded off. The suddenness of the rearing made Sergei start as well, but he got in his shot.

"Take cover!" yelled Obermeier, and dropped into the snow near the sledge. Lohmann stood there helplessly for a moment, then hurled himself forward, and in mid-movement felt a thundering blow against his forehead. He threw his arms up, then plunged headlong into the snow. His hands scrambled vainly around, and his feet stamped on the ground, throwing pieces of ice up. Then his body measured its full length and he lay there motionless.

The horse galloped along the road, with flying mane, whirling legs and neck craned forward. There was foam at its mouth.

Sergei crawled backwards, then sideways behind a telegraph post, and looked cautiously over the snow-heap towards the sledge. A thin crack tore through the dark silence, and the snow flew up like dust. The enemy was firing. He changed his position again; this time he crawled a bit further on, and when he looked out of his cover again, all was quiet. But from here the enemy, who was lying behind the sledge, was also out of *his* observation. Everything lay still and peaceful, the sledge was in the middle of the road, about thirty yards away from him, with the dark extended figure of the dead man in front of it.

Sergei waited. "He'll come," he murmured to himself. "I'm patient, and he will come. He's a German, and he wants to be a hero. All German heroes are impatient, that's why they don't as a rule survive their heroic deeds."

Obermeier, however, had no wish to be a hero. He was only a man in uniform who could also wait, wait to kill.

For almost an hour they lay there in silence quite close to each other.

As the night slowly and imperceptibly gave way to a grey twilight, Sergei knew he would not get his victim. He couldn't wait any longer. There would soon be Germans coming along the road, a patrol perhaps or a supply column. If they caught him here, he was done for. And it would soon be too light for him to run for it. The other man would see him before he disappeared between the bushes of the nearby wood. "I've killed one," he told himself, as he crawled back, stiff with cold, his teeth chattering. Then with head down, he dashed away from the sledge, behind the wall of snow near the road. "That's one dead," he muttered. "Tomorrow there will be two or three, perhaps several of them. One is not enough."

When he thought he was sufficiently far away, he turned

off to the right, raced across the open field towards the wood, and disappeared between the bushes.

Obermeier saw him, but did not fire. It was too far. But even if the running figure had been nearer, he would hardly have been capable of firing; he was freezing cold, his body was stiff, his hands and feet numb. Slowly he stood up, groaning, gazed for a moment towards the vanished enemy, and then began to run round and round the sledge. It took quite a time before some feeling returned to his limbs. When he began to get a sharp tingling in his hands and feet, he carried the dead body to the sledge and laid it in the back seat. Before he drove off, he looked for a few seconds into the expanses of the country, over which a new winter day was slowly breaking. This country was insatiable as a giant sponge. The whole of mankind could have space in it, he thought, and even then it would not be overcrowded.

It began to snow. He drove off towards Barssdovka. Captain Bergen was there to receive him, with Sergeant Major Krull in attendance. They had been waiting for the sledge for two hours, and were already talking of sending a search party to Babinitchi. Now they stood mutely by the sledge, as Obermeier clambered out, limbs still stiff with cold.

"Dead?" asked Bergen, pointing with his chin at the body on the back seat. It was a needless question: anyone could see the man was dead. Only a corpse could lie like that.

"Who is it?" asked Krull, trembling. It was more than the cold that made him tremble.

"Corporal Lohmann. Have his body taken away," Obermeier ordered tersely.

"Come on, some schnaps will do you good," said Bergen; and the two officers went off to Bergen's quarters, leaving Krull to stare wide-eyed at the dead body.

34

Using the medical post as an office, Krull looked through the mail and sorted out some of the letters. He was particularly annoyed to see the name on one envelope: Dr. Ernst Deutschmann. He took a red pencil, crossed it all through, and wrote in clumsy letters: Private E. Deutschmann.

Then he took all the mail to Obermeier, who was sitting in Captain Bergen's room, and laid it before him. "There's one for Schwanecke too. Should he really be handed the letter, sir? Without censorship?"

Obermeier nodded. "Let's have the letter. I will give it to him."

"And Private Deutschmann?"

"Why do you ask? Didn't you notice that letter has been marked Urgent Service Business? Forget your stupid questions, go and distribute the mail."

Krull left the room in a fury. Always these exceptions, he thought bitterly. What has this half-civilian sod got to do with urgent service business! That lot always stick together, even if one's an officer and the other a private.

"I say, Doctor," he said in a mock-posh accent, when he found Deutschmann in the hospital hut, "you have heah a letter from home. Urgent Service Business for the learned Doctor. Here, catch!" He threw the letter to Deutschmann, but deliberately threw it too short.

Deutschmann said nothing. He bent down, picked up the letter, and stuck it in his pocket.

In a room near the barn, Deutschmann sat down on a

stool, and weighed the letter in his hand. He thought at first it was from Julia, and his heart was constricted by a feeling of hot shame mixed with apprehension. But when he saw it was Dr. Kukill, not Julia, whose name was on the back of the envelope as sender, he was disappointed. Why didn't Julia write? What had happened? Air-raid damage perhaps? Why was this Dr. Kukill writing to him? What did *he* want all of a sudden? Was it something about Julia? No, it couldn't be.

Slowly, hesitantly, he tore open the envelope, unfolded the sheet of paper and began to read.

After the first sentences his face hardened. The more he read, the more it paled, till it was soon like the face of a mortally sick man. With a tremendous effort of will he forced himself to read every sentence, every word, right through to the end. When he had finished, he smoothed the sheet carefully on his knees, folded it slowly, stuck it back in the envelope and thrust it into his pocket. Then he sat for a while sunk in his thoughts, unnaturally calm, a man who had had to digest a terrible truth worse than a death sentence.

The same morning Schwanecke stood stiffly to attention in front of Lieutenant Obermeier.

"There's a letter for you, Schwanecke."

A look of incredulous amazement came over Schwanecke's face. "A letter, sir? I never get letters."

"You have this time."

"Oh, dear, that can't be good, sir."

"How do you make that out?"

"Well, how can it be—I mean, if I get a letter...." He stopped, made a helpless gesture with his hand and dropped it back at his side.

"What is it, then" Are you expecting any bad news?"

"No, sir ... that is, my mother in Hamburg, you see, sir. Air raids every day—but she's never written a line to me, so it can't be from her. Someone must have written to me that she, I mean, Mother—after all, she is my mother, even though—do you understand, sir?" He looked up again, into the Lieutenant's astonished eyes, and began to grin. But his grin only made him look the more helpless and bewildered.

"No, you couldn't understand that, sir, could you?" he went on. "My mother always said to me, 'I don't have no son any more, you're a bad lot, a criminal.' That's how it is, sir, where we come from. You grow up like a rat—till you're shot like a rat. That's the way it is, sir."

"Your mother has written to you," said Obermeier, his throat dry.

"My mother?" Schwanecke stretched out his hand, then immediately pulled it back again. "Mother?" he repeated. And now Obermeier saw something he would never have credited if someone else had told him: a tender warm smile came over Schwanecke's hard, sullen face, and his eyes, usually lifeless, like two glass balls, suddenly shone with childlike joy. "Is that right, sir? You're not pulling my leg? Excuse me, sir, but ..." He passed his heavy rough hand quickly over his face, as if he wanted to brush away something that worried him. He wiped the hand on his trousers and hesitantly stretched it out.

"Here you are, then, take it," said Obermeier. "Off you go, and read your letter in peace."

Schwanecke went across to the big barn and sat down on his bed. Kronenberg and Krull, who observed him holding the letter thoughtfully in his hand, sauntered up.

"Love letter from Liesl, Anni, Gretchen—or who?" asked Kronenberg.

"It's from Mummy." Krull grinned.

Schwanecke turned on him. "Get out."

"Hey, you—you've still not learnt how to behave when talking to your Sergeant Major."

"Yessir!" said Schwanecke quietly, and slowly rose. Krull looked into his eyes and moved off again.

"You too," Schwanecke told Kronenberg very calmly, and waited till Kronenberg had also gone. Then he sat down again, and slowly and carefully opened the envelope with his finger-nail.

The first letter for five years. She had not written when he was on remand, she had rejected him when he went to prison, she had kept quiet when the SS collected him from prison and took him to Buchenwald. She had forgotten him when he was drudging it in the quarries of Thuringia, where he had to drag huge boulders with his bare hands and break up the hard basalt in the mountain with a pick. And she had not written when he came to Russia in this battalion of the lost.

But now she *had* written.

You could be on bloody bad terms with your mother, you could have cursed her a thousand times for having brought you into the world—but she remained your mother. And when a letter like this came, all was forgotten, you felt like a small boy who has just been knocked about by someone and now runs to mummy to hear her say that it isn't so bad, is it; and to feel her hand on your head and go on crying for a little—and then it really isn't so bad any more, when she says it and when she strokes your hair.

The envelope was addressed to Private Karl Schwanecke. The letter read:

Dear Karl,

Thursday before last we was bombed out by the terror bombers, everythings had it, the house and the furniture and your sister Irene was in the house when the bomb fell. She didnt die at once and was in great pain and you could hear her screaming but she was dead when they dug her out. Its a terrible time what have we done to deserve it??? now they dont give me a new place to live because everythings so full and people have to sleep at the station but thats had it too. And they say your son is anti-social and a violent criminal, you dont get no flat and so what do I do? I curse the day I bore you and when I think of the trouble I had bringing you into the world!!! Now Im living outside in a stall its very cold and theres no coal and always the bombers and oh I wish this lousy rotten life was over. All because of you. I didnt get a coffin for Irene because her name is Schwanecke and thats a dirty word. But now I dont care about all that my life has had it anyhow I'd just like some peace and quiet perhaps I will get it when Im dead.

Goodbye now from Your mother
Herta Schwanecke."

Schwanecke read the letter slowly, very slowly, word for word. When he had finished, he began again from the beginning, as if he wanted to learn the lines by heart. His lips moved slowly as he read, like a man saying a prayer to himself. The longer he read, the greyer his face became, hollowed, bony, ashen.

When he at last stopped reading and looked up to stare into the void, his eyes were smarting, deep under the bushy eyebrows.

"Cor, what's up with him now?" Kronenberg exclaimed.

"What does darling Mummy write, then?" Krull shouted from the other end of the barn.

Schwanecke didn't hear. One letter after five long years and what had she written? Bombed out—and the name Schwanecke is a dirty word—she'd rather be dead....

"Bastards!" he cried out suddenly. He jumped to his feet, threw back his head, and opened his mouth wide, as if he couldn't get any air. "Bastards!" he yelled wildly, just that one word, over and over again. Then he crumpled up the letter, slung it into the darkness of the room, and stamped on it as if he had gone mad. "Mother!" he cried now. "Mother ... they're all bastards! All of them!"

Krull and Kronenberg rushed up to him. They reached the bed as Schwanecke began to destroy it with his hands and feet, yelling, flailing round him, his face distorted and his eyes crazed.

"I'm going!" he cried. "I'm getting out of here! I'll do you in, I'll do you you all in, the lot of you!"

Kronenberg and Krull exchanged a quick look. He had obviously gone berserk. They hurled themselves on to him, but it needed three reinforcements before they could finally master him, lay him on the half-destroyed bed and tie him down.

Bergen, Hansen and Obermeier came running into the barn. Kronenberg dusted his hands as if he had been carrying a bag of flour. His left eye was beginning to swell up. "Our boy's asleep," he said mildly. "It was a bit of a shock for him. Perhaps over the years he's forgotten how to read and that made him wild."

"Shut your stupid mouth, Kronenberg," snapped Obermeier. He walked up to the bed and looked at Schwanecke's swelling bruised face. "I'll take him with me to Gorki—and you'll come too, Krull."

"B … but my wound … sir," stuttered Krull.

"I've been informed that your behind is now all right again. Anyhow I don't need your behind but your hands, and they're clearly all right again too—or were you hitting Schwanecke with your behind?"

"No, sir."

"Right. One o'clock tonight outside the theatre hut."

"Yes, sir."

"And the partisans?" asked Bergen.

"Don't worry about that, Captain. We do have to go back."

Krull slunk to his bed. Back to the front, he thought. Back again to the ambushes; partisans; …

Bergen gave Schwanecke a morphine injection.

"Think he'll calm down?" asked Obermeier.

"He'll sleep now till this evening. I hope it will be over by then."

"What started it?" Obermeier turned to Kronenberg.

"The letter …"

"Where is it?"

Kronenberg found the crumpled letter and gave it to Obermeier, who smoothed it out and read it. When he had finished, he folded it carefully together, stuck it in his pocket, and left the room in silence.

"What on earth did it have in it?" said Kronenberg. "It seems to have shaken *him* too."

"Who knows? There are letters people just shouldn't send," said Hansen.

When Schwanecke woke up to find himself chained to his bed, he burst into hysterical laughter. "I'm not going to do a bolt, you idiots," he said. "Where the hell would I go to in this Godforsaken country?"

"You never can tell. You had a fine old fit and it's well known, isn't it, that people with fits can do all sorts of stupid things?" Kronenberg sat at the foot of the bed, holding a syringe ready behind his back in case Schwanecke began to rage again. "The SS will catch you and hang you one day anyhow. So you'd really have the best chance if you run away to the Ivans."

Krull gave Kronenberg a kick and said "They'll shoot your ribs out one by one if you go over to them." Captain Bergen himself, Krull's last hope, had declared him fit for service, thereby confirming that his shot in the behind was no obstacle on the road to heroism; and since then Krull had quickly adapted to the circumstances. Only a quarter of an hour after Bergen had examined him and given his verdict, Krull had made a lightly wounded man stand to attention in the hospital barn and then chased him up and down the central passage because, said Krull, lying in a nice warm bed had made him forget how to acknowledge a superior correctly. "I'll damn well help you to remember," he had shouted across the barn. "You lead-swingers, keeping your bellies warm in here, while we lie out in the snow chewing ice. In future I'll take it on myself to deal with everyone that comes back from hospital."

The evening passed without any further trouble from Schwanecke. At the appointed 01.00 hours he and Krull stood shivering outside the theatre hut waiting for the Lieutenant. Schwanecke leant against a wall, looking darkly ahead of him; Krull too was quiet, brooding at the prospect of being near the front again. He thought of the partisans, through whose territory they would soon have to pass. He thought of the trench system with its attacks by bomb-throwers, and the artillery fire ever night.

When Obermeier eventually appeared, he was wearing a scarf bound round his head under the fur cap, like a toothache sufferer protecting his swollen cheek. "All in order, Sergeant Major?"

"Yessir."

"We 're taking Deutschmann along too, he should be here in a moment."

"What's he got to do?" asked Schwanecke disrespectfully.

"Lieutenant Hansen is going to pack up some more stuff for him," Obermeier answered. Then he seemed to realise suddenly who had asked the question and how. He was about to remonstrate, but refrained. Silently and thoughtfully he regarded Schwanecke, who returned his look with a dull indifference.

"Schwanecke ..."

"I know, sir. You don't even need to say it. Any attempt to desert means being shot inmediately. I've heard it a hundred times, I'm sick to death of hearing it."

"Just don't forget it. You will be sent to Orsha the day after tomorrow."

"Why?"

"You know why."

"Oh well, if that's the way it is ..."

A sledge drawn by two ponies came down the village street and stopped outside the barn. A soldier, muffled like a Polar explorer, was squatting on the seat. He put his hand casually to his fur cap, which he had taken from a Russian peasant and was wearing instead of a forage cap. Then Deutschmann came out of the hospital barn, walking very slowly—almost a somnambulist—bent forward, with unmoving, empty eyes.

Obermeier regarded him briefly and wondered for the second time in twenty-four hours what had happened to this man to transform him so completely. Deutschmann had never been noisy and talkative, but to all appearances he had got used to the unit he had to serve in. A quiet, relaxed serenity radiated from him, the attitude of a man who had accepted his situation. But since this morning when he had been given the letter from Germany, that had gone: it looked indeed as if all the life had gone out of Deutschmann. He was like a walking corpse moved by external forces: he spoke like an automaton, he answered questions with the air of one not really there.

Krull climbed in first. He pulled Schwanecke behind him and sat where he could see his movements. He paid no attention to Deutschmann.

Captain Bergen came running out of his hut and called to Obermeier. "Wernher has just phoned. The Russians have broken through near Vitebsk on a front of over twenty miles. He expects that the next push will take place here near us." He stopped and then came up quite close to Obermeier. "In case we don't see each other again, look after yourself. You're one of the last decent chaps there are here, and I—I ..." He turned abruptly away and hurried through the snow back into the theatre hut. Obermeier looked after him, shook his head, went to the sledge and sat down by Krull. "Drive off!" he ordered.

Krull looked at him aghast. "The Russians have broken through."

"So it seems."

"And now—near us?"

"Probably."

Krull swallowed. "What are we going to do if it starts here, sir? We've got nothing. Only three machine guns for the whole Company, four sub-machine-guns, ten rifles, five pistols. That's all. We can't stop the Russians with that, can we!"

"You're right once again, Krull."

Schwanecke gave a broad grin. "Bit of a stink here, sir, I should move away. I'm afraid he's had another accident in his trousers...."

But Krull and Obermeier ignored him. Wide-eyed, Krull looked at the Lieutenant. "They'll shoot us down like rabbits, sir. We can't just let ourselves be shot."

"Why not?" Obermeier rubbed his clammy hands. "What do you think we're here for?"

Just before dawn the horse-sledge got in to Gorki and stopped outside Company Headquarters. Kentrop, who was in command in the absence of Obermeier, Krull and Hefe, came running out of the hut to report. Hefe and Bortke were with the digging squads out in the trenches; and through the field telephone, installed the previous night, they had transmitted the news that a Russian patrol behind German lines had shot up a work party, which had only three rifles and two pistols to defend itself with, and had therefore sustained severe losses: seven dead and thirteen wounded. It was only when reinforcements came with one light machine gun and two sub-machine-guns that the Russians had withdrawn, leaving three of their men dead.

Listening to this report as he got out of the sledge, Krull felt as if the world were caving in on him. What he had feared for so long was now happening.

Obermeier said nothing. He nodded to Kentrop and walked with his head down into the hut. Kentrop turned to Krull and said gloomily: "It looks bloody terrible. And this is only the beginning . They had a fearful pasting at A Company last night."

Deutschmann had registered the conversations as if through a thick wodge of cotton wool. None of these things seemed to concern him. With absent, staring eyes he sat on a board bed in the tiny room where he slept. Nor did he look up when the door opened and someone came in.

It was Schwanecke.

"What the hell is up with you Doc?" he asked, sitting down by Deutschmann and looking at him searchingly. He now regularly called Deutschmann this.

"Nothing. What are you doing here?"

"I'm seeking company, you know? Before they put me up against the wall. . . . "

At first Deutschmann did not make any comment. It was only gradually that Schwanecke's words penetrated into his consciousness. "Do what to you?" he asked.

"Put me up against the wall, I said, Doc. One, two, three, the head's off, and Schwanecke is no more."

"You're mad!"

"The rest are, not me. They'll fix me, you bet. First they stick me here in a penal battalion and say, prove your worth, my boy, if you kill enough Russians, you'll be back in our good books. But then came the stupid business with that cretin . . . "

"Bevern?"

"Who else?"

"But you didn't shoot him, and they can't pin anything on you, can they!"

"Perhaps I did shoot him, though." Schwanecke gave a broad grin.

Deutschmann shrank away. Shocked, he looked at the man sitting by him, who stared back and gave a sly wink.

"You did sh . . . "

"Hell, no, I didn't do anything. But it's like this, if you get me. Once you're in the net, you don't get away from them. Suspicion is enough. And with a suspicion like that it's disastrous. Listen. First man says, He was alone with him in the trench. Second man says, Well, he could easily have shot him. Third man says, He shot him. And fourth men says, 'course he did, no doubt about it, it's a dead cert, nobody else but Schwanecke could have shot Bevern. And that gets added on to previous convictions. Now, as you probably know, my record isn't exactly spotless. Of course not everyone believes I actually killed him. Pity I didn't really."

"Perhaps you did, after all?"

"Oh, to hell with you. Anyhow, now I'm arrested. No probation, I'm an anti-social element. So, firing squad, bm, bm, bm, off with his block, the German people can breath again, Schwanecke is no more. You get the picture?"

"That's terrible," muttered Deutschmann.

"Terrible? Get away. When so many people are copping it … and now I must tell you something I haven't ever told anyone: they may even be right. I mean … you know—I mean I really *was* a bastard. Nothing bothered me. If I saw a girl—up and at her. If I saw a safe—mine for the cracking. I can just imagine everybody else had had enough of me. But now I've seen all this, you understand, I think perhaps—well nobody can promise anything, but perhaps—perhaps I might turn into something else. I've met you, Doc, and Wiedeck and Bartlitz, you're all right, damn it, you people are really all right. I think they'd have to give me a chance. But now it's bleeding well finished, finished!"

He put his head in his hands and wept.

It was incredible. Deutschmann would have expected anything but to see Schwanecke cry. He felt unable to move, unable to say anything. But then he could bear it no longer. He slowly stretched out his hand and put it on Schwanecke's shoulder. "Perhaps it's not so bad, Karl," he said, "perhaps …"

Schwanecke looked up. His eyes were bloodshot and flickering; Deutschmann shrank away from them. "There's no perhaps. I have to help myself, that's all."

"What do you mean by that?"

"What do I mean by that? Stupid question, I shall do a bunk."

"Desert, you mean?"

"That's right."

Deutschmann's face was ashen. "You're mad. If they catch you, Obermeier will have you up against the wall, and we'll have to fire at you."

"Who said anything about my getting caught? No one can catch me here if I don't want them to."

"How are you going to get through the front line?"

"Man, you forget I'm one of your real old front-line rats, I'm up to all the tricks, no one can put anything over me. And I'll tell you something more—get a grip on yourself." He stood up and looked Deutschmann straight in the eyes. "You've always been a decent bloke, Ernst. You're a doctor, man, what the hell are you doing here? Why are you still hanging about? Why are you still hanging about? If you like, I'll take you with me. Honest I will.?

Deutschmann shook his head.

Schwanecke's voice became urgent. "Don't be stupid, Doc. If you come with me, you'll survive. I'll guarantee it. Take your Red Cross flag with you and an arm-band like that and give me one too. Then they'll think on both sides that we're searching for wounded—and we'll go right through the middle.

"I can't do that."

"Why not?"

"It would be a disgusting trick. I mean, the business with the Red Cross."

"Perhaps you're just stupid, I'd like to know what goes on in your head. The thing is crystal clear. The whole war is disgusting. And I'll tell you something. This Red Cross flag is there to—well, to save people's lives. It will also save our lives, why should that be a disgusting trick? If you stay here, on the other hand, you'll have had it, sure as fate, at the next Russian attack. What are you going to defend yourself with? We shall be like fairground targets as we hobble through the snow. They'll get in some good practice shooting us down, and I'll bet you anything you like that'll be happening quite soon—I can feel it in my bones. And you still talk of disgusting tricks and the Red Cross and all that. If you stay here, you've had it: if you come with me, you'll stay alive—and the Red Cross will have done just what it's supposed to do."

"And the others?"

"Who?"

"I mean the others, our mates."

"What about them?"

"What will they do?"

"I can tell you exactly what they'll do. They'll say, Bright lads, at least two blokes who've seen a bit of sense, hope they get through, we'll keep our fingers crossed for them. That's just what they'll say. Wake up, man. Don't you see the way things are going here? We shall be slaughtered like a herd of cattle. It won't be long before you're croaking too. Can't you grasp that? Over there we have a chance. I know it's no joke being a prisoner of the Russians, they won't exactly be friendly, but at least we've got a fifty-fifty chance of surviving. If you stay here, your chances are about one in a hundred. Here you're the scum of the earth if you're in a penal battalion. But over there they might even say, These are martyrs, they've deserted from Hitler's army, long live Schwanecke, Heil Deutschmann, what would you like to eat, and do have a drink on us. Come on, Ernst—come on, my old Doc, take the plunge and come with me."

"No."

"With the armband and the flag we'll get through as sure as anything."

"And the minefields?"

"You still haven't grasped that I've got the bloody knack. I can smell a mine at fifty yards. And they call you an intellectual. I just don't know why you're against it. I have to get away. If I can't find some gimmick like medical orderly or whatnot, it's off with my head—and I'd be a bloody fool to wait for that."

"Well, leave me out of it."

Schwanecke turned round, walked over to the tiny window, and looked out on to the village street. Krull was standing in the deep snow, his greatcoat collar turned up, and shouting at a private. It was the lean, half-starved professor, who could only be employed on light duties within the Company. He had cleared the road of snow and was leaning exhausted for a few moments on the handle of his wire broom. Krull, making a tour of the village, found him in this position. Here was somebody on whom Krull could vent his rage at his own fear. While he chased him to and fro, he could forget where he was, at least for a time, and suppress the forebodings which were constantly harassing him.

"You brainy idle slacker!" he yelled. "Sitting on your bum in universities. Oh, I bet you give a bloody fine lecture, but when it comes to sweeping a road, you're on your knees. Hup hup hup, professor, three times round the office, double march!"

The professor grasped his broom like a spear, and began to run. He was gasping, his eyes popped. He staggered on, with the other hand pressed to his heart. Krull stood in the road, giving orders. "Faster, faster! Keep your feet flying, Head up! Think of wotsisname, Socrates, he was one of your philosophers, wasn't he? Think of Kant, he slept in a barrel in the fresh air—take an example from him, you've got lots of fresh air here! Another round, hup hup hup!"

The professor staggered, stumbled, threw his broom away, flailed with his arms and fell forward into the snow. He lay with his face on the ice in the middle of the village road, a lifeless bundle of clothes, with a lean-grey-haired head coming out of them.

Krull looked down at him in surprise and shook his head. "Well!" he said, and turned round to shout: "Deutschmann! Deutschmann! You're wanted."

Schwanecke swung round from the window with a sour grin on his face. "Out you go," he said. "Your friends have messed up the poor old professor. You go and help, it'll soon be your turn." He went out, as if the affair didn't concern him. Deutschmann ran after him and into the road.

Krull was standing with his legs straddled over the unconscious man. By the time Deutschmann had run up with his first-aid kit, the Sergeant Major had become a bit uneasy. "Is there an injection you can give for this?"

"We'll see." Deutschmann kneeled in the snow and turned the professor over. There was a deep cut over his forehead: the blood had frozen with the cold. When Deutschmann lifted his eyelids, the eyes were distorted and without lustre.

"Is he—is he dead?"

"Not yet. Probably a coronary."

"Talk plain German." With the side of his boot Krull tapped the side of the man laying unconscious on the ground. "What's he got?"

"Oh, measles!" Deutschmann answered furiously, and paid no more attention to the hopeless Sergeant Major standing by him. He looked round for help and noticed Schwanecke, who was leaning against the wall and staring across impassively. "Karl come over and help me!" Deutschmann shouted, and took hold of the unconscious man under the arms.

Schwanecke strolled slowly up. "Leave him," he said. He lifted the professor in his arms, and carried him over to the sick-bay. They put the lifeless body down on a palliasse. Deutschmann unbuttoned his uniform and massaged the lean chest. The professor gradually came to, his mouth opened and closed, and almost inaudibly he rattled: "Air—air—air." Then he lost consciousness again.

"Water!" cried Deutschmann.

Schwanecke ran into a corner, filled a mess-tin lid with water, returned, and began to take a turn in massaging, while Deutschmann percussed the heart area with a flat hand.

"Can't you give him some heart drug?" asked Schwanecke.

"I've got nothing here, only sympathol."

"Then give him that."

"It's won't help."

"Perhaps it will. We *must* pull him through. He's all right, the professor is. That bastard Krull, that bloody bastard!"

Deutschmann took a small flask out of his first-aid kit and poured fifteen drops on to a spoon. Schwanecke thrust a thick forefinger between the unconscious man's tightly clamped lips, and pressed the mouth open. Deutschmann carefully poured the drops in. Then he again massaged the chest and the heart area.

"Shall I get some schnaps?" asked Schwanecke.

"No, there's no point."

"He *must* pull through," Schwanecke repeated. "Krull, that bastard! if I once get my hands on him. . . ."

"He *will* pull through, at any rate it looks like it to me," said Deutschmann, sweating, as the professor began to breathe more regularly and to groan softly. But he was still unconscious.

"Well, are you coming with me now, or not?" asked Schwanecke.

Deutschmann did not answer.

"Do you really want to croak here? Like him? Even if he pulls through now, he'll croak some time soon— when the Russians shoot him, if not before."

"Shut up!" said Deutschmann.

"All right, all right. Go on and die if you want to. I don't care."

They went on working without further talk. When it looked as if there was nothing more to do, they covered the professor with two blankets. Then sat down on either side of him and stared at the floor. They had nothing more to say to each other—or had they? Is Karl right in the last resort, Deutschmann wondered. Is it really just as he says? What's keeping me here? Why don't I seize my chance with both hands. For it *is* a chance of surviving, whereas here....

When Obermeier suddenly came in, they didn't get up.

"Krull?" asked the Lieutenant.

Deutschmann nodded. "He had to do something, didn't he?"

Without a word, his face pale and frowning, Obermeier left the sick-bay.

That night Krull raged round the village like a wild animal—and then he slunk back to his living quarters. Obermeier had given him a terrific hauling over the coals. But that alone would not have been so bad: in the course of his long military career he had learnt to shake off the periodical reprimands of his superiors as a wet dog shakes off water. But far, far more unpleasant was the fact that Obermeier had ordered him to go out again into the trenches, to inspect progress on the earthworks and, worst of all, to measure the half-completed trenches.

"You've developed into a specialist in measuring, Sergeant Major," Obermeier had said to him. "Isn't that so?"

He had clicked his heels and confirmed it hoarsely. "Yessir."

That stupid Yessir hurt him badly inside, and his mood

changed rapidly from one of fury to a sour silence full of foreboding.

35

That evening Captain Barth at Orsha received operational orders from Division. He read them through twice, sat motionless for a moment, then rang up Division and asked for the Adjutant, a captain, who came on the line at once.

"Ah, Barth, it's you," he said jovially. "I was just thinking of you. In fact, to be honest, I was expecting your call."

"Then you know what I want to talk to you about?"

"Of course."

"How exactly do you see this working out? Why must we of all people do it?"

"What a question! Admittedly a unit such as yours doesn't as a rule carry out such tricky assignments, but the General thinks there is sometimes a reason for making exceptions. You see, Barth, we don't want to kid ourselves: the operation is damned dangerous. We know that, too. But what are we to do? The Russians are attacking near Vitebsk, it's only in our sector that things are still quiet. Why?—they're wondering at GHQ. The ground is frozen hard, the best weather for tanks anyone could wish for. And yet nothing is moving, although the Russians must know the west lies open to them if they break through here. It's all flat, there are no great obstacles. We have the suspicion that there's something brewing behind the Russian lines. We've already tried air reconnaissance, but the clouds are too low, and besides they've already shot down two of our planes. The question is, what's going on behind there, behind the Russian lines? And to find that out, your B Company, which is most favourably situated for it, has to infiltrate the Russian lines, divided into several patrols, and see what's up."

"A real suicide squad," said Barth slowly. "I doubt if anyone at all will come back."

"One man must come back. If that one man makes it, he will have achieved more than a whole regiment could do. But that's why I wanted to talk to you. We both know that with your lot there are sure to be plenty of men who would go over to the Russians at the first opportunity that offers itself. That was out only worry about entrusting your probation battalion with this assignment. We're risking it even so, and we will put it in writing that all those who survive the operation intact and come back, will be transferred to their old units and restored to their former military ranks. That should be a terrific incentive."

"I don't find it so terrific."

"I know what you mean: once anyone's over there, the war's over for him. That's true enough, but on the other hand, it's a real probation for your men. If the reconnaisance raid, or perhaps we should call it a patrol operation, comes off successfully, a whole lot of your men will be rehabilitated, and that's quite something, isn't it! If it doesn't—well, that's war, and neither of us started that."

"No," said Barth. "We didn't, did we!"

Not far from Barssdovka there were a few low, half-decayed, dilapidated peasant huts. They were inhabited by old people who didn't want to leave their homes and would rather be shot than flee from the front. In one of these huts old Marfa, a woman in her seventies, lived on the milk and butter from one goat, and spent most of the day staring through the small, half-blind window at the German soldiers and supply columns rattling past. Then at night, when it became quieter, well-camouflaged figures would now and then come through the back entrance, warm themselves, and disappear again, like flitting shadows, as softly as they had come. They were the partisans who had infiltrated through the German front line disguised as peasants.

On one of the silent, white nights crackling with frost, Tanya came to Marfa's hut.

"Ah, Tanyasha, it's you!" said the old woman, blinking at the girl with her bleary, colourless eyes. "It's quite a while since you've been here."

"How are you?"

"I'm well, little daughter." The gnarled rheumatic fingers stroked Tanya's old patched dress. "What are you doing here?"

"I would like to stay with you."

Old Marfa nodded. She did not speak of it any more; and while Tanya came into the house and fitted up a bed for herself in the hayloft, the old woman sat down again in front of the fire and stared with an absorbed expression into the flickering flames.

Tanya was almost happy. From a dormer window in the hay-loft she could see over to Barssdovka. Michael was there, the man from another country who had grown closer to her than anyone before him, to whom she belonged and whom she would follow wherever he might lead her. Perhaps she would see him. Perhaps she could even talk to him. She thought of what she would tell him when she found him. She wanted to tell him how the world was suddenly lonely without him, how she had waited for him and had decided to come here so as to be near him. And she would tell him she had definitely decided to leave everything behind that had before been dear to her, so that she could be with him....

Obermeier came out of the office, one of the men, identical with the rest, in white combat kit, with a sub-machine-gun slung round his shoulder and hand-grenades behind his belt. "Men," he said, "and 'men' means Probation Battalion 999 We are now at last to have our probation; and with a tougher test than usual at that. We are making a reconnaisance raid behind the Russian lines. A dangerous business, I know. The patrol leaders will give you more details about it. This is what I now have to say: everybody who comes back will at once be transferred to his old unit and have his former rank and decorations restored. That'll be the end of the probation battalion, the penal battalion as you—or, to be honest, all of us—call our mob. I know: perhaps we shan't all come back. We don't want to kid ourselves. But it depends on us how heavy our losses will be. Solely on us. I think we understand each other. Since I feel I am one of you, I have no alternative but to come with you. And I shall be coming back too, you can rest assured of that. I hope we shall all meet again here the day after tomorrow, just as we're all standing here now. Then we'll empty a few bottles to celebrate our success—and say goodbye to each other."

"A great guy." Wiedeck exclaimed as they dismissed.

"Who?" asked Schwanecke.

"Obermeier."

"You really think so?" Schwanecke grunted sceptically, but then said on impulse, grinning over his shoulder. "No, you're right. He's a good bloke." Yes, he thought, Obermeier is a good bloke. If I don't get on with him too well, it's my fault, not his. And suddenly, as so often before, and more and more often during the last weeks, Schwanecke felt a pain that was almost physical to think he was an outsider who had to see Obermeier and other decent folk as his enemies. They *were* that, you couldn't alter the fact, and it was a lousy business that things were like that. How much better it would be if they could all pull together—Obermeier, Wiedeck, Deutschmann and so many others—and himself. Damn it, he thought disconsolately, it's a bloody miserable business, Because it's too late....

So B Company, clattering slightly with arms and equipment, moved off through the twilight, like phantoms, hardly rising above the grey-white plain all round.

In front, with Hefe by him, went Lieutenant Obermeier. With the second group Krull. Then Kentrop. And others in a long, long file. Bartlitz, the former colonel. A demoted major. A music teacher. A lawyer. A pickpocket. A Schoolmaster. An architect and again a lawyer. A pimp. A homosexual. A building worker. A butcher. A high civil servant. A burglar. A former district officer. A doctor.

In front of them, where the German front line ran, the

night was dark and silent. Frost. A tracer bullet. And suddenly a machine gun.

Tanya stood at her hayloft window and looked after the silent column long after they were out of sight. For quite a time afterwards she went on looking towards Barssdovka, and a faint, sad smile flitted over her face, as she softly whispered: "Good night, Michael, sleep well … sleep well."

At the front line Obermeier exchanged a few words with the young lieutenant, who knew the form. They compared their watches once more, and then looked in silence for a long time towards the Russian lines.

"Aren't you afraid half your men will desert?" the lieutenant asked finally.

"Why should I be?"

"Oh well, what you hear. After all, they're convicts, aren't they, and communists…."

"You should know, shouldn't you?" said Obermeier and the tone of his voice silenced the lieutenant.

"Twenty seconds more," said Obermeier after a while to a darkly brooding Krull. He held the watch with luminous dial close to his eyes. "15—10—5—off!"

The first figures climbed soundlessly over the edge of the trench, and over the wire. Interval. Second group. Interval. Third—fourth—fifth—sixth group. "See you make it!" Obermeier whispered to Kentrop. "Course we will," Kentrop answered with a grin, showing a gleam of white teeth. Then he disappeared and his men behind him. Seventh—eight—ninth group. Now it was Obermeier's own turn. He looked briefly back at his silent, waiting men, who stood in the trench crammed close together, and said: "off!"

Hours passed, and the men were near to complete exhaustion—when they suddenly found themselves on the edge of the wood.

Obermeier looked at his watch. It was twelve minutes past one.

Ahead of them was a plain, broken up by groups of bushes and isolated trees. Behind it, in the pale light of a Russian winter, the dark outlines of a village could be made out. And in front of them, like huge black shadows, betweeen the edge of the wood and the village, behind the bushes and under the trees, camouflaged with branches and whole bushes stood Russian tanks.

"Cor!" said Schwanecke softly. "A whole army. T 34s. When *they* start rolling..."

"... we shan't even have time to get our trousers down," Wiedeck finished the sentence.

"And all your old first aid stuff won't do us much good either," Schwanecke said to Deutschmann, slanting a grin at him.

"Shut your trap!" said Hefe edgily.

"Don't get so jumpy, man," said Schwanecke. "The question is, what do we do now? We've seen what we were supposed to see, Haven't we?"

"Just about," said Wiedeck.

"So let's be on our way," said Schwanecke. His plan was fixed, the chance had now come. On the return through the wood he could simply stay behind, disappear unnoticed, and then wait for a good opportunity to surrender to the Russians. The plan would not be all that easy to carry out, for the Russians very often wasted little time on an individual prisoner. A burst from a sub-machine-gun was far simpler than transporting him back behind the lines. But on the other hand there would surely be other Russians who would be proud of taking a prisoner, and very pleased to transport him back, as far behind the front as possible—for the Germans were not using pea-shooters either, and were pretty fair marksmen; whether Russian or German, it was always safer behind the front. But anyhow he had time. Under his camouflage suit he had a nice little store of iron rations, which he had "organised" with forethought before they set off. He could wait, and he was not inclined to become involved in any unnecessary danger—not now anyhow, when he was so near his objective.

In the middle of these reflections one— two—three—green very lights rose from the plain, transforming the night sky into an immense green dome, beneath which the faces took on a pale, greenish corpse-like colour.

At the same moment, the steel colossi were set in motion, like ants stirred up by a kick. A howling and rumbling swelled up, became louder and more piercing, filling the whole countryside. The first tanks rolled slowly up, with creaking frozen chains and throbbing engines still cold. The camouflage fell away, the bushes were torn off.

There must have been fifty or more tanks. Faster and faster they rolled along the edge of the wood, past the blankly staring German soldiers, who ducked down hard into the snow-drifts and followed in horror the parade of the steel monsters.

"Well, … me," said Schwanecke. "Now we *are* right in the shit."

"How do you make that out?" said Deutschmann.

"Don't you see, they're making their way through the wood and then on to our front line. When they're through the wood, they'll chop our men at the front into little pieces. We've stumbled right into a tank attack."

"What shall we do, what shall we do?" asked Hefe, trembling.

"The infantry will be coming any minute now," said Schwanecke with apparent relish.

"What?"

"Well, tanks always have infantry following them up. If they catch us here, then. . . ."

"The Lord have mercy on our souls," Wiedeck ended.

"So give us an order, Sergeant," Schwanecke told Hefe.

But Hefe only stared wide-eyed at the tanks rolling towards them. He couldn't move, his powers of thought seemed to be switched off, he had never seen anything like it. This was Russia. It had been different in France, quite different. In France you only occasionally saw French tanks, and they were nothing like those here; when he had seen them, they were mostly shot-up and burnt-out. But these here! As if from a distance he heard Wiedeck say "Run for it!"

With a big effort he took his eyes off the tanks, jumped up, turned and began to run. Now they had to cross the wood again the way they had come. It would have been easier if they could have taken a more or less well-trodden path. But if they did, they could expect an almost insuperable obstacle; the Russian tanks, driving along the wood's edge, would overtake them. On the other edge of the wood the tanks would have spread out widely for battle, and in this formation they would attack the German front line. So Hefe and his men would have to get between the tanks, and more than that, reach their own front line by way of the Russian front line, which would certainly now be fully manned. That was impossible. And yet they ran, panting and stumbling back along the way they had come. They did not stop to worry about what awaited them on the other side of the wood. Not yet. Nor did the other groups in B Company who were in the same situation.

Before daybreak they had arrived back on the edge of the wood facing the German front line. And the other groups arrived there almost at the same time as Hefe's. Equally worn out and panting, they dropped into the snow. Exactly what they could have foreseen had occurred: the Russian tanks had overtaken them and were standing line abreast on the plain between the edge of the wood and the Russian front line.

Obermeier crouched in a hollow with Bartlitz, staring at the tanks. Suddenly searchlights flared up, and with their glaring cones raked the whole field between the German front line and the edge of the wood. They picked out a group of grey figures, who hurled themselves down again and burrowed into the snow, but not quickly enough.

"They're ours," said Bartlitz. "Quite definitely."

"God in heaven," cried Obermeier, "why are they dawdling around as if they were picking blackberries!"

"They don't know any better," said Bartlitz drily, as they both stared at the searchlight cone which stopped just where the little group lay in the snow. "How should they know the way to behave on the front in Russia? They've never been taught that."

Now other dark figures came running out of the wood; they worked themselves quickly through the deep snow, heavily camouglaged with fur caps on their heads, sub-machine-guns with big round magazines in their hands.

"Russians," said Bartlitz.

The frenzied rattle of a German machine gun could be heard. The Russians threw themselves down, some sank to the ground.

"Idiots, now they're shooting as well!" exclaimed Obermeier despairingly.

A tank swung its turret round, and the loud rattle of a Russian machine gun blended with the brief burst of the German, which was soon silenced. Some German soldiers, still in the searchlight beam, stood with hands above their heads, but the machine gun from the Russian tank went on firing. Now the Russian soldiers got up too, and the fierce tack-tack of some sub-machine-guns were heard. The Germans gradually collapsed.

"My God, my God!" groaned Obermeier.

"Now we know what we have to expect," said Bartlitz quietly. "We must have a go. We must go on. Soon the infantry will be spreading out and they'll catch us."

Wiedeck was saying something similar to Hefe fifty or sixty yards away. "No help for it, we must get across. It's still dark now, but it won't be much longer. Where are the others?"

"I don't know," said Hefe.

Wiedeck looked round. "Deutschmann, Schwanecke, Molders ..."

"How should I know?" asked Hefe irritably. "Probably stayed behind, who cares?" At that moment he couldn't be bothered about the others, his only thought was to get out of this witches' cauldron, behind the German lines, only to get away from here. But how?

"Shall I run ahead?" asked Wiedeck.

"Yes, do. You have a go."

Before Wiedeck dashed off, he saw on the left, in the direction of Gorki, a long extended line of Russian infantry coming up. And at the same moment the Russian tanks also began moving again. From the Russian trenches infantrymen stood up and began to charge towards the German front line, with loud cries, firing wildly. The front erupted into a terrible inferno. The German artillery was blazing away. Tank guns barked, and bursts of flame vibrated through the night sky. Two—four—seven tanks exploded and burnt out, glowing as in some immense forge; but the others drove on regardless with howling engines, firing from the long barrels.

A bit deeper in the wood, but so that they could still get some view into the plain, Deutschmann and Schwanecke lay in a hollow behind a thick felled tree trunk. Here they were fairly safe.

"So long as no infantry comes, nothing will happen to us," Schwanecke told Deutschmann. "The tanks can't touch us here."

"They'll be in the German front line by now," whispered Deutschmann.

"Well, of course, what would you expect? Our little lot of Germans couldn't stand up to rolling gunfire like that."

"What do we do?"

"Don't worry your head, leave it to Uncle Karl. The war's over now for both of us. I have the feeling that was out last military operation!"

Krull lay with Kentrop in a flat hollow on the edge of the wood, pressed against the ground and panting with fear. This was the end, how could it have come to this? He was done for.

"We've still got a chance, fatty," said Kentrop, comfortingly.

"Finished, done for!" Krull wailed.

"Pull yourself together, man. We'll have a nice wait here!"

But Krull kept on saying: "Done for, done for, done for!"

Wiedeck was the first to spring up from his hollow and start running in the direction of the German front line.

The searchlights had moved on, and the darkness was impenetrable and grey as always just before daybreak. Wiedeck ran like a madman. And while he worked his way through the snow, he thought of Erna and the children, and then he stopped thinking of anything, and after a time he thought that he must go on, even though he felt his heart was going to burst, he must go on, and then he thought again of Erna and of the baby he had never seen …

Hefe looked behind him, and when he was swallowed by the darkness, he too jumped up and began to run.

Obermeier said to Bartlitz: "Stick by us. I'm going to move now."

"Let me run ahead of you, Lieutenant," said Bartlitz.

"No, I'll go first. And … I'm sorry, Colonel … "

"What?"

"That we're … I'm sorry that a colonel like you should be in a penal battalion, sir."

"Forget it. I'm not a colonel any more, and I'm not sure I want to be one again either."

"I've learnt to respect you very much … I'm …"

A friendly smile came over Bartlitz for a moment. "With officers like you, this—all this—wouldn't have happened. But you called me 'colonel' just now. Did you mean that seriously?"

"Yes. Yes, sir—I did."

"Then I give you the order now to let me run first. You know how it used to be in the old German army: superior officers always lead the way. Goodbye, my boy. Don't start running till you think it's the right moment. And don't forget: one of us has got to get back!" He put his hand on Obermeier's shoulder, then pushed off, sprang out of the hollow, raced over the field, bent forward, with tottering legs and dangling arms—a man who knew it was no good trying to avoid his fate.

Obermeier waited a few minutes. The tanks had now rolled away over the German lines. The partisans and the Russian infantry were combing through the rear trenches. There were no prisoners taken—but then hardly any German soldier capable of running would stay to be captured. They knew all too well what was in store for them if they fell into the hands of the partisans.

Obermeier raced like a sprinter over the snow-covered field, past dark heaps which had once been his soldiers, past still glowing hulks of tanks. He ran as he had never run in his life. He knew he had practically no chance of safely joining his own troops. But if there *was* any chance, it was now, in this confusion, under the protection of the darkness, which was now slowly beginning to lighten. The odds against him were almost infinite, but he had to try: one man must get back.

From the side he suddenly saw a dark howling shadow coming towards him: a tank. A small, piercing bright searhlight shone from the front of it and caught Obermeier in the middle of its beam, rigid like a statue, arms outstretched as if about to dive.

With a few bounds he was outside the beam. He ran zigzagging on, and heard behind him the hammering of the heavy guns from the tank.

A hole, he thought, his heart near to bursting and the sweat running over his face. I must find a hole, a shell crater, a trench.

Wiedeck too saw the lone tank which had been left to bring up the rear. He hurled himself into a flat shell crater and got his head down. Here he was more or less safe, or at any rate the tank crew could hardly discover him. He had completed the first part of the way, he was now already in the former no-man's-land between the Russian and German trenches. Suddenly something dropped on to him, a heavy body, pressing him to the ground and clinging on to his shoulder.

"Get away, you ape!" cried Wiedeck.

"It's me, Bartlitz," panted the man on his back. "Move over ... is it you, Wiedeck? There's room for both of us."

"God, I hope they don't see us!"

A little later a third figure fell into the crater to join them. It whizzed as if shot from a catapult, lay flat over the two bodies, and pressed Wiedeck's head down with both hands when he was trying to see who it was.

"Head down," breathed a voice.

"Lieutenant ...?"

"Yes, keep quiet."

"So—together again," murmured Bartlitz.

"Quiet."

They lay pressed close to each other in the flat hollow, and listened. Quite near them they heard clanking and rumbling, the chains grinding. The searchlight beam from the tank travelled right over them, returned and stopped on Obermeier's flat back, which was just sticking out over the hole.

"He's found us," said Obermeier softly.

"We're done," sobbed Wiedeck.

"Not yet," said Obermeier. "He's not shooting—he wants to roll over us. When he gets quite near ..." He did not finish the sentence, the other two had understood him.

Now the clank of the chains was pretty near. "Off!" cried Obermeier, and all three jumped up and scattered. The tank rolled over the hollow, stopped, turned on the spot. The lid on the top sprang open, and a head looked out. Directly afterwards the machine gun began to rattle.

Bartlitz was hit first. As if riveted, he suddenly stopped, then sank mutely to the ground.

Then it was Wiedeck's turn. He fell on his face, his arms and legs twitched for a while, his body doubled up in two or three convulsive spasms, after which he lay quiet and still.

There was no cover. Obermeier ran and prayed. Bullets were now whirling up the snow round him. He ran. Then the machine gun stopped firing, and a crash near him threw him to one side. He picked himself up again and ran on. Another crash and a dull blow against his arm. The Russians were shooting behind him with the big gun. He was a fine living target, a solitary man laboriously wading and staggering through the snow. A marvellous target.

The third shell scored a bull's eye.

36

Julia woke to see Dr. Kukill's face bent over her. Her empty absent eyes looked to him like two deep dark wells. Her lips moved, but no sound could be heard. Kukill bent still further over her. Breathlessly he listened to the whisper which at last passed her lips very softly and indistinctly: "What—has - happened - where - am - I?"

"You were very ill," he said soothingly. "Now you are better again."

"What - has - happened - with ..."

"Don't talk, Julia. Try to sleep!"

Now memory returned into her eyes, slowly and gradually. She tried to sit up, but nothing came of it except a long tremble which racked her terrifyingly emaciated body.

She said: "Did - the - experiment ..."

"Yes. It was successful. Please relax."

"Will you try—Ernst ..."

"Yes," said Kukill. "I will get him out. I promise you. I—I have already taken all the necessary steps. Have no fears. And if you go to sleep now, then"—he swallowed—"I will tell you something really cheering ..."

But she no longer heard him, she had already fallen asleep.

37

Russian tanks rolled over Barssdovka.

They had overrun the German position on one side, while on the other side, from the wood, Denkov's partisan bands were streaming into the village, led by him and Tartuchin.

Captain Bergen and Kronenberg had got away in time with some of the wounded, racing backwards with the last vehicles, beyond the artillery positions. They were surprised and at the same time reassured by the few signs of nervousness among the artillery men—who had experienced this atmosphere of panic so often before. A Russian breakthrough? Unpleasant but no more. The first hastily scrapped together reserves were already arriving from the rear to mount a counter-attack. And when Bergen, squeezed on to the edge of the road with his convoy, looked into the grim, impassive faces of a storm-troopers' battalion, slowly jolting in their command cars over the rutted street in the direction of the front, with machine-guns, sub-machine-guns, and rifles between their knees, looking fierce and dangerous in their white combat kit with white steel helmets, he wondered a bit sheepishly whether his precipitate flight had been justified.

Lieutenant Hansen had stayed in Barssdovka with the stretcher cases, mostly head and stomach wounds. The wounded of his own battalion had been joined by some from the infantry units which had been driven out of their positions. The barn was half full, the men lay there silently, staring with frightened eyes towards the door, through which the Russians might come at any moment. Hansen walked to and fro between the beds and palliasses, spreading calm and confidence, bringing comfort, releiving pain. Above the entrance hung a big Red Cross flag, heavy and motionless in the quiet still air.

Suddenly they were coming.

For some time now the wounded had heard the roar of tank engines and isolated firing. But now they heard the Russians' voices, brief hoarse cries, and then loud laughter that seemed to go on and on.

With a nod to the wounded, Lieutenant Hansen walked over to the door.

Tartuchin was the first to see the lieutenant in his white apron standing in the doorway. He stopped a moment, then grinned. Here were German soldiers; perhaps among them he would find one particular man, his great enemy.

Intently, with body bent forward, he went towards the barn, up to the short, slender lieutenant, who stood in front of the door, looking calmly towards him, blocking his way into the barn.

"Go! Go!" he said, when he had reached the lieutenant.

"You are ..." began Hansen, who had recognised the former "collab"; but Tartuchin interrupted him impatiently: "Go! Go!"

"No," said Hansen, not stirring from the spot.

"No," echoed Tartuchin, and a quick, gleeful smile flitted over his face. "No? No?"

Slowly, thoughtfully, and—Hansen could see—with deadly resolve, he raised the sub-machine-gun till its barrel was aimed exactly on the lieutenant's chest. "No?" he repeated. "No?"

There was no doubt, thought Hansen: this man will shoot me if I don't get out of his way. But he did not move. In those few brief moments the young surgeon lieutenant rose above himself. He was appalling frightened, but none of his fear penetrated to the surface. Calm and quiet, with impassive and rather haughty-looking face, he stood before Tartuchin, who now began to smile again—a wide, mirthless, murderous smile.

"Stoy!" From the street a loud commanding voice was

heard. Tartuchin's grin stiffened, then he half turned his head and looked over his shoulder.

Sergei Denkov slowly came up, a sub-machine-gun cradled on his arm.

"What do you mean to do?" he asked in Russian, when he reached Tartuchin and Hansen.

Tartuchin shrugged his shoulder.

"Come on, what had you planned to do?" Denkov asked again, and his voice was now sharp.

"He won't let me in," said Tartuchin.

"And you were going to kill him, eh?"

"He is a German," said Tartuchin.

"Have you known him some time?" asked Denkov quietly, not taking his eyes off Tartuchin, who now looked uncomfortably to the side but said nothing.

"Come on, have you known him some time?"

"Yes."

"What do you think of him?"

"He is a German."

"And you're a bastard!? hissed Denkov. "What has he done to you? What has he done to any of us? He has healed our peasants when they were sick, and if I remember aright, he once dressed your wounds. And you want to kill him! Scram! Go on, get going."

Tartuchin moved off in silence with a sour, angry expression on his face.

"Thank you," said Hansen, breathing a sight of relief.

"That's all right," said Denkov, still seething with rage. "Now get out of my way."

"What are you going to do?"

"Get out of my way, I tell you."

Hansen stepped aside and said: "If you hadn't come ..."

Denkov, who was about to walk past him into the barn, stopped, turned round and gave him a long look. Then he said: "Then all of them—" he pointed with his head towards the barn door, behind which the wounded lay "—they would all be dead. I know. Very often nobody comes to stop it. There are all sorts. In your country *and* ours. Come with me.

The wounded went into captivity with Lieutenant Hansen.

The war rolled over old Marfa's house as well. The tanks drove past in a long roaring column. Tanya stood at the window and looked at them with empty eyes. They have taken my Michael from me, she thought with great sorrow. I hate them all, I hate everything.

But she didn't really know who or what was the object of her hate. The Germans? The Russians? The war between the Germans and the Russians? Her fate—or her weakness and her love for the German soldier.

She did not look round when she suddenly heard the door spring open and an icy draught came into the room. But without looking she knew who had come. For a brief moment she had a faint hope she might be wrong. But when she heard Denkov's voice, she knew it was no good hoping she could escape him.

"You?" he asked hoarsely.

Tanya leaned her forehead against the icy window.

"Turn round!"

"Why should I? You have come to kill me. So kill me."

"What are you doing here among the Germans?" His voice trembled. She heard his steps come nearer. His hand wrenched her round.

"Since when has Marfa been—a German?" she asked mockingly.

He stared into her face silently, with hard, merciless eyes.

"Do it then. Don't ask questions!" she asked.

"You ran after him, eh? You've slept with him here, while we...." Now he shook her and shouted into her face. "Why did you do it, why?"

"I love him," said Tanya simply. She closed her eyes and whispered: "Can't you understand that?"

Denkov hesitated. He didn't know what to do. Outside the door his men were storming through the liberated village, yelling and laughing, fanatical haters who at this moment were looking for hidden German soldiers. Now he almost hated them and hated his role as their commander. He was an officer. He was not one of them. It was right, you had to hate the Germans if you wanted to drive them out—but one must never forget for a moment that they too were human beings.

One must punish the guilty, and the harder the better. The guilty, he thought. Tanya too was guilty!

The door crashed open, and the huge Misha Starobin charged into the old house. His eyes gleamed, and there was a grin of delight on his face as he cried: "Comrade Lieutenant—the Germans are finished! We have driven them out—we can leave the woods!" It was only now that he saw Tanya and stopped with open mouth. "You?" he asked, drawing out the one syllable, so that a shudder went down Tanya's back to hear it. She was ready to die, but behind the sound lay something more terrible than death.

"What are you going to do with her, Comrade Lieutenant?" asked Starobin. He wiped his sweat-soaked face.

"What *should* we do with her?" asked Denkov.

"She is a traitor!" cried Starobin; his cold disparaging eyes did not reveal all the disgust he felt.

"Yes," said Denkov heavily. "Yes."

"Give her to me!" said Starobin.

Tanya shrank slowly back to the wall. The looks in the four eyes fixed on her were the cruellest she had even seen. "No," she whispered. "Kill me, but not that, not that!"

"Will you give her to me?" asked Starobin again. "Come on, give her to me. The thing is clear, she is a traitor!"

"Yes, it is clear," said Denkov slowly. He turned and left the room.

Just about then the German counter-attack started.

It was a fairly weak attack, but was carried out with a desperate fury such as can only spring from fear and the urge for self-preservation. With light flak, some assault guns and anti-tank guns, with concentric charges and hand-grenades, the inadequate reserves and a hasty collection of the dispersed units advanced against the Russians. It was all too obvious: if the Russians succeeded in breaking through here, there was not only the danger of large German units being encircled, but also danger for the whole German front. The Luftwaffe even managed to send some dive-bombers, low-level attack planes and fighters in support of the infantry.

The Russians withdrew. Some tanks burned. The rest

rolled back again on their old route over the former German positions, and disappeared behind the woods from where they had come. Severe street-fighting took place for the disputed villages, often house to house. Denkov's fanatical but untrained partisans suffered heavy losses, until the remainder managed to creep back into the protective thickets and earth bunkers of the Gorki woods.

Starobin and his group stayed alive and dragged Tanya with them—behind the old Russian lines.

The old German positions were reoccupied and cleared of Soviet infantry. So the whole thing was like a spectral visitation which had burst forth in the darkness of the night and been dispersed again by nightfall the following day. Only the burnt-out Russian tanks, some German assault guns, and the bodies strewn over the plains, showed that a furious battle had so recently raged here.

Krull was lucky.

When the German counter-attack began, he was lying in a flat shell-hole in the former no-man's-land between the German and Russian front lines. Before that he had worked his way slowly, on all fours, yard by yard, further and further over the plains, which offered him no cover. He had shown a great deal of prudence and patience, but not through deliberate thought; simply out of fear. He was afraid to raise his head and look round him. He was afraid to stand up and run for it, as the others had done. So he went on all fours—and this saved his life.

When the Russian tanks and the infantry began to retreat before the German attack, he was playing possum in his hole. Now and then he heard hurrying steps and excited words from the Russians dashing past him to reach their old positions. He did not stir—not even when a rattling, roaring monster, a tank, drove past quite near him, and everything in him cried out to jump up and run blindly away. But the same fear paralysed him so that he could hardly breathe, and it stayed in his bones even when the roar of the tank engine had faded and finally died away.

He looked a credible corpse: his combat jacket was full of

blood—though the blood came not from him but from Kentrop, who had had half his chest blown away by a German shell, when the Germans were firing a barrage. With his remaining strength he had dragged himself into a shell-hole—and there Krull found him while crawling across the open field. Kentrop was still alive, but Krull, who was seeking cover, pushed him on to the edge of the crater and remained still, half hidden under Kentrop, as Kentrop bled to death. After a while Krull crawled on again, to find a new hole for himself.

When the last Russians had passed him and he had not heard anything for a long, long time, he at last ventured to raise his head.

The plain seemed to be empty. Twilight fell, turning the snow and the sky grey. He waited till it was night, and then crawled on. His feet had gone numb, so there was no pain in them now, as there had been two or three hours before. He was calm, and the fear had left him. But he did not get up to run to the German trenches, now quite near. He crept on, and when he eventually reached them and tried to stand up, he couldn't do so. He collapsed, and whispered with numb hard lips: "What's happened, what's the matter?"

"Nothing's the matter, mate, you're home again," said a soldier, and gave him a drink. Schnaps. It ran like fire through Krull's veins, and he tried once more to stand up. But it didn't work. His legs would not carry him.

He had spent a night and a day in the merciless cold. When he got back, both his feet were frost-bitten; one of them later had to be amputated. Once he had recovered from the amputation, he was not too unhappy: loss of a foot meant he was free from the front for good: the state paid a good disability pension to the war-wounded; and anyhow a good sergeant-major would probably be needed these days, even minus a foot.

Deutschmann and Schwanecke also escaped from the slaughter.

When the Russian tanks disappeared into the distance and new waves of Russian infantry kept moving westward behind them, the two Germans crept deeper into the wood and hid in a hollow, which they cleared of snow as best they could.

"Right, Doc," said Schwanecke. "I think we've made it. We can hold out here."

"How long for?" asked Deutschmann.

"For ever. Till the coast is clear. As you saw, the Russians have broken through, and if they're smart enough, they'll roll all the way to Berlin."

"Don't be absurd!"

"What do you think, then? No, not quite to Berlin," he amended. "Our lot aren't too stupid either, and the Russians are often not very smart, see? They're great fighters, but up here, you know"—he tapped his forehead—"there's a bit missing sometimes. They storm onward, battling through, and then fall like … flies—where a smart general would make a pincer movement or something—you know?"

"I'm not a general," said Deutschmann wearily. He wanted to be quiet and think, but this chatterbox had to keep talking and talking.…

"No, Doc, and you won't ever be," said Schwanecke. "You may be a bloody fine professor, but you'll never be a general."

"That suits me," said Deutschmann. He fished in his pockets for cigarettes, brought one out, and was about to light it. But a violent blow on the hand slung cigarette and matches into the snow, and when he looked up in surprise, it was straight into Schwanecke's angry, threatening eyes. "Are you … mad—you moron? Want to smoke here, do you?"

"Hey, listen!" Deutschmann broke in, but Schwanecke cut him off: "Shut up!" And after a minute of uncomfortable silence: "That's why you'll never make a general, see? Although there are stupid generals too, plenty of 'em! If you smoke here—well, what do you think?"

"Oh, yes, of course." He saw Schwanecke was right. "What are we going to do now? Got anything in mind?"

"We're going to wait," Schwanecke answered. "When the Russians have pushed forward far enough, the supply units will come up, see? Full of old codgers with no fire in their bellies—different from the buggers up forward or those shitting partisans. Then we review the situation, and if it's favourable, we put our hands up and surrender. Just think how proud an old supply bloke will be if he takes two prisoners. Do you know the Internationale, Doc?"

"I know the tune, of course, and a couple of lines. Why?"

"That's about my lot too, but it'll be enough. When we march off with out hands above our head, see?—we sing the Internationale. Then the Comrades will have to stand to attention, and they can't shoot. That's right, isn't it?"

Schwanecke grinned broadly, and Deutschmann could not help smiling too.

But a bit later, in the early afternoon, the situation became less comfortable. They could hear firing from the front, which became increasingly fierce and was rapidly getting nearer. Now they could also hear tanks again, and some German shells were landing in the old Russian positions.

"Well, … me," exclaimed Schwanecke in surprise. "Does this mean our lot are making a counter-attack?"

"Looks like it," said Deutschmann drily.

Schwanecke crawled to the edge of the wood to see what was happening, and when eventually there were Russian infantry as well coming towards the wood, he grew apprehensive. "Let's get out of here," he said. "We must go deeper into the wood, or they'll catch us—and that wouldn't be good at all. They're really cross now they've been chased back. Who'd have thought it?"

They left the hollow.

The wood was very still, deep in snow; now and then lumps of snow dropped from the branches and thudded heavily on to the ground. In the distance, as if from another world, they heard the noise of the battle. Their breath steamed in front of their faces, as they cleared a way through the under-growth, panting and careful, continually stopping to listen. Schwanecke went in front.

Dusk came up.

"Stop!" Schwanecke said suddenly, and came to a sudden halt himself.

"What is it?"

"A few huts, I think, Doc," Schwanecke whispered back, and got slowly on to his knees. Through the branches

Deutschmann could see the dark outlines of some huts sticking out of the snow in a small clearing.

"Think they're inhabited?"

"How should I know? We must have a looksee."

"Come on then," said Deutschmann, and Schwanecke looked at him in surprise, but made no comment. On their hands and knees they worked their way to the edge of the clearing. Now they could get a good view of the three or four huts.

Nothing stirred. All was dead and soundless, they could only hear their own suppressed breathing and the quick thumping of their hearts.

"Maybe there'll be something to eat there," said Schwanecke.

"We've still got some food left."

"A small reserve wouldn't do any harm."

"You don't really believe it yourself. How should there be anything to eat here? Still perhaps ..."

"What?"

"Perhaps we could stay the night here."

"Well, I don't know," said Schwanecke doubtfully.

"Why not? We could get a nice frost-bite out in the snow here."

"That's true, Doc,"

"So let's go!"

Deutschmann had kept trying to dispel his thoughts of Julia and her death. And now he had succeeded. He must stay alive. He had a task to fulfil. He thought he could see some future if they survived now—or at least a glimpse of it.

Cautiously he crept out of the wood into the clearing. Schwanecke followed, sub-machine-gun at the ready.

The huts were deserted.

When they pushed open the door to the first, Schwanecke stopped as if rooted to the spot. "There's been someone here only a short time ago," he said, sniffing the air. "Two or three hours, perhaps only one hour."

"How....?"

"I can smell it," said Schwanecke with conviction. "I can always smell something like that."

The twilight had now grown deeper. When they came out

of the first hut, in which they found nothing edible, they could scarcely make out the outlines of the three others. In the second there was still a small heap of embers glowing under the ashes, but there too they found nothing except three or four empty sacks of grain.

When they rounded the corner of the third and largest, and came to the front of it, they found Tanya.

Schwanecke was leading the way, sub-machine-gun under his arm, alert but by now a little more relaxed. He stopped abruptly. "Man, there's someone lying here," he whispered over his shoulder, and raised the barrel of his gun. Deutschmann came closer, and now he too saw an outstretched human body, lying face downwards in the dirty snow outside the closed door of the hut.

"Christ!" Schwanecke exclaimed. "Look at that, Doc!"

Now they both began to run.

"Christ!" he repeated. "It's a woman."

The dead woman's long black hair lay like a silk collar round her white neck. Her arms were extended along her body, with the palms upwards, the fingers bent, as if in the last seconds of her life she were trying to cling on to something. Across the back of her thick woollen coat ran the trail of death: four small round holes, which the bullets of a sub-machine-gun had made in the quilted material.

Schwanecke got control of himself first. He bent over the dead woman, took hold of her by the shoulder and turned her gently over, as if he thought any movement might still hurt her.

Deutschmann reeled. He came quite close to the girl and looked into her face. Her features were relaxed, and she almost seemed to be smiling. The waxen pallor of her lovely face stood in strange contrast to her black hair. Her full lips were slightly open, as if in her death-throes she had whispered the name she had thought of again and again in those last hours: Michael ...

"Tanya ... Tanyasha ..." gasped Deutschmann.

"What? Do you know her, Doc?"

Deutschmann nodded.

"Could that be why....?"

"Yes."

"Christ!" said Schwanecke. "Christ, such a ..." his voice tailed away.

Deutschmann seemed riveted. Then he slowly shrank back, as it under a terrible spell, with ashen face and wide appalled eyes. He opened his mouth, but could not utter a sound. He kept staring at the four holes where the bullets had come out, forcing the wadding out of the coat like the burst buds of a cotton-bush, and at the sheet of paper pinned to Tanya's breast with a rusty nail.

Schwanecke bent low to decipher the writing on the paper. It said there in Russian, "German whore". He looked blank. "You know some Russian, don't you, Doc? What does it say here?" He looked round for Deutschmann, "Hey, Ernst, what's up, man? What's up?"

Deutschmann pulled himself together. His limbs were stiff, and heavy as lead. They ached at every movement, his whole body ached, but he couldn't he mustn't collapse, he must....

"Come on," he said, in a voice which sent a cold shudder down Schwanecke's spine. "Come on." Only that. But Schwanecke knew what he meant, and leaned his gun against the wall.

The girl could not have been long dead, for her body was not yet stiff. They picked her up and carried her carefully into the hut.

They buried Tanya in the loamy soil of the second biggest hut. An old rusty shovel they had found was their only implement. They took it in turns to dig, and it was almost three hours before the hole was big and deep enough. They did not speak a word the whole time.

The Russian front line was now thinly held. It was bitterly cold, and except for a few widely dispersed sentries, all the troops were in their dug-outs. The Germans never attacked in cold like this. Only the Russians, and besides, when had the Germans initiated an attack in recent months? If they were attacked themselves, they hit back, of course, but otherwise? Also there were too few of them. Far too few. Where now were all the magnificently equipped armies from the first year of war, whose only experience was sweeping further and further east?

Deutschmann and Schwanecke lay in a crater, pressed close to each other.

They had found a place where the edges of the trenches had been crushed by the tanks. Now they wriggled slowly on. About twenty yards away they saw a small dark object—the head of a Russian sentry. A red dot glowed from time to time. He's smoking, thought Schwanecke. He's smoking, the son of a bitch. Hasn't any idea.... I could creep up on him and ... he wouldn't hear a thing.

Behind him Deutschmann's body scraped over the ground, a noise that could be heard for miles, as it seemed to both of them.

But the sentry did not move, and then his head disappeared behind the edge of the trench. They crept on, slowly, very slowly. I must get back, thought Schwanecke briefly, it can't be far now.

Another fifty yards to the dark shadow of the shot-up tank. Only forty now. Schwanecke waited till Deutschmann was laying at his side, then pressed his mouth against Deutschmann's ear. "May be mines. We must watch out. Stay right behind me. All right?"

Deutschmann nodded. His breath came in quick gasps.

"Right, let's go."

They crawled on. Schwanecke tested the ground ahead of him with his hands. There were no mines here. Perhaps on this hump. He must go round the hump. Stay in the hollows all the time. He must remember the way. He must imprint in his memory every rise in the ground. When he returned, he might not have so much time to look out for mines. There!

He again waited till Deutschmann had caught up with him, and whispered: "There—a mine." His hand grazed over a small rise in the snow, which looked in no way different from any others. "I can smell them, see? And there, on your right—there's another. Look out! Through the middle—right, Doc, on we go."

Twenty-five yards.

Tangled and riddled remains of a barbed-wire fence stretched into the night on both sides. "Don't move!"

Schwanecke whispered back to Deutschmann as he crept on. But Deutschmann did not hear him. His heart was beating in quick throbs that went right up into the throat. He looked at the soles of Schwanecke's boots swaying in front of him, sometimes vanishing in a passing patch of mist—and then reappearing if he closed his eyes for two or three seconds and quickly opened them again. By the tank I'll be able to rest, he thought. By the tank. How much further is it? The few yards left to get there seemed an infinite distance away.

His face hit the cold barbed wire, and he jerked back. He had not seen it, and he suddenly realised that for a few seconds, which seemed to him a very long time, he hadn't seen anything, and that he was crawling as if through deep darkness. I must pull myself together, he thought, gritting his teeth, I must ...

Schwanecke's shadowy body dodged between the wires, and Deutschmann stayed right behind him. Sometimes Schwanecke's body touched a stake or the wire, then he was through, round, grinned, showing a gleam of white teeth, and crawled on. Then Deutschmann too was half over the wire, the tank was quite near now, only ten or fifteen or twenty yards away. There he would be able to rest.

One leg was caught by the wire, and he pulled impatiently to get clear. The jangle of empty food-tins hanging on the fence sounded as loud in the silent night as sudden pistol shoots. Schwanecke turned round in horror: "You fool! Quiet" But Deutschmann did not near him; in desperation he tore at the wire his trousers were caught in. The tins jangled, he got clear, crept on—and in that moment the front awakened from its sleep.

A Russian machine gun began to fire, the trenches came to life, hoarse excited shouts could be heard, and tramping steps; the firing grew denser, it came at them from all sides, Mortar fire. Very lights whizzed up and illuminated the foreground with a white glittering light. Then it started on the German side as well. Soldiers crept from the bunkers and hurried into the trenches—Schwanecke could picture the scene as vividly as if he were lying in the midst of it—German tracer bullets, the frenzied rattle of a 42 machine gun, rifle grenades; and right in the middle, the two men, pressed as deep into the snow as they could burrow.

"Quiet, just stay quiet!" hissed Schwanecke. "It'll pass, they haven't seen anything. Just stay quiet!"

They could find splendid cover behind the tank. All that mattered was to get there and then wait.

Now the firing increased, and grew fiercer. In the distance they heard faint artillery fire. And probably the Russians had seen something after all, for the firing became more accurate, it concentrated with more and more precision on the place were they were lying; it could only be moments before it caught them. Schwanecke looked behind him, cried: "Run! To the tank!" jumped up as if shot from a catapult, and with a few great bounds covered the distance to the tank, where he hurled himself down and burrowed into the snow under his steel helmet, panting hard but already fancying himself more or less safe. Only a direct hit from the artillery would catch him here.

Then he looked back.

Now Deutschmann jumped up too. Bent low, a running, gasping shadow, tracer bullets whizzed past him. Now he was quite near, only a few steps more, and now Schwanecke saw it, he really saw it, he wasn't just imagining it—he saw the reddish line of a phosphorus bullet going through Deutschmann's head, at eye level; he saw it pulling Deutschmann back in mid-jump and also sharply upwards, as always with head-shots; and at the same time a mine went off quite near, surrounding Deutschmann with a cloud of snow and flinging snow and dirt into Schwanecke's face.

He wiped his eyes, passed a hand desperately over his face, and cried: "Doc—hey—Ernst—doc!"

And again: "Doc! Ernst!"

Nothing.

Schwanecke crept back quickly, on knees and elbows.

Deutschmann was groaning, babbling, scarcely intelligibly; hoarse gurgling noises came from his wide open mouth: "Head—Karl—Karl—" And now he cried aloud, a long-drawn-out shrill cry: "Kaaaarl! Kaaaarl"

"Yes—I'm here—I'm here—I'm here!" gasped Schwanecke, and looked aghast at the bloody pulp above Deutschmann's mouth. There was no nose left, no eyes, no eyebrows, only shreds of flesh, slivers of bones, and from the midst of it came whistling, gurgling noises and babbling incomprehensible words.

Schwanecke looked round desperately, and after a moment's hesitation straightened up, gripped Deutschmann under the arms and pulled him behind the tank. Deutschmann screamed, and his screams cut like a thousand knives into Schwanecke's brain. He looked at Deutschmann's trailing legs and said: "Oh Christ, that too, that too!"

The left leg was wrenched half round and much longer than the right. Below the knee the trouser leg was shredded and bloody.

"I'll get you back, Doc, I'll get you back!" gasped Schwanecke, "never fear, I'll get you back."

"Leg—what's—my leg ... !"

"It caught you a bit, Doc, wait a mo ..."

"Leg—I—I—I ..."

With flying hands Schwanecke undid Deutschmann's belt, and tied off the shattered leg above the knee. Then he tore in pieces the shredded cloth of the trousers and closed his eyes for a moment when he saw the dreadful wound: the leg hung by only two or three shreds of skin. The head-wound could wait. But this—he could bleed to death.... He said: "I'll get you back, Doc, it's not too bad, Ernst, it's not too bad at all, I'll get you back, never fear!"

"Yes—no—you must—get across...."

"Shut up, Doc!" Schwanecke said gently. Field dressing! Where was the field dressing? "Does it hurt, Doc?"

"Yes—the eyes...."

The Russian gunners' fire was concentrated on the tank. But Schwanecke didn't bother about that. "The eyes, that's just the blast, Doc," he lied. "It's only the ... blast, I bet." And while he spoke, he pulled out of his pocket a secret jack-knife he had "organised" from the Pioneer Corps. He turned his eye away from Deutschmann's leg as he opened the knife, and said: "Just a bandage, Doc, never fear, be over in a minute. Then I'll get you back to our...."

"The eyes—the eyes ..." whimpered Deutschmann.

"Yes—in a moment," said Schwanecke. He applied the

knife, and with two or three quick strong cuts slit through the shreds of flesh and skin by which Deutschmann's leg was hanging.

Deutschmann screamed. Schwanecke thought he had never heard a man scream like that before, but it was over already, and he said soothingly: "It was only a bit of skin, mate, only a bit of skin, it had to come off, see? See.... I ... It's over at once!"

"Yes—yes—the eyes...." groaned Deutschmann.

Schwanecke bandaged the stump of the leg as well as he could, then took his own field dressing and attended to the head-wound, which had almost stopped bleeding. It was finished, anyone could see that it was all up with Deutschmann's eyes, they were gone, torn out, the root of the nose shattered, the bone at the forehead, it was a wonder the brains weren't coming out of it, but perhaps the wound didn't go so deep, such things always looked worse than they were at first sight, of course, and perhaps....

When he had finished, he half straightened up and yelled across to the German lines: "don't shoot—don't shoot! Hey, you fools—don't shoot!" He yelled it out over and over again, till the firing from the German trenches really stopped, and then he cried: "Covering fire! Do you hear?—covering fire!"

They gave it.

He hoisted the now unconscious Deutschmann on his shoulder, staggered to his feet, bent down once more, picked up Deutschmann's severed leg as well, and stuck it under his arm.

Then he ran for the German trenches.

He was half way there and everything was as bright as day from all the Very lights—when he suddenly felt there was something missing. It took some time before he realised what it was: the firing had stopped. The front was dead quiet, the silence only punctuated now and then by the brief sound of Very pistols being fired.

As it should be, he thought grimly. That's the ticket. As it should be.

Slowly, step by step, he went on, fully erect, through the lit up night, casting a furtive shadow on the white expanse of snow. He didn't bother about mines. Perhaps—perhaps he even wanted to tread on one. He was on the way back. He was going to his own death, and knew it. But he went on. He did it although he did not think the man he was carrying would live. Perhaps he was even dead already, as dead as this leg he was carrying under his arm. But he had promised to get him back, he had said, I'll get you back, Doc! And now he was doing it, never mind whether Ernst was still alive or already dead, although by doing it he was almost certainly going to his own death.

A young lieutenant took charge of him, when he climbed over the trench revetment into the gun position. Two medical orderlies were also waiting at the ready with a stretcher. Slowly, carefully, gigherly, Schwanecke laid Deutschmann's body on the stretcher and straingtened up again.

One of the stretcher-bearers bent over Deutschmann.

"Is he still alive?" asked the lieutenant.

Schwanecke shrugged his shoulders.

"What are you going to do with that?" Shuddering, the lieutenant pointed at Deutschmann's leg.

"Oh, that." Schwanecke laid the leg on the stretcher. "I've got him back," he said then. "Do you understand? Complete!"

"He 's still alive," said the stretcher-bearer.

"Hurry then!" said the lieutenant. Then he asked Schwanecke: "Where do you actually come from?"

"Over there. We're—Penal Battalion, see? 999. We had a little outing."

"Yes—yes, I see" The lieutenant, nodded gravely. He had heard of the tragedy of the probation battalion's B Company. It was said that only one man had come back, and he had frost-bitten feet? And now these two as well—it was a lousy business. He said: "I'll have you taken back. You can have a rest then. I think you've deserved it."

Deutschmann was immediately transported back via Babinitchi. The M.O. of a reserve unit now occupying the positions gave him anti-tetanus and anti-gangrene injections, and shook his head doubtfully when a medical orderly looked enquiringly at him.

"Both eyes and the leg ..." he said softly. "I don't think ... but one never knows. Give me a morphine ampoule."

The M.O. at the advance dressing station also sent Deutschmann on at once; he had meanwhile regained consciousness. "You will be taken to the base hospital at Orsha. There they'll see what can be done."

Deutschmann groped for his eyes and felt the thick bandage that had been put on. "What's happened to my eyes—and my leg? I don't know...."

"What?"

"I remember..."

"The leg's gone." The M.O. tried hard to make his voice sound casual. He took Deutschmann's groping hand from the bandage and laid it on the blanket. "As for the eyes, that's only half as bad. We'll patch you up, nothing has happened to the nerve, you know, and that's the main thing, of course."

"I was a doctor—I've often—told white lies—like that," whispered Deutschmann. The M.O. was silent, not knowing what to say now—to a man who had been a doctor.

"And what about Schwanecke?" Deutschmann asked.

"Who's that?"

"The man with me who ..."

"Oh yes. He's all right as far as I know."

"Is he—he isn't...."

"Isn't what?"

"Where is he?"

"I think he's with one of the companies that are staying on."

"Yes," said Deutschmann. "He saved my life."

38

A Company had sustained very severe losses from the Russian flank attack, but it had not, like B Company, been completely wiped out. Wernher received by telephone a report from the lieutenant in whose sector the drama in no-man's-land had taken place, and asked to have Schwanecke sent to him under escort.

"Why's that?" asked the lieutenant. "Has the man got a black mark against him?"

"Yes."

"He behaved magnificently …"

"I'm sure he did."

"You're a funny mob," the lieutenant said with a sigh. "Still, all right, I'll send a sergeant with him."

Now Wernher stood at the window watching Schwanecke saunter up under escort, grinning to his mates on all sides. When he entered Wernher's room, he did not salute; he stood at ease, and went on grinning. Wernher dismissed the escort sergeant.

He found it hard to look at Schwanecke. The man's combat jacket was flecked with blood, his hands were brown from congealed blood, even his face showed streaks of blood.

"I have heard," Wernher began hoarsely, "that you behaved magnificently. You saved Deutschmann's life …"

Schwanecke said nothing.

"It's very difficult for me. My orders from Orsha were to have you arrested and taken there. That's if you came back. Your conduct in this operation will not doubt be taken into account. Obviously I cannot disobey my orders. Have you anything to say?"

Schwanecke shrugged his shoulders, put his head to one side, and continued to grin. Wernher took a few steps up and down, then turned abruptly and gave Schwanecke a long appraising look. "Why did you actually come back?" he asked. "You knew that ..."

"Sure."

"Why did you come, then?"

"I was pining for you, sir."

Wernher ignored this. "You, Deutschmann and Krull," he muttered, "are the only ones left. All the rest, Lieutenant Obermeier ..."

"Krull?" asked Schwanecke. "He's ...?" The grin had now left his face.

"Yes. He's in hospital in Orsha."

"Bastards like that have all the luck."

"You're talking of a sergeant major, Schwanecke."

"So what? Where does it say a sergeant major can't be a bastard?"

I ought to bawl him out for that, thought Wernher, though of course he's quite right. Anyhow it would do no good. You can't deal with this man like any ordinary chap.

"What exactly have you done?" he asked. "Is it the business with Lieutenant Bevern?"

Schwanecke shrugged his shoulders again.

"Or is it the law about dangerous criminals?"

No answer.

"What do you think they'll do to you?"

Schwanecke passed the side of his hand lightly across his throat, made a noise like "Hrrk", winked, then reverted to his broad grin. Wernher was baffled. This man was obviously joking about his own death, although he had brought back Deutschmann, his mate. He could have deserted, stayed alive, and hoodwinked the Russians with tales of being a politically persecuted martyr, a communist sent to a penal battalion, Heil Stalin ... and yet he had come back and ... It didn't make sense.

"I shall have to lock you up tonight," Wernher said

eventually. "And tomorrow I'll have you taken to Orsha." He shook his head. "I wish I didn't have to—that's all I can say."

"Suppose I scram?"

"What do you mean, scram? You'll be under lock and key."

"Ah well, sir, perhaps you didn't know, but I'm a … Houdini, if you'll excuse the expression. King of escapers, I've got quite a reputation for it. No wall will hold him, no ropes are tight enough—it's even been in the papers."

"Really?"

"Oh yes, I could go into a circus. You know, blokes that escape from chains, that sort of thing. I saw a real genius once, he was properly trussed, and then abracadabra, he was free. Maybe you'll see the same—hey presto and I'll be gone, vanished."

"I shouldn't try anything," said Wernher wearily, doubtful now whether Schwanecke meant him to take all this seriously or whether he was still playing the buffoon. "Don't do anything stupid, my lad. You've still got a chance with a courtmatial, but—you don't want to get shot straight off, do you?"

"No one will hit *me*," grinned Schwanecke. "Hey presto, he's vanished."

"Off you go," said Wernher, as two guards came for Schwanecke. He ran his eye over the prisoner. "Oh, and clean yourself up first."

"That's right, vanished," said Schwanecke, nodding. He winked at Wernher over his shoulder as he went out.

He was locked in a barn, with a guard in front and behind. Wernher did not mean to take any chances. However, when the reliefs came on at 2 a.m. they found both guards lying unconscious in the barn, obviously knocked out, and one guard's rifle had been taken, together with all the ammunition from both rifles. The sergeant major's pistol with three full magazines had also disappeared, and a long butcher's knife from the cookhouse.

"Perhaps he wants to start an offensive," said the soldiers cheerfully, as they talked over the mystery of what had happened that night. Nobody ever found out how he had managed it, or what became of him after his escape. A bloke like that was unlikely to die in his bed, in Russia or in Germany—but then you could never tell. Perhaps *he* would survive the war if anyone did.

39

Deutschmann was taken in a Rumanian hospital train through Russia and Poland to Berlin. He heard only the names of the stations, which the other wounded called out to him: he heard the voices of the Red Cross nurses who distributed tea and coffee, sandwiches and fruit, at the windows.

"Are you thirsty?" one of the others would ask him now and then: he was slowly learning to distinguish them by their voices. "Like some tea?" Then he would nod. He couldn't speak. Blind, he thought, blind and one leg gone, what's to become of me? He drank the tea.

"Tomorrow we'll be in Berlin."

What was Berlin to him?

"Are you looking forward to it?"

What had he got to look forward to? But he nodded. He scarcely spoke, mostly he nodded or else feigned sleep.

What shall I do when I've recovered, he brooded continually. Yes, if Julia were still alive—then I could dictate, think, work, go on working, in spite of everything.

It was pointless to think about it. She was dead. Tanya was dead. Schwanecke was probably dead. Obermeier, Bartlitz, Wiedeck, all of them—why must he still live on?

He lay in a base hospital somewhere. How long have I been here, he wondered. The nurses say four weeks, surely it must be much longer.

He heard the door opening. It squeaked a little. Who had come into the room? One of the nurses, Dr. Bolz—or perhaps his old friend Wolfgang Wissek, who had apparently called soon after he had been brought here, when he wasn't well enough to receive visitors.

He listened, but could not hear steps, nor the clatter of instruments or glasses, which usually meant the nurses were there, nor the rough, good-natured "Hullo there, how's our patient?"which Sister Hyacinth—funny name—would always say when she entered the room.

Silence.

"Who's there?" he asked.

At the door stood Dr. Wissek, Dr. Kukill—and Julia. They did not move. As if petrified, they looked at the pale thin man lying flat on the bed with the thickly bandaged head and the bloodless mouth only just visible over the strong chin. Long, lean, ashen hands, with fingers which suddenly came to life and groped over the blanket....

Dr. Kukill lowered his head. Blind and a cripple, he thought—she had him back, a blind cripple, oh God! She had him back, but like this, like this. He turned and slowly went away, with back bent, dragging his feet. He had no reason to stay here any longer. His part in all this was over, over for good—or evil, and alas it seemed more like evil. He had seen Julia's eyes when she looked at her husband in bed. Anyhow he could feel quite clearly that his presence was not required.

"Who's there?" Deutschmann asked again in a nervous uneasy voice.

"It's me," whispered Julia, leaning against the door-post. "It's me, Ernst, my darling, it's me!"

Dr. Wissek too had seen the look in her eyes; to him it presaged a love which could overcome all the trials ahead. Now he went out as well, closing the door softly behind him. For a moment he listened—and heard slow steps, then suddenly very quick ones, running to Deutschmann's bed.

He smiled.

WAR

0426 Universal/Tandem

	Theodor Krancke and H. J. Brennecke	
164911	**POCKET BATTLESHIP**	60p
	Gordon Landsborough	
149122	**BATTERY FROM HELLFIRE**	40p
161254	**LONG RUN TO TOBRUK**	45p
149041	**PATROL TO BENGHAZI**	40p
177509	**THE DEAD COMMANDO**	60p
166949	**THE GLASSHOUSE GANG**	60p
176464	**BENGHAZI BREAKOUT**	60p
170997	**DESERT MARAUDERS**	60p
	Heinz Schaeffer	
165047	**U-BOAT 977**	60p
	A. V. Sellwood	
170059	**THE WARRING SEAS** (NF)	60p
	Brigadier Durnford-Slater	
16475X	**COMMANDO**	60p
	Michael Crichton-Stuart	
164830	**G. PATROL**	60p

0427 Tattoo

	Edwyn P. Hoyt	
003024	**THE GERMANS WHO NEVER LOST**	60p
	Heinz Konsalik	
003016	**DOCTOR OF STALINGRAD**	60p
003059	**HIGHWAY TO HELL**	60p
003008	**STRAF-BATTALION 999**	60p
003113	**THEY FELL FROM THE SKY**	70p

† For sale in Britain and Ireland only.
*Not for sale in Canada.
♦ Film & T.V. tie-ins.

THRILLERS

0352	Star	
	Georges Arnaud	
397012	**WAGES OF FEAR**	75p ♦
	David Axton	
395184	**PRISON OF ICE**	85p
	Paul Boncarrère	
396474	**ULTIMATUM**	75p
	William F. Buckley Jr.	
396962	**SAVING THE QUEEN**	60p*
	Richard Butler	
396059	**WHERE ALL THE GIRLS ARE SWEETER**	60p
	Henry Denker	
300523	**A PLACE FOR THE MIGHTY**	75p*
	Burt Hirschfeld	
398582	**FATHER PIG**	60p*
395176	**SECRETS**	85p*
398590	**MOMENT OF POWER**	75p*
398604	**BEHOLD ZION**	85p*
	Tony Kenrick	
396253	**THE SEVEN DAY SOLDIERS**	60p
	Hugh C. McDonald	
396849	**THE HOUR OF THE BLUE FOX**	60p*
	Graham Masterton	
395982	**PLAGUE**	75p
396911	**FIREFLASH 5**	60p
	Michael Maguire	
395818	**SCRATCHPROOF**	70p
397853	**SLAUGHTER HORSE** (also see Tandem Thrillers)	70p
	Lawrence Sanders	
300078	**THE FIRST DEADLY SIN**	95p

† For sale in Britain and Ireland only.
* Not for sale in Canada.
♦ Film & T.V. tie-ins.

THRILLERS

0426 Universal/Tandem

	Nick Carter	
183584	**ASSASSIN: CODE NAME VULTURE**	60p*
173635	**BERLIN**	50p*
174437	**CAMBODIA**	50p*
174275	**THE CHINESE PAYMASTER**	60p*
173554	**THE COBRA KILL**	50p*
128028	**CODE NAME WEREWOLF**	60p*
174003	**THE DEATH STRAIN**	50p*
173988	**THE DEFECTOR**	50p*
174518	**HOOD OF DEATH**	50p*
173201	**THE HUMAN TIME BOMB**	50p*
180836	**ICE TRAP TERROR**	60p*
18470X	**THE JERUSALEM FILE**	60p*
180917	**MASSACRE IN MILAN**	60p*
173716	**THE MIND KILLERS**	50p*
173120	**THE LIVING DEATH**	50p*
176898	**THE MAN WHO SOLD DEATH**	50p*
180089	**THE N3 CONSPIRACY**	50p*
179889	**THE PEKING DOSSIER**	50p*
180674	**THE SIGN OF THE COBRA**	60p*
184467	**SIX BLOODY SUMMER DAYS**	60p*
176545	**THE KATMANDU CONTRACT**	60p*
181042	**VATICAN VENDETTA**	50p*
184114	**THE Z DOCUMENT**	60p*
	David Chandler	
183908	**THE GANGSTERS**	95p*
	John Gardner	
184548	**THE LIQUIDATOR**	60p
	Michael Maguire	
172914	**SHOT SILK**	70p
	(also see Star Thrillers)	

† For sale in Britain and Ireland only.
*Not for sale in Canada.
♦ Film & T.V. tie-ins.

GENERAL FICTION

0352	397403	Robert Stone **DOG SOLDIERS**	75p*
	395427	Peter Upton **GREEN HILL FAR AWAY**	95p
	30157 0	Margaret Walker **JUBILEE**	95p*
	301562	N. Richard Nash **EAST WIND, RAIN**	95p*
	395540	Gail Parent **DAVID MEYER IS A MOTHER**	70p
	300809	Molly Parkin **LOVE ALL**	50p
	397179	**UP TIGHT**	60p
	396288	Erich Maria Remarque **BOBBY DEERFIELD**	85p* ♦
	396946	Judith Rossner **TO THE PRECIPICE**	85p*
	302089	**NINE MONTHS IN THE LIFE OF AN OLD MAID**	75p*
	398892	Alan Sillitoe **THE GENERAL**	50p
	300965	**THE LONELINESS OF THE LONG-DISTANCE RUNNER**	50p
	300949	**MEN, WOMEN AND CHILDREN**	50p
	300981	**SATURDAY NIGHT AND SUNDAY MORNING**	50p
	395141	**THE WIDOWER'S SON**	85p
	397144	**THE FLAME OF LIFE**	70p
	398809	**THE RAGMAN'S DAUGHTER**	50p
	396415	Hubert Selby Jr. **THE ROOM**	75p

† For sale in Britain and Ireland only.
*Not for sale in Canada.
♦ Film & T.V. tie-ins.